CAPTIVATED BY HER CONVENIENT HUSBAND

Bronwyn Scott

MILLS & BOON

First Published in Great Britain 2019
by Mills & Boon, an imprint of HarperCollins*Publishers*
1 London Bridge Street, London, SE1 9GF

© 2019 Nikki Poppen

ISBN: 978-0-263-26922-2

MIX
Paper from
responsible sources
FSC® C007454

This book is produced from independently certified FSC™ paper
to ensure responsible forest management.
For more information visit www.harpercollins.co.uk/green.

Printed and bound in Spain
by CPI, Barcelona

For Rowan, who loves *Martin Guerre* the musical.

The world likes to define who we are,
but I think it's always best to simply be yourself.

Chapter One

Indigo Hall, Sussex—Friday, October 26th, 1855

Avaline Panshawe-Tresham could put off her entrance and all it would entail no longer. She had to get out of the carriage, had to go inside, had to dance with the men, smile at the women, suffer the solicitations of her well-meaning in-laws, who had already arrived, and not least she had to endure the dubious charms of the evening's host, Tobin Hayworth, all the while pretending she was as oblivious to his intentions as she was to the disappointment she'd brought the Treshams—all seven years, three weeks, one day of it, and counting.

There seemed no end in sight when it came to her association with disappointment, not that the Treshams had ever said as much. They were far too kind. Still, Avaline knew and that was all that mattered.

She drew a steadying breath and smoothed her ice-blue skirts. She checked to see that her pearl and gold earbobs were fastened securely, that her slender pearl pendant wasn't twisted, that her matching combs were secure in the folds of her artfully arranged hair. She was stalling, of course, as she'd stalled at home at Blandford Hall, dragging out her departure with an inane debate with herself over wearing the blue or the pink silk. Now, there wasn't anything left to hide behind. There wasn't a hair out of place, or a creased wrinkle to be found. She was out of excuses and out of time in so many ways, and she was furious.

Tobin Hayworth had held his harvest ball tonight on purpose. He knew very well the import of October twenty-sixth to her. It was one day after the anniversary of the Battle of Balaclava; a year and a day after her husband, Fortis Tresham, fell in battle, never to be heard from again. His body had never been recovered. He'd fallen and he had vanished, as if he'd never been. But he *had* been and perhaps he still was. It was a small hope she clung to and one whose odds grew smaller by the day. It had been a year since he'd fallen, making it seven years since he'd married her and promptly departed England. It was a long time to be gone.

That was the great failing that confronted her daily. She'd been a dismal wife, unable to keep her young, restless officer husband home. It was the one thing the Treshams had hoped she'd do by whatever means necessary. Marriage was usually a great domesticator of men of Fortis's station—sons of dukes. Once a man married, he settled down, looked after his estate, his wife and his nursery. The plan should have worked. It had all the trappings of success. His parents and hers had arranged it. What could be more perfect than an alliance between neighbours, one of whom claimed the title of the Duke of Cowden, and the other an ailing baron, who claimed a large, unentailed tract of failing land that abutted the Duke's estate and an eagerness to see his only child wed? Their marriage had been accomplished during Fortis's leave. It had ended when he left three weeks later. She'd not conceived a honeymoon heir for him. She had hardly kept him in their bed long enough to do more than make the marriage binding. He'd been off, riding, hunting, shooting, and fishing with his friends for the duration of the honeymoon. She'd not tamed Fortis Tresham. If anything, she'd made him wilder.

She'd written dutifully, one letter a month to wherever he was posted, telling him of the estate, of the family, hoping her stories would invoke a sense of nostalgia, a longing for home, for her even. But not once had he written back. Now, he might never write. He might be gone for good, despite the Treshams' latest sliver of hope that he'd resurfaced in the Crimea. They'd sent his best friend and fellow officer, Major Camden Lithgow haring back to Sevastopol to vouch for the man who'd walked out of the pine forest claiming Fortis's name.

Avaline wasn't sure how she felt about that. To have Fortis back would solve her current problems, but it would also certainly create others. How did two people pick up the pieces of a marriage that had hardly existed, after all this time? Still, they might have an indifferent marriage, but she didn't wish him dead for it. She hardly knew the man who had so briefly been in her bed, in her life.

That was a new sort of guilt she carried these days. While the Treshams hoped desperately for the possible return of their third son, she couldn't remember what he looked like. The picture she carried of him in her mind had begun to blur years ago. She remembered dark hair, blue eyes, a broad-shouldered physique, a handsome visage, a man pleasing to the eye. Was she exaggerating these features now? Was he as broad-shouldered as she recalled? Was he as tall? As handsome? As callow? He'd not been the most attentive of husbands, or had that been her fault? Would he have been more attentive if she'd somehow been different? Would it matter if she *did* remember it all aright? Did those memories of seven years ago still represent the man who might come home to her? War changed any man and this one had been lost for a year. How might war and this unaccounted year have changed him? Who knew what sort of man had walked out of the forest?

Avaline's more practical side argued that it hardly mattered what he looked like or what he'd become as long as it protected her from Tobin Hayworth's avarice. Fortis's name was all that was safeguarding her now and its shield was wearing thin. A body to go with the name would take care of Hayworth for good.

There was a sharp, impatient rap on the carriage door. 'My dear, you must come in before you catch a chill.' The door opened without her permission. It seemed the knock was not a request for entrance, but a warning of intrusion. Such officiousness could only mean one thing. Hayworth had found her.

He stood outside, framed in the carriage doorway, resplendently dressed in dark evening clothes, pristine white stock impeccably tied, blue silk waistcoat severely tailored, grey eyes like steel. The man was the epitome of ice and control. Just looking at him made Avaline cold. He held out his hand without the slightest qualm that he'd be refused. He was a man who was obeyed. Always. 'I cannot leave my mother alone in the receiving line for long, so I must ask you to hurry.' His tone implied hurrying would not have been necessary if she had come in with the Treshams upon arrival. 'I was concerned when I saw you were not with Cowden and the Duchess.'

'I needed a moment alone to gather myself,' Avaline replied coolly. She might be required to take his hand, to go in and put on a show, but he needed to remember she was not his to command. 'Today has been difficult for me. I was tempted to beg off this evening and not come at all.' She would have done just that if she hadn't feared him coming after her and having to face him alone at Blandford. Far better to confront him here, surrounded by people and with the Treshams for support. There was safety in numbers. 'I may not stay long,' Avaline warned him as she stepped down. 'I am not sure it's appropriate to be out revelling on such a day.' She did not bother to keep the scold from her voice.

Disapproval flickered flinty and hard in his gaze. Hayworth had made his opinion on harbouring hope that Fortis be found alive plain several months ago. 'The heights of feminine fancy and womanly foolishness,' he'd called it.

'Has there been news, then? Is it official that he is lost for good?' Any concern one might detect in the enquiry extended only as far as how the news would affect him and his plans.

'No, there's been no news.' She knew the response would needle him. As long as there wasn't news one way or the other, Hayworth could do nothing. She still had some power, some control.

Hayworth patted her arm. 'Your loyalty does you credit in theory only. But it does not serve you in practice. As I have pointed out before, your estate needs a firm hand, as do your finances. You cannot lean on Cowden's benevolence for ever, any more than you can go on pretending your husband is out there, somewhere. It's been seven years with no direct word from him and now there is this issue of "being lost". To be blunt, this does not sound like a man who wants to come home and he is dragging you down with him. We can handle this as abandonment, push it through court and free you so your life can start again. We needn't wait any longer.'

We. He made it sound as if this was something she wanted done when nothing could be further from the truth. Hayworth was wasting no time this evening. Usually, he made his appeal towards evening's end. But why wait? Now that the case had been made, why pretend towards subtlety? It was no secret he wanted to be that firm hand on her family estate, on her finances, and on her, if they were being blunt. He sought nothing short of marriage—an audacious claim considering she already had a husband.

Inside Indigo Hall, the opulence of Hayworth's East India Company fortune was on full display, a reminder to all in attendance that his star was in the ascendancy. Tobin Hayworth didn't have a title *yet*, but it was only a matter of time before the Crown recognised him with a knighthood. Avaline understood marriage to a baron's daughter such as herself would certainly smooth that path for him and, in exchange, he would smooth her financial hardships. Blandford would be restored. That message was on display everywhere she looked tonight. He led her up a wide, curving staircase done in the same polished marble of the floors and the strong, thick columns in the entrance hall. Enormous cut-crystal vases brimmed with expensive hothouse bouquets from discreetly carved niches while footmen abounded, waiting to assist with any trivial detail, dressed in autumnal velvet livery for the express purpose of this harvest ball.

'All this could be yours to command, my dear. Luxury at your fingertips, your cares erased. You'd want for nothing,' Hayworth murmured the temptation at her ear. 'Make no mistake, tonight I am laying my world out for you so you can make an informed decision.' He gave away his antecedents with such flagrant talk of money. The inherent subtlety of a gentleman eluded him and always would. No matter how well dressed or how wealthy he was, Tobin

Hayworth would always be *nouveau riche*, a nabob to the bone.

'I don't think there's any decision to make,' Avaline responded with a bluntness of her own. 'I am *married*, Mr Hayworth.'

He chuckled affably at her rebuke, his mouth at her ear. Anyone watching them ascend the stairs would think this was a flirtation, not a coercion. 'Are you? You don't really know, but you *should*. I would think marriage is not something that possesses an in between. Either one *is* married or one is not. You cling only to technicalities now, to your detriment, when you should be preparing yourself for the worst and accept you may very well have been a widow for over a year. If you'd accepted that a year ago, you'd be out of mourning by now and this whole ordeal would be past us.'

'You dare too much, Mr Hayworth.' Avaline felt a chill move through her. The depths of his roguery were revealed increasingly to her each time they met, a sign of how confident he grew with each passing day. In truth, she could not argue with his facts. Her position on all fronts, including her continued defence of her marriage, was weak indeed and growing weaker each day there was no word about Fortis.

'Don't look so glum, my dear. You are about to be rescued,' Hayworth said through gritted teeth before breaking into a smile as the Duchess of Cowden approached. 'Ah, Your Grace, what a pleasure to see you.'

The Duchess of Cowden met them at the top of the stairs, elegant and cool in lilac silk. 'Mr Hayworth, what a splendid little party. There you are, Avaline. Come, there are people to meet.' Without further preface, the Duchess looped an arm through hers, effectively removing her from Hayworth's side. The Duchess had effectively insulted him, too. Did Hayworth know? His grand harvest ball was nothing to the Duchess, whose town house ballroom in London held four hundred and even then was always a crush.

'That man is odious,' the Duchess whispered as they walked away. He was more than odious, though. He was dangerous. He'd not made a fortune in the East India indigo trade because he talked a lot. He'd made it because he was a man of action. He did what he said. If he thought he could dissolve her marriage and coerce her into another, Avaline was quite concerned he actually could.

'Thank you for coming tonight,' Avaline offered sincerely to her mother-in-law. It would have been easy enough for the Treshams to stay in town to await Major Lithgow's return and his news of Fortis.

The Duchess dismissed the effort. 'Major Lithgow knows where to find us. It could be days yet depending on the Channel crossing. We'd rather be here, supporting you. Today is a difficult day for all of us, made no less difficult by Hayworth's event. He planned this on purpose and it is poorly done of him.'

Avaline smiled, grateful for the support. Fortis's family had stood beside her all these years, treated her as a daughter when her own parents had passed within a year of each other, leaving her alone with Blandford and its debt. Would they continue to stand by her if Fortis were truly dead? That, too, would be decided when Major Lithgow returned. Her future hung in the balance as did her freedom. Regardless of Lithgow's news the freedom she'd known would be at an end. She would be a wife or a widow. She'd either have a husband or she'd need a husband—a woman's lot in a nutshell.

'Try to dance and forget for a little while,' the Duchess encouraged, reading her thoughts. 'There's nothing else to be done until Major

Lithgow returns. I've arranged partners for you. Here's Sir Edmund now.'

Sir Edmund Banbridge claimed her for the first dance, another family friend of the Treshams claimed her for the second. The Duchess had done her job well, peopling Avaline's dance card with those who'd understand how emotional the evening was for her and wouldn't press her for small talk. But eventually, the list ran out and Hayworth, as host, could not be denied for ever.

'I believe supper is mine.' Hayworth took her arm, brooking no prevarication as the supper waltz ended. Avaline understood her reprieve was over. She would not be allowed to refuse, but on principle, she had to try.

'I find I have no appetite tonight.' She would not have him believing she was in favour of his company.

'Then we'll walk outside. You needn't stay indoors.' Hayworth reversed direction, taking them away from the crowd moving towards the supper buffet.

Avaline saw her mistake immediately. He was punishing her. If she would not eat with him publicly, she'd be forced to walk with him privately where anything might be said or done.

The French doors leading outside to the veranda closed ominously behind them, the temporarily deserted garden spread out before them. This was not a situation she wanted to be in. 'We have our seclusion, my dear. Just the two of us. Perhaps now you'll tell me why you resist my offer so vehemently? Or do you need some different form of persuasion?' Something dangerous glinted in his eyes. His body shifted, moving closer to hers, crowding her against the rail, a predator stalking his prey, a horrifying reminder of how alone she was out here with him.

'I don't consider cornering a woman on a dark balcony persuasion of any sort,' Avaline replied staunchly, trying to ignore the fact that to keep herself from touching him, her back was pressed against the hard wrought-iron of the balcony. She could physically go no further.

The knuckles of his hand gave a possessive caress of her cheek, his touch leaving her cold while her mind debated the plausibility of what he might venture here in the dark. Would he truly go so far as to *force* attentions on her? Admittedly, it was difficult to conceive that he would. She'd been raised in the belief that gentlemen knew the limits of propriety and abided by them, yet that very assumption was being challenged before her eyes. 'You're a beautiful woman, Avaline, who has been on her own too long, you've forgotten certain pleasures. You need a man to remind you.'

'I have a man.' Avaline was starting to panic now. He was giving no sign of retreating.

He gave a harsh laugh. 'You have the memory of a man. It is not the same, I assure you.' His mouth bent to hers in a swift move meant to take her by surprise, meant to render her helpless. The moment his mouth caught hers, she shoved, hard and certain. There could be no hesitation on her part or he would see it as acceptance. The shove bought her space, enough of it to rush past him and gain the door. She fumbled with the handle, struggling with it in her haste. She slipped inside, but not before he got his hands on her again, his grip punishing about her wrist.

'Don't be a fool, Avaline. I like a good, hard chase,' he growled, 'and I always win.' As if to prove it, he dragged her to him and then danced her back to the wall until she was trapped between him and the damask. 'I don't mind if we play rough. I will have my answer.' His mouth was inches from hers, his body pressed to hers, giving no quarter. 'Tell me again, why do you resist?'

Then he was gone, miraculously pulled away from her, a fist crashing into his jaw with enough force to send Hayworth sprawling into a Louis XV chair too brittle to take his weight. He went down and the chair splintered with him. A man was on Hayworth like a wolf on its prey, straddling the prone figure, one hand gripping his collar, the other forming a ready fist to finish the job. No, not a man, an avenging angel, Avaline thought, taking in the dark hair, the broad shoulders beneath the soldier's blue coat and the ripple of muscle as the man bent over Hayworth. Another blow landed, galvanising Avaline. Avenging angel or not, she couldn't allow him to continue even if Hayworth deserved it. Violence was violence.

She ran forward, gripping her rescuer's arm. 'Stop! Please, stop!' The arm tensed, muscles flexing beneath her touch, iron hard and rigid.

The man turned his face to her, blue eyes lethal, mouth set grim. 'Are you sure, my dear Avaline? I will only stop if you say he's had enough.'

He let go of Hayworth's collar, dropping him on to the floor. Hayworth rolled to his side, curled in a ball, nursing his jaw. 'Allow me to answer your question. Perhaps the lady resists your proposal on the grounds of bigamy, Hayworth.' His growl was pure, primal possession and it sent a trill of excitement down her spine. 'Looks as though I've come home just in time.'

Avaline's breath caught. She did not remember that voice, the rich rolling timbre of it behind the growl or the sound of her name on his lips as if it belonged there. How could she forget such a voice? But the hair, the shoulders, the blue eyes, the uniform… Her mind started to grasp the details, the realities. This must be what it felt like to see a ghost, the impossible made real. The world spun. She instinctively reached for him in a desperate attempt to steady herself against the overwhelming realisation.

'Fortis. Oh, my God, you're back.'

Chapter Two

Blandford Hall— the next afternoon

Fortis sat on a sofa upholstered in rose silk, his back to the wainscoted wall, his sight line trained on the wide double-doored entrance of the drawing room, his peripheral vision aware that beyond him to the left were French doors and beyond that a manicured garden bursting with autumn colour. He was aware, too, that he was surrounded on all sides by luxury, safety and people who loved him. Beside him on the sofa sat Avaline, keeping respectful—or was that wary?—inches between them, making sure not to touch him. Perhaps she was unsure what to make of his return? To his right sat Her Grace, the Duchess of Cowden, his mother, clutching his father the Duke's hand against the joy and the shock of her son's return. Across from him on a matching sofa were Helena and Frederick, his oldest brother and his wife. In the last chair sat his newest sister-in-law Anne, with his other brother, Ferris, standing protectively at her shoulder.

Everywhere he looked there were reminders that he was safe. He was returned to the bosom of his family. But what his eyes could see proof of, his mind struggled to accept. *This was his life?* Wherever he turned, this was what it always came back to. This was all his: Blandford Hall, his wife's home—*their* home, the place they'd spent the first three weeks of their marriage; this family full of graciousness and warmth and unbounded love, this family who'd held him close in turns and cried openly at Hayworth's ball when he'd made his appearance in the supper room, Avaline in his arms.

He supposed, in hindsight, his entrance had been rather dramatic—dramatic enough to make Avaline swoon. All he'd thought about when he'd caught her was getting her away from Hayworth, finding his family and going home. The result had been somewhat more. Upon their arrival today, Anne and Ferris had reported that romantic tales of the hero returned were already circulating the neighbourhood. His return had not been the private affair he'd envisioned on the journey from Sevastopol with Cam Lithgow. Today, however, it was just the eight of them, just the Treshams. He was missing Cam sorely. He hadn't realised how much he'd counted on Cam to smooth the way, to be the bridge between his long absence and his sudden return. Cam had been a godsend last night, shooing people away, putting himself between Hayworth's gawking guests and the Treshams' emotional reunion. It had been Cam who'd ushered them all to carriages and sent them home—he and Avaline to Blandford and his family to the Cowden estate at Bramble. But he couldn't rely on Cam for ever. Cam had his own business to see to, which left Fortis with tea poured out, no one to ease the conversation and an awkward silence settling over the room.

Fortis supposed he should be the one to say something, to take charge, but what did one say after having been gone for seven years? 'How are you? What have you been up to?' It seemed too trite, too open ended. Even if by some stretch of the imagination such a question wasn't impossible to ask, it was impossible to answer in a decent amount of time. It would take Frederick alone at least an hour to tell him of his nephews—all five of them now—and Ferris another hour to tell him about falling in love with Anne, let alone anything else that had happened in his absence.

The enormity of that swamped him. He'd missed so much: births, weddings, deaths. Avaline's parents had both died. He knew that much even if he couldn't remember them. That was embarrassing in itself. He could not remember his in-laws, what they looked like, sounded like, what they had said to him. He knew he had them. But knowing was somehow different than remembering. Knowing was fact and he suddenly found facts weren't enough. Was that how his family felt looking at him? That they didn't know him? Or that what they remembered of him was somehow lacking when faced with the reality of him sitting in the room? He was not the only one for whom this was awkward. They didn't know any more what to say to him than he knew what to say to them. Maybe this first conversation wasn't about telling, but asking. He needed to give them permission to ask their questions.

Fortis cleared his throat. 'You must have things you want to know,' he said, taking up that train of thought. He'd been sprung on them as an impossible surprise. There'd been no time to send word ahead. Any letter sent would have arrived on the packet with him. Surely they would want explanations. Perhaps they might even have doubts now that the euphoria of their reunion last night had passed. He hoped he had answers. There was still so much that was a fog in his brain. He'd tried to explain as much to Cam on the journey home.

The discomfort of giving those explanations must have been evident on his face. Ferris, the physician, the brother who'd studied medicine and dedicated his efforts to serving the medical needs of the poor, leaned forward earnestly. 'No, Fort, you needn't tell us anything yet or ever. Cam made a thorough report and we understand.' Fortis knew what 'we understand' meant. It meant the family knew he hadn't been entirely in his right mind when he'd come out of the woods, that he'd displayed signs of confusion, displacement, that he'd been unsure of who or what he was. Cam and the army had sorted that out *with* him and *for* him thanks to the letters from Avaline in his coat pocket dated from the day before Balaclava almost a year prior, along with the miniature of her, the tattered remnants of the uniform that proved his rank and identity, his pale blue eyes and other sundry details despite the overlong dark hair he refused to let Cam cut. Even now, he was wearing it long, tied back in a ponytail like lords a generation ago.

'I don't need your pity,' Fortis answered Ferris sternly. He didn't need to be patronised or felt sorry for. Poor broken Fortis—did they think he was a shell of his former self? Did they think he couldn't function in the world? Beside him, Avaline shifted, uncomfortable with the sharp tone he'd taken. Is that what his wife thought, too? His pretty, surprised wife who'd swooned in his arms? Did she believe her husband was not capable of fully returning? All because of Cam's damned honest report that had labelled him confused? It wasn't untrue, he was confused. He felt confused right now sitting amid all this love and luxury, knowing it was his, but not remembering it as his. He just preferred that confusion be private, that it remain his to manage, *alone*. He wasn't used to relying on others to carry his burdens with him or for him.

Frederick intervened, smoothing the tension. 'We know you don't, Fort. We just need you to know we don't expect you to disgorge everything all at once. Being home is enough for us. All else will come. It has been a long time. None of us must assume we can all pick up where we left off as if nothing and no one has changed. We've all changed, but we will all find our ways back to each other if we're patient.'

Fortis nodded and took the olive branch, moving the conversation on to safer ground. 'Helena, tell me about the boys. Five boys all under ten—are they a handful?' That brought a round of laughter. It was a good choice of topic. Helena was a proud mother and Fortis let talk of the boys'—his nephews'—escapades swirl around him, wrapping him in laughter. He felt himself relax a certain degree. There was no pressure here. There was nothing for him to recall. He'd not known the boys. Helena had been pregnant at his wedding with her first. It was easy to laugh and smile along with the rest of them, to feel as though he was home. And yet, the feeling couldn't quite settle, like clothes that were just the tiniest bit too small—a trouser waist too tight, a coat stretched too snugly over shoulders so that every move was a reminder that the fit was not effortless.

After a while, Ferris rose. 'Fort, come walk with me in the gardens.'

'Is this your idea of rescuing me?' Fortis asked once the glass doors were shut behind them. 'If so, I don't believe I was in need of rescue.' He couldn't seem to help himself from being defensive with his brother today.

Ferris shook his head, unbothered by the surly tone. 'No, you didn't. It was me being selfish. I wanted a moment with you. Will you allow me?'

'As my brother or a physician?' Fort was instantly wary. All his battle senses were on high alert, ready to protect himself.

'As both, I hope. War changes a man. I see that change in you.'

Fortis lifted an eyebrow in challenge. 'Do you? You haven't seen me in seven years. I am sure everyone looks different after such a long time apart. I don't think that makes it remarkable or worthy of study.'

Ferris nodded, doing him the credit of contemplating his thoughts. 'True, your hair is longer, your muscles more defined. You've come into your full build. Nothing of the little brother remains. I shall have to get used to looking at the man my brother has become instead of looking for the boy he once was,' Ferris acceded with a physician's eye for anatomy. 'But there are other changes as well. Mental changes.'

Fortis baulked at that. No man liked having his sanity questioned any more than he liked discussing his emotions. 'What are you suggesting?'

'Please, Fort. There's no need to be defensive. I've been working with soldiers on their returns from India, the Crimea, wherever Britain has the army posted these days. In places where the men have seen violence, your condition is not unusual, nor, unfortunately, all that rare. War takes a toll on a man we're just beginning to acknowledge, to say nothing of understand. But I hope in time we may.'

Fortis scowled. 'And what condition is that?'

'You sat with your back to the wall today, so you could see the entire room, so you had clear visual access to points of entry and perhaps escape?' Ferris added with wry insight. 'That is something men do who live on the edge of danger, on the edge of life. You have the tendencies of one who has lived under stressful conditions where the need to fight is always an imminent possibility.'

Fortis wished he could deny his brother's conjecture, but he could not. He could not recall anything to the contrary and what he did remember—the smoke, the cannon fire, the rush and riot of battle—certainly upheld Ferris's assertions. But Ferris wasn't done.

'We've also found that these soldiers have unclear memories, difficulty explaining their time away to others. They have a reluctance to integrate back into their old lives, back into their families. There are other symptoms, too. If I could ask you a few questions?'

'I'm not sure I like being a specimen under a microscope or an object of study.' He did not want to answer any questions. He felt ridiculously vulnerable standing here in the garden with Ferris, his brother's assertions stripping him bare.

'Not an object, Fortis. A man. I don't want to study you. I want to help you, if you need it and if you'll allow it. Cam's report suggested...'

'Damn Cam's report. Thanks to that blasted paper, you've already decided I do need help. You're all convinced I'm on the verge of craziness.' Fortis gestured towards the house, anger acting as his best defence. 'That's what all of you were thinking in there, too afraid to ask your questions because of what I might say. It's far safer to not ask, isn't it? Then everyone can pretend I'm all right.' A dark thought welled up from deep inside him. Perhaps *he* was the one pretending he was all right when a part of him knew he hadn't been all right, not for a long time, not for months, well before he'd walked out of the forest. It was something he wanted to keep to himself like his confusion. But his brother had seen his failings so easily. Did the rest of them? Did Avaline?

'I am asking now.' Ferris folded his arms across his chest, the quiet steel in his voice issuing his challenge. His brother was daring him to tell the truth. 'Do you have dreams? Nightmares? Trouble sleeping? Periods where you lose track of time, where your mind wanders or where you juxtapose reality with a remembrance and your mind thinks you're there, reliving it, instead of in the present?'

'I might have dreams on occasion.' Fortis shook his head. Ferris looked as if he wanted to press for more detail, his physician's mind hungry for information, but this was all he was willing to offer today. He didn't want to confess to dreams that left him waking in a sweat, wrapped in a sense of foreboding with nothing to cling to but vague images he could not call into focus, dreams in which he watched himself from other points of view, or wasn't even himself but some other nameless person. Perhaps he'd admit to those dreams if he could remember them. Perhaps it was best he didn't remember them. Maybe he should be thankful he couldn't. Maybe his mind was protecting him.

Ferris nodded, something in his brother's face easing. There would be no more interrogation today. Ferris clapped a hand on his shoulder. 'Well, if you do have such dreams or experiences, I want you to know not to fear them or feel you have to hide them, not from me. They're normal for men who've been in your position. They're nothing to be ashamed of. You can come to me, Fortis. I can help and I can listen.' Ferris paused, searching for the right words. 'Sometimes there are things a man may not want to tell his wife, but he can always tell his brother.'

'Married less than a year and already you have secrets from Anne?' Fortis teased. It was easier than being serious, easier than having Ferris examine his soul.

Ferris smiled wryly and said frankly, 'No, I

am afraid Anne knows all my transgressions to date. She's seen me at my worst, in the dark of night after I've lost a young patient for no good reason except poor living conditions society chose not to rectify.' Bitterness flashed in Ferris's eyes for just a moment.

'Then we are both soldiers of a sort,' Fortis offered in sombre comfort. 'I appreciate you telling me that.'

Ferris nodded. 'That's what brothers are for.' He gestured towards the French doors. 'We should go back in. Helena will want to be getting home to the boys.'

Inside, everyone was calling for coats and carriages, the flurry of activity making the drawing room into a scene of warm, familial chaos, a scene that was almost normal as husbands helped wives into autumn wraps until the Duke looked about the room, his eyes landing on Fortis with enough fatherly force to silence the chatter. 'You three…' He gestured to his grown sons and something inside of Fortis froze. 'Stand together over there in front of the fireplace.'

The three of them did as they were told, never mind Frederick was thirty-eight and a father of five, or that Ferris was thirty-five and a physician, or that he was thirty-two and a soldier who'd returned from the grave. Apparently, a man was never too old to obey his father. *His father.* Something warm and unlooked for blossomed in Fortis's stomach, melting away the ice. He'd not thought of his father for a long time. *Father.* The concept made his eyes sting.

The tall, white-haired Duke of Cowden stared hard at the sight before him, perhaps seeing the physical differences in him that Ferris had noted. Perhaps his father saw not only the length of his hair in contrast to Frederick's and Ferris's shorter lengths, but the hue of it, too. His was a walnut brown while theirs was a dark chestnut. Still nuts, though, Fortis thought to himself. Perhaps he saw, too, that Fortis was more muscled in build than the lean handsomeness of his brothers, another consequence of war and constant activity. Did his father see the brokenness inside as well? Fortis found himself standing taller as if such an action could hide whatever deficiencies he possessed inside.

Whatever the Duke saw or didn't see in his sons, there was mist in his eyes, too, as his gaze lingered on each of his tall, handsome, dark-haired sons in turn. 'I never thought to have all three of my sons under the same roof again.

What a blessing this is. I shall never take the sight of it for granted.' He gestured to the ladies. 'Wives, join your husbands, I want to see my family altogether.' He smiled. 'If only the boys were here, Helena.'

Helena laughed as the women came to stand with them. 'Then we'd all be herding cats. They'd never stand still.'

Avaline stood beside him, but he noticed how careful she was to leave a little space between them, not like Anne and Helena who had taken their husbands' hands. Except for carrying her into the supper room last night, Fortis had not touched her. He had sensed a reticence, an uncertainty in her. It was to be expected. They hardly knew each other. Was she wondering even now how one should behave with a husband one hadn't seen in seven years? And yet a part of him yearned for her to slip her hand into his as Helena had done with Frederick, to look on him with the warmth Anne looked upon Ferris when he'd re-entered the room after only being gone a few minutes. He needed to be patient with Avaline as Ferris and his family was being patient with him. What was it Frederick had said earlier? They were all changed?

There were hugs and farewells in the hall, the

women exchanging plans to meet for sewing together the following week. Frederick embraced him. 'We'll talk about the estate soon, eh? Once you've got your boots on the ground here.' With a last surge of noise and well wishes, his family departed.

Avaline closed the door behind them and turned to face him. She smiled too brightly as she stood in the wide, now-empty entrance hall of Blandford Hall. Their home. Just the two of them, a fact emphasised by the overwhelming silence surrounding them. They were alone for the first time that counted. They'd been alone last night, but there'd been the excuse of the late hour, the need to sleep and the promise of talking tomorrow to smooth over the immediate awkwardness of surprise and shock. Now tomorrow was here and there was no more family to hide behind. Here they were, Lord and Lady Fortis Tresham. Husband and wife. In broad daylight, a seven-year chasm gaping between them. 'That went well,' Avaline said.

'I thought the last bit was odd.' And touching.

Avaline's bright smile softened, making her even more beautiful. 'The loss of you aged your father greatly. You cannot imagine what having you back means to your parents, especially His Grace. I think one reaches a certain age where one comes to grips with their own mortality, but never the mortality of a child. To lose you was for your father to lose part of his immortality.' She blushed and looked away. 'You're staring.'

Damn right he was staring. The most beautiful woman in the world was his wife. 'You're lovely. I was thinking the miniature doesn't do you credit.' Fortis fished in the pocket of his waistcoat for it. He'd put it there first thing this morning when he'd dressed. He brought it out now and flipped it open, studying the comparison.

'You have it with you?' Avaline asked, surprised.

'Yes. I carry it with me always. It's never left my pocket, except of course when I look at it.' He felt sheepish over the admission. 'I suppose it's a silly habit now that I can look at you every day.' He put it back into his pocket.

'You never use to stare,' Avaline ventured, the intensity of his gaze causing her to flush.

'I'm making up for lost time.' Fortis smiled.

'You didn't use to do that either. Smile,' Avaline commented, a little smile of her own playing on her pink lips. He'd made a study of those lips over the past hours. His eyes knew intimately the enticing fullness of her bottom lip, the symmetrical perfection of the upper. It was a mouth that invited kisses and he wanted to oblige, although he wasn't certain how that might be received, how *he* might be received by this wife who'd been glad of his presence last night, but who had retreated in the light of day.

'I imagine there will be a lot of things I didn't used to do. I've been given a second chance to be a better husband, a better man, and I intend to make the most of it.' Whatever he remembered or didn't remember, he knew that much at least. He'd been lucky. It was nothing short of a miracle he'd come out of that forest. He could agree to that, but he could see that his words had taken Avaline by surprise. She didn't know what to make of them or of him. But they couldn't sort that out standing in the middle of the hall where servants might overhear them.

'Take my arm, Avaline, and walk with me. Give me a tour of all the improvements you've made.' He smiled encouragingly and he hoped calmly, all the while his heart thudding in his chest at the prospect of this angel's fingers on his sleeve, of her skirts brushing softly against his trouser leg as they strolled. Yet Avaline hesitated. 'I am your husband and you are my wife. You needn't be afraid to touch me, Avaline. I will not break like glass nor dissolve in a heap like ash.'

Slowly, Avaline took his arm, her fingertips ever so light on his sleeve. It was a start.

Chapter Three

His arm was as strong and as real beneath her fingers today as it had been last night, yet losing him was exactly what Avaline feared. Not in the sense that he'd dissolve physically, but that another, less tangible, piece of him would indeed evaporate if held up to scrutiny, the piece that had played the hero, who'd swept her up into his arms, who'd been solicitous of her needs, aware of the shock she must feel over his reappearance. He'd not pushed her to consummate their reunion last night, which hadn't surprised her. Fortis had never shown interest in her bed beyond his wedding-night duties. What had surprised her, though, was the concern he'd shown for her well-being when he'd left her at her bedroom door. That was the man she didn't want to lose, not before she could discover him, this more mature, less self-centred version of the husband who'd come home. Yet it was this very newness that hindered her now as they walked in the garden, silence between them once more. What should she say? There was so much *to* say, but none of it seemed quite the right place to start.

'Shall we start with last night?' Fortis ventured as they turned down a path lined with oaks that formed a vibrant canopy of changing leaves overhead. He was taking charge just as he had in the drawing room. It had been courageous of him to invite his family's questions, to offer himself openly, and it had cost him something. She'd sensed he hadn't been entirely comfortable with it.

She'd wanted to reach out and take his hand in the drawing room, to let him know he wasn't alone. But the Fortis she'd married wouldn't have wanted such sentiment. He would have seen it as an assault on his strength, so she'd not risked it. Perhaps she had not risked it for herself either. She could not allow this heroics-induced empathy she felt for the man who'd swept her up in his arms, who'd come to her aid against Hayworth, also sweep away the realities of their marriage.

Fortis had made his position on wedding her very clear before he'd left. So clear those words were still burned in her mind seven years later.

'This is a marriage of convenience, Avaline, to secure for you an unentailed property of your father's and eventually join it with my father's. I have done my part. The property is secured. Now, if you'll excuse me, I promised to meet the boys this evening.'

He'd left with the army the next day. She could not let herself forget her place, for fear she would again fall victim to the fantasies she'd once harboured about their marriage.

She had to stay strong. Fortis could not come home after seven years of not answering her letters, miracle from the grave or not, and take her for granted again. She was stronger now, smarter now, no longer the fresh-from-the-schoolroom miss straight from Mrs Finlay's Academy, no longer the child he'd once accused her of being. But the man who walked beside her seemed oblivious to her inner turmoil. He was more concerned with the present than the past. 'Is it safe to assume Hayworth has been making an idiot of himself?'

'Ever since news came from Balaclava.' Avaline paused, gathering herself against the emotions of that awful day in London when Cam Lithgow had told them Fortis was missing. Her reaction had been part fright and part an overwhelming numbness. All Fortis had left her was his name and with Cam's announcement she'd stood to lose even that. She'd felt exposed, the very last of her protection against Hayworth ripped away. But another part of her had been shockingly numb, emotionally empty. While family members around her had wept openly, she'd not been able to conjure such a depth of feeling over the loss of a husband who had not wanted her and whom she had not seen in years.

That lack of feeling had compounded her guilt. The loss of Fortis was *her* fault. She'd not been enough of a wife to make him stay and now he was likely dead because of it. Last night, all that had changed. She had a second chance to keep him here if she chose to take it.

'Hayworth wants—*wanted*—' she corrected herself '—to have you declared dead and, if not that, he wanted the courts to declare abandonment.' She was clearly not abandoned now. Fortis was here. Her protection was restored simply by Fortis being alive. He needn't stay and perhaps he did not intend to, yet another reason for withholding her heart. She didn't need to engage it in order to have what she needed from him—the name of a living husband.

'Abandonment? That's ludicrous.' Fortis laughed at the notion. 'He never could have won that.'

'Couldn't he? There were six years of unanswered letters,' Avaline argued quietly, not for Hayworth's sake but for hers. It was proof Fortis cared so little for their marriage, for her. That disregard had nearly cost her everything.

'Well, I am here now,' Fortis answered gruffly, his jaw tight. She immediately felt terrible for making the accusation, yet she couldn't help riding that little crest of anger she'd allowed herself. He'd endured years of war and a year of who knew what hardships. But so had she. In her own way, she'd gone to war, too, alone and unarmed against Hayworth, against a world that talked about her behind her back without knowing the whole truth; that she'd married a man she didn't know when she was little more than a girl in order to save her estate and herself from marriage to Tobin Hayworth years ago. The marriage hadn't been a love-match as the Treshams had put about, painting it as a whirlwind romance during Fortis's leave to explain the haste. It had been a marriage of convenience, pure and simple. Only it wasn't so simple any more. Fortis was back and the past must be dealt with. Resuming a marriage with a man who didn't want her was the price for thwarting Hayworth.

'Yes, you are here now. For how long?' The question came out sharply. Other than putting her beyond Hayworth's intentions, what else did his appearance mean for her? For *them*? Was he home to stay? Or simply to lend her the protection of his name once more before he was off on new adventures?

Fortis's brow knit in perplexed question or maybe shock that she'd asked such a thing. 'I am home to stay, Avaline. I am resigning my commission, of course.' He was staring at her as if he couldn't believe she'd not already concluded such action was a natural progression of events. 'I am home to share the running of the estate, although I dare say there is much you'll have to teach me. The army isn't keen on imparting estate management skills.' He gave a soft chuckle at his humour. 'I am home to be a husband to you, to have a marriage with you, a real marriage this time.'

He was acknowledging the imperfections of what had lain between them in the past and his part in that. It was her turn to stare, all her girlish hopes surging to the fore, refusing to be held back. Oh, what she would have given to hear those words from him years ago! Now, she didn't know what to make of them. If her question about his intention to stay had hindered *him*, his answer had positively stunned *her*. A *real* marriage? With this handsome man who both did and did not resemble the man she'd married in looks and deed?

What did he think a real marriage involved? Sex? Children? A family? Running an estate together? All of it or just some of it? As she stood in the autumn garden, surrounded by the vibrant colours of the leaves, the sun out, the autumn air crisp, it was easy to be swept away by his declaration, easy to dream. Even now, a nugget of hope blossomed at his words. Was the kind of union she'd always dreamed of within her grasp; one of love and mutual respect, one where husband and wife shared daily life together? The possibilities of what that marriage could hold were endless and tantalising. And frightening. To achieve such a thing would require great risk on her part, a risk she would not contemplate blindly. Broken hearts were not blithe considerations. Did he know what he asked of her with his declaration? How like the Fortis she'd known to consider only his wants without understanding the cost to others. She'd already paid the price once.

Avaline stepped back. They had drifted together as they talked and now she needed distance. She needed to remind herself she was not a green girl any longer. She'd given her innocent heart to this man once before, naively thinking that marriage inherently included love. She'd been proven wrong. She'd already seen what marriage had meant to Fortis Tresham. Nothing. It had meant absolutely nothing. It hadn't been worth a backward glance before going out hunting with his friends, or worth a single letter home. To trust that man again would be an enormous leap of faith, one she would not take carelessly.

He did not miss or misunderstand the movement. Hurt flashed in his blue eyes along with realisation. 'Avaline, are you sorry I am home?'

She did not answer immediately. He wished she had. He found himself wishing for many things in those critical seconds. He wished she'd flung herself into his arms and kissed away his doubts, that she'd murmured a rush of reassuring words. *No, no, no, how could you think such a thing? I'd never want you dead.* She'd done neither of those things. Instead, she'd moved away from him, separating herself from him, and that one step back communicated volumes long before she spoke the words, 'I don't know.'

It occurred to him the answer might have been different, better if he'd answered those beautiful letters he'd found in his campaign trunk. What a cad he must have been. But her answer might also have been *worse*, if Tobin Hayworth hadn't posed a threat to her. She might have said, 'Yes.' Yes, that she was sorry he was home, that he was a disruption to the life she'd carved out. He'd been gone for seven years and his wife wasn't sure if she was glad he was home, safe and mostly sound.

'You're honest, I appreciate that.' But, damn, the honesty hurt, like tearing off a scab and re-opening a wound, an all-too-apt metaphor, Fortis thought. Now that the family was gone and the first sweetness of homecoming past, it was time to get down to truths. The first truth was this: he had hurt her. He had hurt this lovely creature with his neglect and his absence. That he had done so was unconscionable. There was no question there. The real question was why had he done it? And why didn't he know?

The strength of those realisations sent him stumbling backwards to the stone bench set on the pathway and he sat down hard from the shock of it, the consequence of it. Avaline's dark eyes were shuttered and wary when they should have been full of warmth and hope. That's what he wanted to see when she looked at him. The intensity of that desire surged in him, strong and powerful, a testament to how much he wanted it. He wanted, he *needed*, his wife's approbation.

'I'm sorry, I shouldn't have said that.' Avaline looked suitably horrified. That was some consolation, he supposed, but he didn't want it at the expense of a lie. He wouldn't let her undervalue her own feelings to save his.

'Of course you should have. What you should *not* do is pretend that everything between us is suddenly perfect after a seven-year absence, any more than I should simply absolve myself by saying we never had a chance.' It would be so much easier if they could, though, if they could just start afresh as Fortis and Avaline. 'But this, my dear, Avaline, is an apology, if you'll accept it. I'm sorry I hurt you.' He was sorry, too, for why ever he'd done it. He hoped in time he might understand his reasons. 'We'll take this homecoming slowly. We will figure out what we can be together if you are willing to let me try again, although I'm bound to make mistakes.' He gave her a hopeful smile. He would try to make her happy. He would try to be a better man than the one he'd been before, a different man, one whom she'd be proud to have at her side.

Who the hell did Fortis Tresham think he was, crashing a party to which he was not invited and then assaulting the host? His actions were nothing short of barbaric. Tobin Hayworth nursed his jaw with a juicy slab of raw steak while he gingerly sipped an afternoon brandy. Eating luncheon had been out of the question. His jaw hurt twice as badly today as it had last night—something he'd not thought possible. He'd barely slept from the pain and he certainly hadn't attempted to chew anything. He still wasn't convinced his jaw wasn't broken, although the doctor, whom he'd roused in the middle of the night, assured him otherwise.

The only benefit to the pain was its clarifying properties. It brought into sharp relief the import of Fortis's return and all it meant. Blandford and its mistress were no longer accessible to him. He'd hoped to capitalise on Avaline being a baron's daughter to help solidify his candidacy for a knighthood. A living breathing husband was far more problematic to deal with than one who didn't come home. But Fortis Tresham had come home and at the crucial moment. For Avaline and the Treshams it couldn't have been more *fortuitous*, one might say, all puns aside. There was nothing funny about how conveniently Tresham had appeared just when he was starting to make his push with Avaline and with the courts. He'd begun the paperwork to declare Fortis Tresham dead a few days ago.

Tobin's stomach growled, rebelliously acknowledging it hadn't been fed since dinner the night before. He'd even missed the midnight supper on Avaline's account and now there was only soup to look forward to for supper tonight. He readjusted the steak. His jaw was eating better than he was. Of a certainty he'd have to withdraw his claims, but only temporarily. He did not think for a moment Tresham's return merely a coincidence. It was anything but. It was far too convenient after a year missing, after Major Lithgow's reputedly tearful meeting with the family in London last spring informing them that he had searched diligently for Tresham and come up empty-handed, that suddenly a man claiming to be Fortis Tresham had walked out of a Crimean forest and Lithgow had brought him home.

No, it reeked of rotten and he knew why. The Duke of Cowden despised him. On the surface, one might think the two neighbours would be bosom friends. Both were shrewd businessmen. Both had made fortunes through a series of lucrative, successful ventures. Cowden sat at the helm of an exclusive investment group known as the Prometheus Club, a nod to setting the world on fire with innovation or some such literary drivel Tobin didn't pretend to understand or enjoy. Tobin didn't have time for such niceties. He only had time for money and for people who made him money.

Therein lay the difference. He was well aware the Duke did not share his values or morals when it came to how money was made or how business was conducted. The Duke felt him to be a man with no scruples. Well, so be it. Scruples didn't keep one warm or fed. Only money did that.

Tobin drummed his free hand on the polished surface of the small table beside his chair, his feet resting comfortably on the fireplace fender. At least some part of him was comfortable as his facile mind went to work on this latest scheme. A missing man was home after an over-long, unsubstantiated absence. Perhaps someone should question that if Cowden didn't? By rights, Cowden ought to be the one questioning it. The son of a duke, even a third son, came with enormous advantages. Fortis Tresham, through his marriage, had an estate and a pretty wife. Through his birthright, he had access to the Cowden coffers, entrée into the highest echelons of society. Whatever he wanted to do, he could do it without much effort at all: diplomacy, politics, or simply do nothing. Tresham could afford the latter, too.

Surely Cowden was sharp enough to understand the temptation such a plum posed, or was Cowden too honourable to contemplate the allure? Perhaps Cowden believed too much in his unassailability to think that someone would attempt to grab Fortis's seat at the Cowden table. Cowden might be above envisioning such contretemps, but Tobin wasn't.

He could easily imagine someone doing just

that. He just needed to make Cowden imagine it as well and he would, as soon as his jaw healed sufficiently to pay a call and, in the most genuinely concerned way possible, voice his misgivings. After all, he didn't want anyone taking advantage of his dear neighbour, especially if the one taking advantage wasn't him. Meanwhile, if he couldn't talk to anyone, he could write. He could begin making polite enquiries about the nature of Fortis Tresham's return. He couldn't ask directly, of course. He wasn't family. No one was required to tell him anything. But he had friends on the inside, people whom he'd had contracts with and who would like to do lucrative business with him again. They could access information he could not.

He smiled to himself and poured another drink one-handed. It would be the scandal of the Season come spring if it came to fruition. Cowden would never live it down, especially if Tobin could prove the Duke had done it wilfully. Still, even if the man was a fraud and he'd swindled Cowden on his own, Cowden would look like a fool. It wouldn't do the old man's business reputation any good. People would finally think he was losing his touch. That all assumed the news came out. If the opportunity arose, Tobin would give Cowden a chance to keep the secret. Tobin was very good at keeping secrets, for a price, and this, if it were true, would be a secret that kept on giving.

He toasted himself in victory. It seemed every cloud did have a silver lining. Now, he had to prove it. All of this was merely conjecture until he had evidence. But if the evidence was there, he would find it. A dog with a bone could hardly compete. Tobin Hayworth was nothing if not tenacious.

Chapter Four

He was nothing if not tenacious and tenacity was what would get him off this battlefield alive. He was not going to die here in the muck and blood of Balaclava. He'd not survived this long to give up now. He crawled, all elbows and hips, belly to the ground in an ignoble undulation as he dragged himself towards what he hoped was safety. His arm hurt, his leg ached and he had to admit that some—no, a lot of the blood on him was his own. He was wounded. There'd been ample opportunity; the musket ball that whined past his ear could have grazed him after all, the sabre that had sliced at him could have caught him in the arm, the bayonet he'd dodged might have stuck his leg before glancing off. He was lucky to be alive and he knew it. But luck meant scrabbling through

the remains of battle, looking dead men in the eye and keeping his own fears of joining them at bay, which was a very real possibility each moment he remained on the field and the sun sank closer to the horizon.

Panic threatened to grip him. He was fighting it as much as he was fighting to make his way forward. Panic would swallow him whole if he allowed. It was near dark. The scavengers would be out soon and they would show no mercy as they rifled the pockets of the dead and the near dead. They'd kill him for his boots and his coat, which miraculously still had all its buttons. For people who had nothing, he was a slow, crawling, easy target of a gold mine and he had no strength left to fight them if they came.

He dragged himself forward, another inch, another body length, and another again, each effort sending a shooting pain through his arm. He fought back the stabbing agony in his leg. He'd nearly reached the edge of the battlefield, the sun almost gone from the sky, when he heard it—the faint, hoarse rasp of a desperate man. 'Help me.'

He should ignore it. He was wounded and barely able to help himself let alone someone else. He'd lingered too long on the field already. Even now, he could hear the voices of scavengers. There would be no mercy for him, a British soldier far from home, if he were caught. But because he did know the danger, he turned back. He could not doom someone else to that fate. He began to crawl awkwardly towards the plea... Someone was on him. Oh, dear God, he'd been found. The scavengers had found him—no, no, no. He kicked and grappled, trying to get hold of his attacker. He would not go down without a fight. Never mind that he was already down. This would be a fight to the death...

'Fortis! Wake up. You're home, you're safe.' The frantic words penetrated the fog of his brain, but still he grappled, unwilling to release his foe, unwilling to take the chance that the battlefield was the dream and home the reality. It would be a fatal mistake if he were wrong. He had his assailant now, his fists were full of white cloth.

'Fortis! It's me, Avaline!' At the desperate words, the dream let go, his eyes flew open in horror and recognition. Avaline was beneath him, her dark eyes wide with incredulity and fright. She had not understood what she'd walked into when she'd tried to wake him.

He let go of her at once and rolled on to his back, his mind taking stock. He was sweat-drenched and breathing hard, but he was home and alive, and he'd attacked his own wife. He pushed a hand through his hair. What must she think of him? 'Avaline, I'm sorry.' He was so *damned* sorry. Beside him, Avaline lay breathing hard, her gaze riveted on the ceiling as she collected herself. This was hardly the way to get back into his wife's good graces. She would think him every bit the fragile man Cam's report suggested he might be. Any moment, as soon as her shock settled, she'd realise that and bolt from the room.

Instead, Avaline turned her head and looked at him. 'I'm the one who should be sorry. Ferris warned me the dreams could be dangerous, but when I heard you call out…well, I couldn't just leave you alone.' She was kindness itself and it had cost them both.

'What did I say?' Hopefully nothing embarrassing. This was awful enough as it was without sounding like a whimpering fool. His wife was courageous. He didn't know many men, let alone women, who willingly ran towards trouble, yet despite her misgivings over his return, she'd come to him in his need. The gesture overwhelmed him with its implicit generosity. Perhaps she wasn't as indifferent to him as she'd tried to be in the garden. She'd been guarded then, her mind alert and on full defence. She'd made it clear that beyond protection from Hayworth, his return was met with reserve.

'Help. You simply said help.' But he hadn't just *said* help, he'd *yelled* it, loud enough to be heard through the adjoining door between their rooms. Great. He'd called out in his sleep like a frightened child. New, waking panic gripped him at the thought. Who else had heard? Had he awakened any of the servants? Would they all be staring at him at breakfast? Whispering behind his back that the master was home and not right in his head?

Avaline stroked his cheek with the cool back of her hand, a soft smile on her face. It felt good, comforting. He wanted her to go on touching him. Did she realise she was touching him? That they were lying side by side in bed in nothing but their nightclothes? She'd been very conscious of their closeness today in the drawing room and in the garden. Did she only touch him now out of pity? He would not take her touch of pity. Fortis closed a gentle grip around her wrist and pushed her hand away. 'Avaline, I am not an invalid.'

She stiffened—the rejection, though politely done, had clearly stung—but she was not defeated. 'I know. But you are a soldier returned after a harrowing experience. You are not entirely yourself. Yet. But you will be, in time.'

How much time? he wondered. It had been three weeks since he'd left the Crimea with Cam and it had been nearly three months since he'd walked out of the forest in July. He felt just as confused now as he had the day he'd walked into camp, the missing blocks of his memory still as jumbled, sometimes even more so after the army had filled in the missing pieces. He would have thought that would have helped, not make it worse.

'Let me help,' Avaline soothed, her hand back at his brow, and this time he let it stay, craven fool that he was. He told himself it was only because he'd gone so long without female companionship. 'Tell me your dream.'

'No.' He would not tell her. He did not want her burdened with the horrors of his ghosts. One did not tell an angel about hell. An angel was what she was, in her white nightgown, her blonde hair loose and spilling over her shoulder and by some miracle she was *his* angel, one he did not deserve. He would not sully her with tales of battlefields and dead men.

She gave a nod. 'Then, perhaps you'll tell Ferris or write them down.'

'Perhaps I will.' He could give her that concession. 'I'm fine now, Avaline. You can go back to bed.' He doubted he'd sleep the rest of the night. He seldom did once he dreamed. He'd sat up more than one night on the journey home, on the deck of the ship looking up at the stars until the sun rose. Sometimes Cam had sat with him. Cam had dreams, too. His wife, Pavia, had herbs that helped. Cam swore by them, but Fortis had been too proud to take them at the time. Now that there was Avaline to consider, he might need to rethink Pavia's offer. He couldn't go around assaulting his wife at night. Tonight it had just been wrestling. Heaven help her if he ever got his hands on a weapon.

Avaline got out of bed without protest. She smoothed her nightgown, seeming flustered. Perhaps the intimacy of their situation had dawned on her. 'I am just next door if you need anything.'

'Goodnight,' Fortis said firmly. 'I'm fine. I'm sure it was brought on by nothing more than the rigours of recent events.' He wanted to reassure her. 'After all, it's not every day a man is reunited with his family and his wife. This is nothing sleep and hard work can't fix.' If he was busy, it would take his mind off the past. The journey home had allowed him too much time with his own thoughts. Frederick was right. He needed to get his boots on the ground. He'd start tomorrow with a tour of the estate. He'd have Avaline show him around. A man who worked until he was exhausted didn't have time for nightmares. He would show her his strength. He would not be a burden to her. Most of all, he would make sure she wasn't sorry he'd come home.

He'd dismissed her! Avaline sat down hard on the edge of her bed, sorry she'd ever raced to his side. His cries had awakened her. They'd been dreadful in their desperation, the sounds of a man who'd reached the edges of his sanity and was about to lose hold. In her haste to comfort him, she'd forgotten everything in-

cluding Ferris's warning. She'd raced recklessly
to his side, her one thought being that no one
should be so tortured. Her empathy had not
been enough armour.

She'd not been prepared for what she'd en-
countered; a raging bear of a man whose mind
had seen her as an enemy. He'd attacked the
moment she'd touched him, his war-taut body
tight-sprung. She'd been no match for his
strength. She'd found herself beneath him,
crushed between the hardness of his body and
the mattress, and when she had managed to
wake him, he'd not been glad to see her. No
matter how polite he'd tried to be about it, the
message was still the same. He'd sent her away
as soon as he could.

Avaline lit the lamp beside her bed and
picked up a book. She wasn't likely to sleep
any time soon. Her mind was too full of disappointment. She hadn't realised how much hope
she'd inadvertently put into his words from the
garden today. He'd said he wanted a real marriage and, despite her best attempts not to, she'd
wanted to believe him.

But in a real marriage, husbands and wives
told each other everything: the good, the bad,
their hopes and their fears. Tonight, he hadn't

been able to tell her his dream. Tonight, he'd turned her away when she'd brought comfort. Tonight in his room was not that different from the last time she'd been in there…

'You're going out?' Avaline stood in the doorway connecting their two rooms. She'd not been in his room since he'd taken up residence. It seemed empty, devoid of personality, and he hadn't even left yet. But he was already packed. His trunk stood strapped and ready for departure in the corner. She had the sudden sensation that maybe he'd never unpacked.

Fortis turned from the mirror where he was straightening his stock. 'Yes. You needn't wait up for me. The boys and I are going to make a night of it at the tavern in the village. One last hurrah before I am off again to parts unknown. You understand. It will be ages before I see them again.'

'But you leave tomorrow,' Avaline stammered her protest. What about her? It would be ages before he saw her again, too. 'I thought we could have supper together, just the two of us.' She'd had the cook prepare all his favourites: jugged hare, fresh vegetables and bread. They hadn't had an evening alone since their

wedding, three weeks ago. Every night had been filled with a never-ending round of dinners given in the newlyweds' honour in lieu of there being time for a proper wedding trip.

What there hadn't been time for was getting to know her new husband, but she seemed to be the only one bothered by this. Fortis appeared perfectly happy with the arrangement and, if he'd expected to spend his leave in bed with his new bride, he gave no indication he was disappointed it had turned out otherwise. After the dinners, he'd sent her home alone while he'd gone out with his friends. Tonight was her last chance to make up for whatever failings he might have found in her on their wedding night.

'I'll wait up. We can have a nightcap together.' Avaline tried once more.

'No need. As I said, the boys and I will likely make a night of it. I'll be home with the sun, long enough to get my trunk. The train leaves at eight.' He was all brisk efficiency, not a single note of remorse in his tone.

'Perhaps you might manage a goodbye kiss if you can spare the time,' Avaline said testily, her anger and disappointment getting the better of her. She hadn't known what to expect of

marriage, but she hadn't expected to be disregarded.

Her tone got his attention at last. 'Avaline, are you going to act like a spoiled child?' He shook his head in a mild gesture of despair. 'I told my parents you were too young. But they insisted. Your parents insisted. Now it seems I'm right. I am married to a child who expects her husband to stay home and play with her, a child who knows nothing of the world.'

The words stung. He thought her a child? A spoiled child at that, all because she'd wanted a piece of his attention? She raised her chin. 'I am not a child. I merely thought things would be different.'

'How so?' He pulled out his pocket watch, irritated that she was making him late. 'Let me spell this out for you. This is not a fairy tale where we suddenly fall in love.' He strode from the room without a word of apology, without even a chaste kiss on her cheek. The message could not be clearer. Her husband wasn't interested in loving her.

She'd been dismissed then, too. Not much had changed, after all. She'd been right to reserve judgement about the man who'd returned to her, right to protect her heart from making a fool of herself again. She blew out her lamp, finally exhausted, one last thought lingering as she drifted to sleep. Maybe the old adage was true. The more things changed, the more they stayed the same. That was certainly proven tonight, although a part of her wished it hadn't. Part of her wanted to believe the man in the garden wanted the same things she wanted and that he was capable of giving her those things.

Chapter Five

~~~~~~~~~~~~~~~

He was going to exhaust himself before supper at this rate. Avaline stopped long enough from helping with lunch preparations to watch her husband with the tenants as they thatched a roof. Perhaps that was his plan. Work hard, sleep hard in order to avoid the bad dreams by night and perhaps his wife by day.

For all the differences she saw in Fortis, that one hadn't changed. Last night had driven that home. He'd never had time for her and it seemed he still didn't. No doubt he'd brought her today to tour the estate because he'd needed her to make introductions. The sooner she could accept that, the sooner she could move forward with constructing what her new life as Fortis's wife would look like.

The sight of him working made it difficult

to harden her heart entirely. It had pleased and surprised her to see his willingness to join in. He'd never shown an interest in the estate before. Perhaps he'd meant that piece at least when he said he'd come to home to help with Blandford. It gave her a different kind of hope. The new life they could have together might not be the fairy tale she yearned for, but perhaps neither would it be as disappointing as their past. They might be able to use their dedication to Blandford to build a foundation between them, one that in time would give way to respect and friendship. Many marriages were built on less. She could learn to be happy with that if she could just keep her fantasies in check. Something that was easier to say than to do, when one's handsome husband was up on the roof, flexing his muscles in shirtsleeves.

Avaline used a hand to shield her eyes against the sun. At some point in the morning, Fortis's coat had come off along with his waistcoat, his shirt open at the neck, the once carefully laundered garment now sporting splotches of sweat and grime. His trousers were dusty from hauling up the bundles of straw. He paused on the roof, straightening for a moment to wipe the sweat from his brow. It was heated work, hard work, even beneath an October sun. The day was clear and crisp, the not-so-subtle hint of oncoming winter in the air, yet the efforts of labour were evidenced in the steam off his body.

What a body it was. Even at a distance, she couldn't help but be aware of it, of him. Shoulders strained tirelessly beneath his shirt; long, booted legs strode confidently on the flat of the roof with athletic grace, old buckskin breeches showing well-muscled thighs, never mind that most men of his class had eschewed breeches for trousers. 'No sense in ruining perfectly good trousers,' he'd told her this morning when she'd raised a questioning eyebrow at his attire. That was new, too, another piece of reality the military must have drilled into him: thrift, frugality. The Fortis she'd married had been fashion conscious. Not a dandy, certainly, but always well-turned-out. Too bad breeches weren't back in fashion. She liked the look. He wore them well. Extremely well. Well enough to make a girl forget quite a lot of things, ranging from helping the women lay out a luncheon to the risks of wagering one's heart on a fool's prospect. Perhaps she wasn't beyond such foolishness as she thought. If so, she would need to be on her guard.

'Let me take those.' Mrs Baker came to help her with the basket of apples on her arm and she felt silly for standing about gawking at a man who'd dismissed her from his bedroom last night.

'I'm sorry, Mrs Baker, I was just bringing the basket to the table,' Avaline apologised hastily.

The woman smiled knowingly, following the recent trajectory of her gaze. 'You must be thrilled to have him home, such a handsome man, and the two of you only married a short while before he had to leave. You can make up for lost time now.'

'Yes, of course,' Avaline replied automatically and hurried off to put the apples on the table. Perhaps she should take a cue from Fortis and immerse herself in work as well. Then she, too, would be less inclined to spend so much thought on his return. Perhaps it would indeed be possible to simply go on from here without confronting the past. Perhaps she should just accept Fortis as he was. She could not make him love her and it was hardly his fault that once she'd thought to love him. That had been her choice.

It was clear that was what Fortis meant to do. He'd been congenial at breakfast, stating his intention of meeting the tenants. He'd asked questions about the estate while they ate, showing a considerable interest in how she'd run things. That interest had been both welcome and unnerving. On the one hand, she was grateful to be able to lay down the burden. Estate management had not come naturally to her, but she'd learned. She'd had no choice. There'd been no one else. Between herself and her land steward, Mr Benning, they had managed admirably. On the other hand, as relieved as she was to surrender the burden, there was a sense of loss, too. She *had* done admirably. She'd come to take pride in how she'd made ends meet and kept the estate going against considerable odds and debt. She would miss that challenge. Her role now would be reduced back to playing Lady Bountiful and delivering baskets. After seven years of free rein, it was something of a demotion.

A long arm darted around her and grabbed an apple in a lightning-quick move. 'I'm famished!' Fortis laughed when she whirled around, startled. He took a big, crunchy bite of the fruit and finished off the apple in four bites. He reached for another, looking entirely boyish. He might have been any one of them instead of a duke's son. She liked the notion of that—*one of them*, a part of Blandford in a way he'd never been a part of it before. Before, Blandford had been a nuisance, merely a piece of land he held for his father, not a home as she saw it. She'd grown up here. It was all she knew. Yes, perhaps her earlier thought was right—with Blandford between them, they could build something together out of their marriage.

'There's meat and bread, too,' she offered, smiling back. It was hard not to. His smile was intoxicating, his good humour contagious and, as long as she was honest with herself about the limits of what this marriage could provide, it was safe to indulge. This man was easy to be with, perhaps even easy to work with. The men seemed to like him. She'd heard them joking up on the roof, bits of their conversation and laughter floating down to the ground. That was new, too, or was it that she'd not had time to discover it? Had all this good will and good humour been there and she hadn't noticed? Perhaps she'd been too wrapped up in her own needs and disappointments to truly see him? 'Let me make you something,' Avaline offered.

'I can make my own bread and meat.' He grinned, stretching around her again. The action brought his body close to her, the smell of morning soap and afternoon sweat combining for a masculine appeal all its own. He assembled a stack of bread and meat and gave her a wink. 'Come on, let's find a place to sit before John has us back up there slaving away again.'

'John?' Avaline asked in surprise. A duke's son was on first-name basis with a tenant farmer?

'John Wicks.' Fortis found them a piece of grass and sat down without ceremony. She joined him, tucking her skirts beneath her.

'I know Mr Wicks. He's a good man. He's a leader among the tenants. He worked with me and Mr Benning to take care of those who needed it most while you were gone.' Something nudged at her arm and she looked down to see Fortis holding out bread and sliced ham. 'What's this?'

'Your lunch. You didn't think I grabbed all of this for me or that I would eat it all in front of you?' He laughed. 'Take it.'

'Thank you, that was very…thoughtful.'

He stretched out long legs that drew the eye. 'John speaks highly of you. He says you've done a masterful job of keeping the estate going. He says Benning is a good man, too.'

'You'll want to look over the ledgers and decide where to go from here,' Avaline offered generously, blushing from the praise. He would never know how much it cost her to make that offer, to begin turning the estate over to him, the running of her home handed over to a veritable stranger, never mind they'd grown up as neighbouring families. Fortis was seven years older than she was. It wasn't as if they'd roamed the fields together. He'd already had a commission in the military by the time she was thirteen.

Fortis knit his brow. '*I'm* to make the decision? It seems I might be the worst possible person to do that at this point. I'm the one who knows the least what the estate needs. It seems that perhaps Mr Benning and yourself, myself, and perhaps John Wicks and others like him should make those decisions. I'd appreciate it, Avaline, if we handled the reins of the estate together.'

He paused and she almost choked on the ham. 'You want my input?' she stammered.

'Yes,' he answered simply. 'Unless you don't wish to offer it? Perhaps you want to lay it all down?'

'No. Not at all,' Avaline said firmly lest she accidentally throw this unexpected gift away.

'I would be pleased if you would consult me. I will help in any way I can.'

'Good.' He gave her an infectious grin and swallowed the last of his lunch. 'It looks as though John wants to get back at it.' He rose and held out a hand to help her up. It was a natural enough gesture, a casual one. But Avaline hesitated, feeling as if taking his hand signalled something more, a sealing of their partnership, or at the very least, an acknowledgement of it. Was she ready for that? She supposed she didn't have a choice. Ready or not, Fortis was here, offering his hand, and, in time, perhaps he might offer her something more. Avaline reached up and took it, aware of all the flaws and hope that came with the gesture.

Chapter Six

⚬⚬⚬⚬⚬

That little flame of hope flickered doggedly throughout the week, tempting Avaline with possibilities of what might be with its persistence as she began to reconcile the old with the new. The days took on a pleasant pattern not unlike that first day. Fortis rose early. He breakfasted with her and discussed plans before he rode out—that was new. Never once had Fortis sought her opinion. New, too, was his interest in the estate he'd disparaged early in their marriage. He spent his days with the tenants, working feverishly against the weather to complete the necessary autumn preparations before winter arrived in force and he came home each night, exhausted, retiring to his chambers and falling asleep almost immediately after dinner, only to rise the next morning and start it all over again, as did she. That piece was old. The avoidance he'd once evinced in their marriage still remained. It was merely more politely done than it had been before. War could change a man in many ways, but war could not change a man entirely, it seemed.

Fortis was not the only one with patterns. She had her own regimen, too, her own attempts at establishing normalcy. After breakfast and seeing him off, she spent the mornings in the estate office, reading through correspondence, meeting with Mr Benning and going over accounts. In the late morning, knowing that Fortis wouldn't be home for lunch, she often rode out for exercise, for visiting or, like today, for sewing at Bramble with her sisters-in-law and the Duchess. She loved needlework and she loved her sisters-in-law. Together, the calm concentration of needlework and the comradeship of other women had been her lifeline as a new bride, then an abandoned bride, then as a potentially widowed bride. Through all the rigours of her marriage, the Tresham wives had remained steadfast in their friendship, supporting her, without ever once criticising her or their husbands' brother.

Avaline secured her sewing box to the saddle and accepted a leg up from the groom as she mounted her mare, a pretty chestnut with a sweet disposition who didn't mind the bouncing of the sewing kit against the saddle. She settled her skirts and took the reins, revelling in the sight of her frosty breath in the crisp morning. Winter was coming; indeed, it might already be here. Icy frost coated the green fields this morning, making them shimmer like diamonds beneath the sun.

Fortis and the men would be glad to finish the roofs today. Soon, it would be too icy to be climbing around without fear of slipping. She hoped it wasn't too slippery today. Avaline nudged her mare into a comfortable trot and set off for Bramble, determined to enjoy the beautiful morning ride. Good weather and time outdoors would be rare in the months ahead and contentment was always to be savoured, also being a rare commodity. She would spend the afternoon with her sisters-in-law and return to Blandford in advance of Fortis to make sure all was prepared for dinner and to change her dress.

Her days, like Fortis's, were full and that should be enough for her. His re-entry into her life had gone smoothly thus far. She should not ask for more of his homecoming. She should accept the pleasant, if superficial, pattern of their days. She should not poke the sleeping dog of their short but miserable past, nor question the internal workings of their current marriage. She should simply accept, as Fortis seemed to have done.

He seemed perfectly happy to simply go on from here and she ought to take her cue from him. If he did not wish to discuss the intimate status of their marriage, she should let it be. If he did not wish to share with her any of the last seven years, she should let that be as well. After all, this new version of Fortis was an improvement over the groom she'd known. Yes, this new Fortis still rode out every morning and was gone all day. But this new Fortis also waited for her to rise *before* he rode out. He consulted her, he took an interest in making her family home *their* home. He took an active part in estate life and was winning the respect of their tenants day by day with every roof he thatched. This new Fortis empowered her to keep looking after the estate business. This new Fortis still went to bed without her, but he also looked on her with a blue-eyed intensity that said he was aware of her, that he found her beautiful.

It was these differences that fed that tenacious little spark of hope. While much was the same between them, much was also different.

That difference made her greedy. It made her wonder—if things could be this good with having expended very little effort, how much better could things be if she and Fortis broached the difficult topics that lay between? How much fuller would her life be if she had a husband in truth like her sisters-in-law? Men with whom they shared everything, men with whom they did not lead separate lives while living under the same roof? But such a wondrous thing came at great cost. In truth, Avaline was not sure she was ready to pay that cost. She did not want Fortis to break her heart again, yet the temptation dangled like a carrot before a reluctant horse, urging it onwards as the week went on. It was hard to not like her husband and she feared liking would soon become something else if she gave in to the former.

Avaline turned into the drive at Bramble and tossed her reins to a groom. A well-trained servant stood by to retrieve her sewing kit and show her to the sitting room where the women were already assembled. 'I am sorry I'm a little late, I took some extra time to enjoy the morning.'

'We're sure you did.' The women exchanged knowing smiles that made Avaline blush at the implication. Heavens! They thought she'd spent the morning in bed with Fortis.

Avaline smoothed the skirts of her riding habit. 'It's not what you think!' she gasped. 'I was just admiring the scenery.' But that only made it worse.

'As you should be, dear Avaline. You've had little scenery to admire for years and you have quite a handsome "landscape" on which to feast your eyes.' Anne laughed.

Helena took mercy and patted the seat beside her on the cosy sofa. 'Then we're disappointed for you. Come, have some tea before we sew and tell us all about life at Blandford now that you and Fortis have had a week to settle in. I hear he's been working hard.'

Helena pressed a painted china cup in her hands and she gave them the sanitised version of the week, very similar to the version she'd told herself on the ride over. But in the telling, in hearing the words out loud, she was achingly cognisant of all that was missing. She made no mention of the nightmare, or of Fortis's reticence to discuss anything that wasn't estate related. He'd dismissed her from his bedroom and not invited her back. It was the only blemish on an otherwise amicable week.

'It sounds as if you've established a very pleasant pattern between you,' Anne offered encouragingly. Did she imagine pity beneath Anne's encouragement? She didn't want their pity. 'A very pleasant pattern' seemed to be a polite euphemism for something empty. Sitting with these women who were in love with their husbands shed a different light on the definition of her days. She'd been so sure she could live with 'pleasant patterns', up until now. Those patterns wouldn't force her or Fortis to acknowledge a distasteful past. But in exchange for that peace, there was a limit to the future they could have.

'Have you decided what you're going to make Fortis for a Christmas gift?' Helena asked, getting her own sewing out of her basket. It was a Cowden family tradition that the wives all made a handicraft for their husbands. This year, she'd be able to participate in full. She had an actual husband to give a gift to.

'A shirt,' Anne said naughtily. 'Then you can

have the pleasure of putting it on him and taking it off.'

'I should think she wouldn't need to wait until Christmas to undress him,' Helena replied with a laugh.

'And I should think,' the Duchess put in, fixing her beloved daughters-in-law with a friendly but stern look, 'that Avaline and Fortis will find their own way in their own time.' Avaline gave the Duchess a thankful look. These women were her friends. They had supported her through seven years of difficulty, never once blaming her when Fortis left when it would have been easy to do so. Yet she didn't want to share intimate, uncomfortable truths with them for fear that they might think she was complaining about her husband.

To voice her worries seemed disloyal to both the Treshams and to Fortis. Avaline picked up her sewing and asked after Helena's boys instead. Perhaps the Duchess was right. It was up to she and Fortis to find their way together, alone. Without family intervention, friendly as it was. She glanced out the window to the sunny, cold afternoon. If she wanted to see what kind of intimacy was possible, she'd have to take the risk and be the one to make the first move, the one to reach out with a toe and test the proverbial ice, to see what sort of weight it would hold before it cracked.

The beams of the roof structure would crack under too much weight. Fortis balanced carefully on top of the last roof, cognisant of shifting his weight to avoid snapping a beam as he shaded his eyes against the last rays of sun. They had a half-hour of daylight left and the roof would get slippery again as it had been this morning, when the temperatures dropped. 'We have to work fast, John. If we don't finish by daylight, we'll be forced to break out the lanterns,' he called down. He didn't like the idea of flames, it posed its own dangers to thatch. Hopefully, they'd finish before that was necessary, though. The beautiful but cold weather had conspired against them today, making speed impossible this morning with slippery rooftops, and they were paying for the delay now.

'I'll come up and help. Two of us up here will make the work go faster.' John was already climbing.

'Just be careful, I don't like this structure. It's weaker than I'd prefer,' Fortis cautioned. There hadn't been time or the resources to replace some of the worst beams. The frame would last the winter and in the spring they could replace the entire roof instead of doing it piecemeal now. But Fortis was regretting that decision. He wanted to get this roof finished and get off it before someone went sailing into Mrs Dabner's stew pot in the fireplace below.

The only supper he was interested in was whatever Avaline had on the table tonight. If they didn't speed up, he'd be late for dinner, arguably one of the best parts of his day. He loved riding up the drive to Blandford at twilight, seeing the warm lamps welcoming him through the windows and knowing Avaline awaited him within. It felt unnervingly like a fairy tale that could be snatched away at any moment, that he'd wake up and discover his home, his wife, was all a dream, that somehow he didn't deserve this.

Despite all that he couldn't remember of his life up to this point, the life he lived now was unbelievably good and full, more than he'd ever imagined, and he was reluctant to test the limits of that goodness, to see how far it extended. Although he was tempted.

Was Avaline? He'd promised to take it slow,

not to rush her. She was cautious about him and for good reason. He understood he had to earn her trust. He had to prove himself worthy of her. But he wanted more than conversations about the estate. He wanted to follow up their long conversations with even longer kisses. He wanted her in his arms, in his bed.

They were nearly done when Fortis heard it: the ominous crack of a beam. He turned to shout a warning to John, but it was too late. The man was already slipping, the very footing beneath him falling away as he struggled for purchase. 'John! Take my hand!' Fortis threw himself across the roof, extending his arm in a flash of movement. He grabbed for John, gripping his hand. 'I've got you. Hold on!' Fortis offered his other hand and hauled him up until the two men lay side by side on the roof, breathing hard. It wasn't until they were both back on the ground that Fortis started to shake.

'Tresham, are you all right?' John asked amid the congratulatory backslapping. The men had surrounded them, praising his quick thinking.

'No, I'm not.' He had to get away, had to get

off the battlefield. 'We have to go, we have to get out of here, the scavengers are coming.'

'Tresham, it's all right. You're safe.' Someone was talking to him, then to someone else. 'Send to Bramble for Dr Tresham.'

No, the scavengers were sending for reinforcements. He was frantic now. He pushed through the crowd, desperately seeking out space, a place to run, a place to hide. He had to get to safety. Fortis broke away and started to sprint. He was nearly free of them now. The scavengers were behind him, still coming. He could hear them. He threw himself on his belly. He had to save himself, he had to get to the wounded man. He wouldn't leave the man to face the scavengers who would surely kill him.

He crawled awkwardly towards the plea. A man lay on the ground, half of his body pinned beneath an enormous horse. The half he could see was bloodied from a cut to the temple, not unlike his own. 'I'm here. Help is here,' he reassured the man, although he wasn't sure how much help he'd be with an aching arm and wounded leg. 'Can you walk if we get this horse off you?' There was no question of moving the entire horse, but perhaps if he could lever the body up just enough for the man to wriggle out from underneath? He glanced about, looking for something to use. The Russians had been loading the cannons with anything they could find at the end and firing on anything that moved, even their own men.

There! A plank, just a short distance away, perhaps from a supply wagon or an ambulance. He crawled to it and retrieved it. 'Help me slide this beneath the horse,' he instructed. 'Now, be ready to wriggle out. We won't get many chances, I haven't the strength.' He had to get up on his legs to apply pressure to the lever and his own injured leg wouldn't hold for long. Even now as he rose into position, he could feel his leg tremble from the effort. 'On the count of three.'

One. Two. Three. He put the full force of his remaining energy into the lift. The body elevated marginally. 'Come on, now!' he encouraged the man between gritted teeth. One wriggle, then another and the man was free. He collapsed beside the wounded man in the dirt, breathing hard. 'Can you walk?' he asked again, this time more for himself. He was going to need this man's help now. Other than the horse landing on him, the man looked unhurt where it counted: arms, legs. All the things one needed to escape a ruined battlefield.

Together, supporting each other, they got to their feet and began a slow stumble towards shelter and safety. Once they'd cleared the field, it was obvious something more was wrong with the man, something unseen. His own leg might be unreliable, but he could treat that. Given time, that would come out aright. An unseen injury meant internal damage. That was dangerous and often untreatable. The man was breathing hard by the time they found a cave in the forest with a small creek nearby. A cave meant they could risk a little fire. Water meant they could treat their injuries. 'It's going to be all right,' he told the man, 'I'll take care of you. We're safe here.'

He settled the man against a wall and set up camp as best he could. There was just his pack between the two of them and whatever was on their persons. He took stock as he unpacked: a tin camp cup, a tin dish and utensils, a small pot. Three days' worth of rations, a bedroll and his flint. He half-limped, half-crawled his way to the creek for water and managed to drag back enough wood for a small fire.

'Treat yourself first,' the man ordered

*hoarsely when he knelt to tend him. 'I can wait.'
The man was in pain, but not from anything he
could easily see.*

*He nodded at the advice and began to strip
out of his clothes. His stock would have to be
sacrificed for bandages and his shirt would
have to double as a towel. He began to wash
his cuts, wincing as water found the vertical
red line running from shoulder to elbow. His
arm would need resting for a while, but it would
heal. He'd fashion a sling for it once he'd taken
care of his patient. The slice on his leg was
deeper, but God willing it wouldn't leave him
with a permanent limp.*

*Bandaged and clean, he turned his atten-
tion to the wounded man, cleaning the blood
at his temple. 'This is just a graze. I'll ban-
dage it and it should be fine. Where else are
you hurt?' He worked open the man's coat and
shirt and sucked in his breath. 'Your horse fell
on you?' It was mainly a rhetorical question.
The man's torso showed signs of severe bruis-
ing. 'Is it hard to breathe? I imagine your ribs
are...compromised.' He chose his word carefully. Compromised could mean sore, bruised,
cracked, broken. A broken rib was dangerous,*

deadly even. But he would not say so to a man who'd survived today's debacle of a battle.

The man's eyes, blue eyes the colour of pale lapis, like his own, a woman had once told him, met his gaze, soldier steady. The man wasn't fooled, having seen enough of battle to know what was being held back despite the careful words. 'Compromised? You're being delicate, I think. I suppose we'll know soon enough how bad it is.'

'I'll bind them. It will help.' Matter-of-factly, he tore his shirt into strips. He'd have to rely on his coat to keep him warm. Thankfully, the weather was still pleasant in the Crimea even if the military climate was not. 'Then I'll see to dinner and getting you moved to the bedroll.'

'Thank you,' the man managed to say, his eyes on him as he went awkwardly went about the chores, sometimes limping, sometimes crawling. 'You will be rewarded for your gallantry, sir...'

'I didn't drag you from the battlefield for reward,' he answered gruffly. 'I wouldn't leave anyone to those scavengers.' A noise outside had him on alert and he held up a hand to silence the patient. They were in no condition to defend themselves if anyone came upon them

now. He reached for his rifle and prayed there wouldn't be more than one intruder. His muscles tensed. With his arm wounded, he might only be able to hold steady long enough to get off one good shot. But by the heavens, he would go down fighting.

'Fortis! Fortis! You're safe. Let me take care of you. Brother, please, wake up.'

He couldn't move, couldn't fight. The words made no sense to him. They were only repeated. He struggled, but succeeded only in opening his eyes. The world spun. He felt nauseous and cold. He made an incoherent noise in the back of his throat. He was going to be sick. Hands that had held him down supported him now, lifting him into sitting position. Just in time. He retched into the dirt and grass of the forest floor. The world started to settle. Someone wrapped a blanket around his shoulders. His vision focused. Ferris squatted in front of him; John and Avaline were there, Avaline ghostly pale.

'You're in the forest on the edge of Blandford village,' Ferris said softly, searching for the pulse at his wrist. That didn't seem right. He'd been in the Crimea, on the battlefield. 'Do you know how you got here?' Ferris asked, moving his hand to his forehead, checking for signs of fever.

'No.' His answer was straightforward. He had nothing more to add. Should he?

Avaline knelt beside him, taking his hand. 'What is the last thing you remember?'

He looked at John, questions filling his answers. 'We were on the roof? You fell?' How could that be when he was in the Crimea? How could he be both here at Blandford and there in Russia? He looked about at his surroundings. 'Where's the other man? The wounded man?'

Ferris held his gaze, firmly, calmly. 'There is no other man, Fortis.'

He shook his head violently. 'No, there was a man. I pulled him off the battlefield. We limped into the forest. I found a cave and a stream where we could tend our wounds. I can't leave him, Ferris. Please.' He was begging now. 'I told him I'd take care of him.' He struggled to his feet, shaking off John's restraining hand. 'Please, Ferris, we cannot desert him. I gave my word.'

Ferris had a hand on his chest. 'Fortis, you had a flashback. Listen to me. You were thatching a roof. You saved John from falling, but it seems the event brought back memories of the battlefield. Balaclava took place a year ago.'

Fortis furrowed his brow. Was there really no wounded man here in the forest? It had seemed so real. Something wasn't right. He gripped his brother's sleeve. 'Ferris, there was a second man. I wasn't alone in the forest,' he insisted. 'Not this forest, I mean. The Crimean forest. In the cave.'

Avaline stepped forward, fragile and strong all at once. 'Let's go home, Fortis. A hot bath and a hot meal will have you feeling better.' He sensed she said it as much for himself as she did for her. Worry was etched in her eyes and he saw how much he'd frightened her. Again. First the nightmare, now this.

'I'm sorry, Avaline.' What a poor husband he was turning out to be, a man who couldn't separate the present from the past, dreams from reality. Surely, a man of strength should be able to do so. Suddenly, he was seeing himself through her eyes, John's eyes, the eyes of the men of the village. He'd run off into the forest like a mad man, screaming God knew what nonsense about scavengers and invisible wounded men. He was filthy now, covered in pine needles and dead leaves. Good Lord, had he crawled through the dirt? Why the hell couldn't he remember anything useful?

Avaline looped her arm firmly through his, lending him her strength. 'Don't be ashamed, Fortis. Absolutely do not be ashamed. I won't have it. We're going home.'

He drew a deep, steadying breath. Home, where the lamps would be burning in the windows, welcoming him back.

Chapter Seven

It was an incomplete homecoming—a fact driven home to her by the sight of Fortis curled up in a ball beneath a tree in the woods, affirming the incompleteness that had niggled at her since the sewing circle earlier that day.

Avaline shut the door to her chambers behind her and leaned against it, eyes closed, searching for peace. The last hour and a half had been horrifying from the moment a message had come to Bramble, short and terse, saying only, 'There's been an accident in Blandford,' to the moment they'd found Fortis and even the moments after that when it had become shockingly clear just how deep Fortis's trauma ran. But more than the sight of him, the story he'd told with such passion and intensity had shattered any illusion that her husband was acclimatising well to being home.

The misgivings and hopes she'd mulled over as she'd ridden out this morning under blue skies, spirits high, seemed petty by comparison to what had happened. There was so much more to Fortis's homecoming besides their marriage. She could not pretend he rode out every day and worked to exhaustion just because he wanted to prove himself to her, to the estate, or because he wanted to take up his new role as a full-time landowner. He worked to exhaustion in an attempt to forget, an attempt to avoid his nightmares. But those nightmares had found him anyway in the waking light of day.

What did she do with this husband of hers, a man she'd never really known and knew even less now? Be patient, Ferris had said. Love him. It was easy for Ferris to speak of love. He had Anne and anyone could see the love between them. But she and Fortis? Ferris didn't understand what he was asking of her, yet she was not without compassion. She'd be lying to say that her husband, the man who'd returned to her, didn't raise any feelings, despite her better judgement.

How many times over breakfast this week

had she caught herself staring at him when he filled his plate and then offered to fill hers? Studying the strong line of his profile, the line of his nose, the curve of his jaw, the definition of his body beneath his clothes: the broad shoulders, the lean hips and firm buttocks. Most of all, that smile that lit up his face, that twinkled his eyes. She remembered his eyes with a little less light in them, eyes that were always fixed on something other than her. Not so now. Those blue eyes were all hers and far merrier. It was hard to not be attracted to that man.

There were the niceties, too. She wasn't so shallow as to think attraction was all about looks. He remembered what she liked, he'd eaten lunch with her that first day in the village instead of going to stand with the other men. These were the actions of a considerate gentleman. But they came as part and parcel of a man who was also broken inside, tortured by memories and by the lack of them, his world a kaleidoscope of fragments. It would take courage to love him.

Her maid entered and helped her change into a loose gown and she gave instructions to have supper brought to Fortis's room. They would dine together there tonight, surrounded by candlelight and solitude and maybe that would bring her husband peace. Maybe it would bring her peace. Before she could help him, she needed to beard her own ghosts in the very chamber that made them.

When she was ready, Avaline opened the connecting door and stepped into her husband's chamber, a place she had not visited since the last night Fortis had been home. She'd been prepared to fight back unpleasant memories. Things had not ended well that evening. But she'd not been prepared for this: he was naked. And wet. And gloriously fresh from his bath.

Whatever she'd imagined when she'd undressed him with her eyes over the breakfast table paled in comparison to the reality before her. This man was all warrior. The smooth, broad expanse of his chest gave way to a defined atlas of muscled abdomen and long, muscle-moulded legs, whose perfection was marred—or was it enhanced?—by the white scar running from hip to knee, perhaps a mate to the scar on his arm. But instead of distracting, it served only to draw the eye to that most male part of him. She should look away, but Avaline found she could not. His member, even in a partial state of arousal, was as strong, large and potent as the rest of him.

'Do I still look the same, give or take a few scars?' He turned his leg, looking down at the scar. 'I got that from a bayonet.' He lifted his arm. 'This one from a sabre-slice,' he joked, but it only served to make her blush. There'd been a hasty wedding night, a neutral coupling accomplished half-clothed in nightwear. He'd been gone in the morning, off fishing. Fortis smiled and reached for a towel. 'Well? Do you see anything you like?'

'I am hard-pressed to say,' Avaline confessed. Best to begin as she meant to go on. Tonight they would discuss the hard things, starting with how it used to be between them. 'The truth is, I've never seen you naked in the light.'

His wife had never seen him naked? Had he seen her? He stirred beneath the towel and sat down in an attempt to tame his desire or at least hide it. 'We'll have to rectify that.' It was only partly said in jest. He patted the space next to him. 'Will you come sit or have I frightened you too much today?' He hoped not, but it was a small hope. The last time she'd been in his bedroom, he'd fought her in his sleep. Now, he'd surprised her by walking around his room naked, *after* she'd found him curled beneath a tree raving about a man who wasn't there. It was probably miracle enough she was still speaking to him. His conscience whispered the plea, *Please come to me, Avaline. I probably don't deserve it, but please come to me.*

She came, hesitantly—whether her hesitance was a remnant of today's episode or a response to his nudity he didn't know. But she came and that was all that mattered. It meant she hadn't given up on him.

'Was I so bad as a husband before?' What sort of husband *had* he been? One that had not shown her pleasure, he feared, if she hadn't seen him naked. He had regrets, he knew that much. But why? He'd hurt her in some way, he knew that, too. But how? He hated these gaps, even more so when they concerned his wife. How was he to build a marriage with her when there was so much he didn't know about them, but also about himself?

'No, not bad, Fortis, just apathetic,' Avaline answered quietly as if a softer voice could also soften her words.

'Apathy can hurt as much as blatant disapproval.' A memory tugged at him, all feelings and echoes; of people passing him by, ignoring him. *Look at me, see me*, he'd cried, but no one did. Everyone kept moving. The sensation was gone before he could grab on to it. 'I am sorry, Avaline.' He was saying that a lot these days. The more he learned about himself, the less he liked himself. He found her hand and slid his fingers between hers. They were good at holding hands. He liked feeling her close, liked the physical connection of touching her.

'Do you know what you're apologising for?' Her gaze was fixed on their hands, linked together.

'For neglecting you with my attentions. For not being the husband you needed. For riding off to war and not looking back.' He knew that much. In his trunk he had six years' worth of her letters, letters he hadn't answered, proof enough that he'd never looked back and that, when he had, it had been too late. 'Is there more? I hope not, because that sounds like a daunting enough list of wrongs. I can't go back, Avaline, and change the past, but I can change what we are to become.' He ran his thumb over the back of her palm. Would she understand that, for all his flaws, he was in earnest on this?

She smiled, always the angel. 'You have, Fortis. You're different now. You're more caring, less self-focused, less reckless with others.'

'War changes a man, physically and mentally if Ferris's hypotheses are to be believed.' He'd been what? Twenty-four or twenty-five when they married? Still very young to be a husband by the standards of the day, and she'd been even younger; eighteen without a debut. What had either of them known about loving another? It was no excuse for his neglect, but it did offer a context for understanding it.

'I like it.' Avaline met his gaze, her words swift. 'I like this new Fortis.' Her praise warmed him, encouraged him.

'Even if he runs around the forest rescuing invisible men?' They had to deal with that, too.

'Yes. We'll get through it. I have great hope that some day your memories will come back and, when they do, the past won't haunt you. You will be able to fully accept that you're home and you're safe.'

'I could ask you the same, Avaline. When will you be able to fully accept that *I* am home and *you* are safe? Not just from Hayworth, but you're safe *with* me? That our past and its mistakes need not define us any longer.' Safe enough to do more with him than discuss the estate. It was a bold question, one which she was saved from answering by the arrival of dinner. But he'd made his point, he'd seen it in her eyes.

Servants brought in the supper, laying a table with china and silver and efficiently withdrawing as if the lord of the manor dined bare chested and wrapped in a towel every evening. Their level of detachment was impressive, really. Still, Fortis reached for a robe and slipped it on as Avaline poured the wine and filled their plates. 'Jugged hare and baby potatoes. They used to be your favourites.'

He sat down across from her at the little table, watching the candlelight play across her face. 'After military rations, I think any food is my favourite. Military food was regular, I'll give the army that. A man could count on three meals a day, although a man couldn't always count on it being good.'

'Not even the officers' mess?' Avaline queried, looking up from her potatoes. 'I thought officers always ate well.'

Had they? He'd have to ask Cam the next time he saw him. Food had been in short supply when he'd made it back to camp. There had been supply-line issues that had nearly starved the army, but that was not the norm. Fortis swallowed a piece of the jugged hare and smiled to cover the lapse. '"Well" is a relative term, my dear. Nothing compares to a meal at home with charming company.' Charming company, beautiful company, forgiving company. His wife was all those things. The candlelight turned her blonde hair to deep honey, her brown eyes to polished obsidian, the curve of her jaw to soft, shadowed mystery.

It was a face that combined both strength and feminine welcome, a face that invited a man's attention and his protection whether she needed it in truth or not. He wanted to touch her, to stroke her cheek, to run his hand down the long column of her neck, to rest his fingers where her pulse beat at its base. He wanted to push her lavender gown off her shoulders and caress the creamy curves of her, curves of shoulders, curves of breasts. Fortis shifted in his seat, accommodating his growing arousal. He wanted to touch her, taste her, this beautiful wife of his. She was everything the miniature had depicted, a woman who carried her soul in her eyes. She had not disappointed.

Avaline refilled his glass. 'You're staring again. Do you find me vastly changed?'

How to answer that? He found her perfect in every way, but how could he say that when there had apparently been a time when he hadn't? And yet, if he had to say one more time today that he simply didn't remember, he would go truly mad. He was so damned tired of not remembering, of defining himself by what he didn't know instead of what he did. 'I find you to be exactly what I need.' He lifted his glass. 'To my wife, to our future.' The toast pleased her and surprised her. She blushed as they drank and he took the opportunity to move the conversation into more useful territory. 'We finished the roofs today. Just in time, too, if this morning was any indicator. Winter has arrived. Is there anything else that needs immediate attention before the cold hits in force?' Other than himself, that was. His erection was not subsiding. Not even talk of cold mornings and roof repairs could dim its insistence.

'There are a few stone walls that need repair if we're to keep the sheep and cattle in, but there are men to see to that, you needn't worry about it personally. You can spend the winter going over ledgers and crop rotations.'

She smiled, laughing. 'Scintillating prospect, isn't it?' Then she sobered. 'I'm afraid country life isn't as adventurous as the military.'

'Well, it is certainly safer. I'm looking forward to that,' he assured her. For all her strength, Avaline had her vulnerabilities, too. It was plain she worried he would leave her again. Well, he had all winter to convince her of his intentions. He leaned across the table with a smile. 'Tell me what we do for Christmas. I've never had holidays at Blandford before.'

It was just the right subject for a frosty night and Avaline warmed to it as he poured out the last of the wine, dividing it between their glasses. She regaled him with plans to decorate the front hall and banister with greenery and the red bows kept in boxes in the attics, the lists of foods, and the games. 'Of course, we'll go to Bramble for Christmas Eve and Christmas Day to spend it with your family.'

He squeezed her hand. 'I can hardly wait.' Between them on the table, the candles sputtered, each burned down.

'I suppose that's my cue to go.' Avaline was suddenly self-conscious. She slipped her hand from his and rose from the table. 'I wasn't aware it was so late.'

He rose with her, filled with a sense of disappointment. He was not ready to let her go. 'Does it matter? We have no claims on our time. Why shouldn't we stay up all night talking if we wish?' Or something else. He let his gaze linger on the fullness of her lips. Nights were good for other things besides talking. For once, she didn't have an answer. He reached for her then, his touch gentle but resolute. It was time for the future to start if there was any hope of them outpacing the past.

Fortis cupped her face where the slim column of her neck met soft jaw, his fingers sliding beneath the heavy depths of her hair. His mouth moved to capture hers, swift and insistent in its possession. He kissed her, drinking hard at her lips. Had he ever wanted anything as much as this woman in his arms?

'Fortis?' She breathed his name against his mouth.

'Let there be no doubt as to my lack of apathy tonight,' he whispered fiercely. 'Let me make up for any wrong I've done you.' God, he wanted his wife, with all his body, his mind, his very soul. He craved her and yet he sensed the reticence in her surrender even as her mouth consented, even as her hand slipped behind his neck. She was in uncharted waters, unsure what to think of this overture from a man who'd shown her nothing but neglect for the short duration of their marriage. He'd had a month to think about this moment, waiting for Cam and the journey home. She'd had barely a week and there was still so much unsettled between them.

'Fortis.' She shook her head, readying her excuses.

'Shh, Avaline.' He pressed a finger to her lips. 'Say nothing. Say only that you'll stay with me tonight. We needn't do anything. Just lie with me, just sleep by my side.' He held her gaze, willing her to see the truth of his words in his eyes. 'I will not press you for more, not tonight, not until you're ready.' He felt her body relax against him. 'Those are my terms, Avaline, if you want to come to bed with me.'

Chapter Eight

Avaline's first thought upon waking was that something was wrong—different. The bed didn't *feel* like hers, the room didn't smell like hers. It smelled masculine, all sandalwood and spices like Fortis. Her eyes flew open as she remembered: She'd spent the night in Fortis's bed! And she was still in it. But he was not. She squinted, letting her eyes adjust to the daylight as she scanned the room only to find it empty, too. She pushed herself up on her elbows and tried to get her bearings. She'd fallen asleep in her gown, lying next to Fortis as he told her about finishing the roofs in the village. She'd meant to stay awake until he'd fallen asleep and then slip off to her room, but she'd failed miserably. Outside, it looked clear and frosty, the day well advanced. She'd not only slept away the whole night, she'd slept late as well.

The door opened and Fortis appeared, tray in hand laden with sausage, toast, eggs and a warm pot. He flashed her a warm smile as he set the tray on last night's dinner table. 'Breakfast is served,' he said with flourish. Fortis reached for a cup and poured, a whiff of the beverage wafting in her direction.

'Is that hot chocolate?' Avaline was out of bed in an instant. There was nothing she loved better than chocolate in the mornings.

He'd been paying attention during a week of breakfasts together.

'Yes, it's a hot chocolate kind of day. It froze outside last night. I think that means winter is officially here.' Fortis held out a chair for her and served her cup. 'It's a good thing we finished those roofs yesterday.' He dug into the bowl of scrambled eggs and heaped them over a layer of toast. Avaline sipped at her chocolate, watching him eat with gusto. Fortis was in high spirits this morning, a sign he'd slept well, that he hadn't been plagued by any further nightmares or remembrances. He seemed fully recovered from the upset of yesterday. Ferris would be pleased when he came to check on his brother.

'Did you sleep well?' Fortis asked, working on a second helping of eggs over toast. 'I slept spectacularly.' He gave her a boyish wink when she nodded that she, too, had slept well. 'Perhaps you and I should sleep together more often. We'll be the most well-rested couple in Sussex.' She blushed and his grin softened into an expression of sincerity. 'I mean it, Avaline. I liked having you beside me last night. Even if you did fall asleep in the middle of my roofing report,' he teased. 'I know you may need time before you're ready to resume that particular part of our marriage and I will give you that time. But you should know you needn't wait on me. I will be a husband to you in all ways, Avaline, when you're ready.'

'Thank you.' She blushed furiously, shocked by the frankness of their conversation and the very fact that they were having it at all. This handsome man wanted to take her to bed, wanted to make love to her, and he wanted her permission to do so. She could not imagine the Fortis she'd known ever consulting her on such a thing, or ever being intuitive enough, selfless enough, to know that he should. It both warmed her and worried her. The all-too-familiar question niggled once more. What had wrought the change in him? She pushed back the question. After last night, she needed to stop questioning it and merely accept it. War changed men. It had changed Fortis and for the better. This was what she wanted in a husband. She needed to accept it, not question it. They would both be happier if she did.

Fortis leaned close with a secretive whisper. 'Be warned, though. I will do my utmost best to woo you into bed for more than sleeping, my dear,' He held up the pot with a wicked spark in his eye. 'More chocolate, darling?'

'I see your game, now. You think the way to my heart is through chocolate.' Avaline laughed and held up her cup, enjoying this lazy morning. It was the sort of morning she'd once imagined having with a husband. It was the sort of morning, the sort of easy banter, she'd given up ever having with Fortis. But that was all in the past. Fortis was home and reformed. They had a second chance to turn this marriage of convenience into something more.

They lingered over their late breakfast and might have lounged about until lunch if Ferris hadn't arrived. Even then, Fortis might have sent his brother away if it hadn't been for the pressing business of yesterday that needed discussing. Fortis dressed quickly and met his brother in the office downstairs.

Ferris took one glance at him and noted the haste. 'I hope I am not interrupting?' he asked with a cheeky grin.

'You are interrupting, but our discussion is important,' Fortis scolded him as he retrieved a folder from his desk before taking a seat in front of the fire, gesturing for Ferris to do the same. 'Do you need a drink?'

Ferris waved away the offer. 'No, it's too early for that.' His smile sobered. 'How are you this morning? No ill effects?'

'None. Only questions.' Fortis cut straight to the heart of the matter. He tapped the folder. 'Yesterday, when I was dreaming, or whatever you want to call it, there were two of us. There was a man on the battlefield. The two of us crawled, staggered, our way to the cave but there is no mention of a second man in Cam's report.'

'There was no one with you when you returned to camp, Fortis. Cam would have said so,' Ferris confirmed, but that didn't solve any mysteries, it only created more. There had been someone.

'There's something else. In the flashback, I wasn't myself, or maybe I was, but I wasn't in my own body. Does that make sense? I pulled a man out from under a horse.'

'You were under a horse, according to Cam's report,' Ferris answered. 'It's not unrealistic to think in your flashback that you were watching your own rescue. In our dreams, we are not always ourselves. Our dreams are not always in the first person.'

'So, again, I ask, who was the other man?' Fortis pressed with the question that continued to plague him. 'Let's assume someone pulled me out from under the horse and got me to safety. What happened to him? Where did he go?'

'He may have made his own way back to British lines, once you were safe,' Ferris said, recognising the weakness of that reasoning before he even finished the thought.

'And left a fellow soldier in a cave for months? He didn't think to send help back?' Fortis shook his head and Ferris agreed.

'You're right. If he left and he didn't come

back, then perhaps he was killed or perhaps he died of his own injuries.'

Fortis nodded, considering the new theory. That made sense. They'd staggered, unsteady on their feet. They'd both been hurt.

'A little while ago you said "let's assume someone pulled me out". Do you think someone didn't?'

'No, I wonder if I was under the horse at all. Is it possible Cam was wrong? That the horse didn't fall on me? Why I do remember crawling through the mud? Why do I remember the agony in my leg and my arm? And I have the scars to prove it. Avaline saw them last night.'

'I don't need to know what you're showing to Avaline.' Ferris chuckled.

'Seriously. I have two scars and I remember them. The man under the horse had no visible wounds in my flashback. I am wondering if maybe I was thrown clear when I fell. I'm not disputing Cam saw me fall. I am, however, disputing what happened after that. Cam admits he doesn't truly know.'

'Fine.' Ferris was willing to concede. 'It's possible you weren't pulled from beneath a horse, that you were wounded and left for dead on the battlefield and as you crawled to safety, you found a man who had been trapped beneath a horse and you rescued him. That's all very plausible, which would explain how you remember it.'

Fortis nodded, the knot of confusion in his mind easing.

'It's also possible your mind is jumbled and you received those wounds somewhere else and your memories are blurring together. That wouldn't be in the least unusual. We all have dreams that mix experiences,' Ferris assured him. He leaned forward and put a hand on Fortis's knee. 'You are home now and you are safe. Everything will sort itself out in time. Be patient and all will make sense.'

It was as good of an answer as he was going to get today. Fortis let it go at that. It did make sense. It did help. But he did want to know who the other man had been and what had happened to him. Had he rescued the man or had it been the other way around? Had the man lived? Or was Ferris right and the man had died of wounds or of going for help?

'I came to see you today to make sure you were well, of course, but there is something else,' Ferris said. 'Tobin Hayworth has been to see Father.'

He didn't get any further with his news. A rustle of skirts announced Avaline's presence in the doorway. She was dressed for the outdoors in a blue-wool walking ensemble and looked entirely fetching. 'Are you two planning to take over the world?' she teased.

'We've been talking about the things I remembered yesterday,' Fortis confessed hesitantly. There was so much to settle between them yet that it hardly seemed fair to burden her with his personal problems. He paused—the other piece of news concerned her as well. 'Tobin Hayworth has been to see Father. You're just in time to hear about it.'

He watched Avaline's smile fade. 'What can he possibly do now?' she asked, her voice edged with a concern she couldn't hide.

Ferris spoke up, arms crossed against his chest. 'He came to Bramble under the guise of concern that the family, and most especially you, Avaline, were being hoodwinked by an impostor who was taking advantage of the situation and playing on your sympathies.'

Avaline glanced at him in disbelief. 'That's ludicrous. Why would he even think such a thing?'

'Because the man's besotted with you.' His

response was nothing short of a growl. 'Hayworth had his hands all over you at the ball.' Fortis felt a surge of primal protection as he spat the words out. He should have been more careful. Avaline blushed, embarrassed that he'd made the revelation in front of Ferris.

'I did *not* invite his attentions. I've spent years fending off Hayworth's neighbourly advances with nothing more than a name for a shield,' Avaline was quick to point out and he realised she thought his anger was directed at her, that he thought she'd encouraged him. Is that the sort of marriage they'd had? A jealous one? A one full of blame? If so, it was not well done of him.

'No,' Ferris put in, looking uncomfortable about being caught in the middle of a potential marital quarrel. 'The estate did that. But he's after more than the estate now.'

Fortis felt the full weight of his brother's meaningful stare as Ferris explained, 'He's after you, Fortis, because you stand between him and Blandford, and between him and Avaline. He even believes you stand between him and a knighthood.'

Fortis scoffed at the idea. 'The man's deluded. How could I prevent him from getting a title?'

'He hoped to use Avaline's connections and her family pedigree to elevate himself,' Ferris summed up. 'He told Father he found your return far too serendipitous for the Treshams' benefit to be believable.'

'What did Father say?'

Ferris grinned. 'Father had Hayworth escorted from the premises.' Then Ferris frowned. 'But that won't be the end of it.' He nodded to Avaline. 'I've delayed your walk long enough. I'll be off, but I thought you should both know Hayworth was on the prowl.'

'He wouldn't dare come here,' Fortis said confidently, walking his brother to the door.

Avaline wondered if that confidence was misplaced. Fortis didn't know Hayworth the way she knew Hayworth. The man stopped at nothing to get what he wanted: an estate, a title, another man's wife, revenge for public humiliation. There was plenty he wanted from Fortis Tresham and he could only get it if Fortis wasn't Fortis. As unlikely as it sounded, Avaline had to wonder what had led Hayworth to believe he could attempt such a thing. He would not have tweaked Cowden's nose for no reason. Did he have more than doubts to go on? Or was this a gamble built on bluff alone? That latter seemed uncharacteristic of Hayworth. He never gambled without surety.

The worries she'd so recently put to bed woke once more. If Hayworth had doubts, it meant she wasn't the only one who'd noted the differences, who perhaps hadn't accepted the differences as a matter of course, a consequence of war and long absence. Was there a chance Cowden held doubts, too? What did those doubts mean? She only wished it wasn't her enemy who'd raised them.

'Ready for our walk?' Fortis took his coat and gloves from the butler and slipped them on, cheerful once more as she took his arm and they headed out into the crisp day. They walked in silence past the little stone chapel where they'd married and down to the duck pond where a few intrepid ducks braved a swim. Avaline fished in her pocket for crusts of bread and handed one to Fortis.

He took the bread and tore off crumbs for the ducks, noting her distraction. 'Are you worried about Hayworth? There's no reason to be. I don't think the world has gone so mad yet as to make a man prove he's really himself.' He shrugged off the situation as ridiculous. 'Everyone knows Hayworth is all sour grapes over having his agenda thwarted. Anything he says now will only make him look like a poor loser.' Fortis tossed a bread piece between two ducks who each immediately grabbed an end and fought for it.

She was feeling rather like that piece of bread, a potential prize to be fought over by two stubborn men whether she wanted to be or not. Unlike Fortis, she was not ready to dismiss Hayworth's threats, but she had to suggest caution carefully if Fortis was to take her seriously. 'Hayworth is not a man who takes risks he's likely to lose. Today, he was just testing the waters to see what sort of response he'd get. Perhaps he heard about yesterday's accident.' Or perhaps he'd heard about a week's worth of Fortis's exploits in the village thatching roofs with the common farmers. Perhaps like her, he had been surprised by the arrogant Fortis Tresham rubbing elbows and rolling up shirt-sleeves with commoners. *Unlike* her, he'd questioned that behaviour. What she had chalked up to a change of heart after years away, Hayworth had seen as suspicious and deceptive.

Fortis sighed. 'What if he did? I had an episode. That only proves I'm a troubled soldier. It doesn't prove I am not Fortis Tresham. In fact, I'd say the opposite, that it proves I most certainly am. A man can't disappear into the woods for a year and come back unchanged.'

But what if that wasn't all Hayworth had to go on? She offered Fortis another piece of bread. 'What *do* you remember after Balaclava, Fortis?' Avaline asked quietly. She'd not pressed him on that point and neither had his family. But that missing year was becoming more important in light of these new developments.

'Very little,' Fortis replied. The strong line of his jaw tightened, an indicator, she'd learned, that he did not like discussing it. 'Bits and pieces that don't always make sense. I can't explain them to myself let alone someone else. Ferris helped quite a bit this morning.'

'Hayworth may use that confusion to his advantage,' Avaline put forward the thought tentatively. 'How can you prove what you don't remember?' She tossed the last of her bread to the ducks. 'We need those memories, Fortis. It would make things so much easier.' She gave him a soft smile and slid her gloved hand inside his.

Chapter Nine

～～～～

Fortis didn't want to talk about memories any more. He had other, more immediate concerns than a temperamental neighbour and a past he couldn't recall. He had a wife to woo and marital amends to make, something that was driven home yet again when she'd mistaken his concern over Hayworth's attentions for blame. She looked pretty this afternoon in her blue wool, the sun on her blonde hair, but he thought it would be a while before an image rivalled the one of her last night, sleeping peacefully beside him, her hair loose on the pillow.

He'd watched her sleep awhile, mesmerised by the peace on her face, the quiet rise and fall of her breast. It had taken all his willpower not to wake her with a kiss and coax her into lovemaking. But he'd given his word. He could not risk breaking it over something as insignificant as mere carnal intimacy, especially when it was clear from all the signs he'd previously failed her in that regard.

They walked about the pond, making a loop that would take them back to the house, Avaline pointing out the nest of a song thrush high in a bare tree as she chatted about the winter birds. She was an engaging conversationalist, well versed in all aspects of her property from its crops to its ecology. Of course, she'd had twenty-five years to learn it, this sense of home and roots that went so deep as to be an intrinsic part of her. She was Blandford and Blandford was her.

'I envy you your connection to your home. I've never had that.'

'No, I suppose that's the bane of being the third son and in the military. You're always on the move. It was for Frederick, the heir, to know the Cowden lands.' She smiled at him and his world felt warm. She could light him up with a single look. How was it that he'd failed her so miserably where passion was concerned? 'Have I bored you with talk of thrushes and house sparrows?'

'Not in the least. I like listening to you talk,'

he assured her. When she talked he could set aside his troubles, stop sorting through his tangle of memories and simply be in the moment. The house was coming back into view and he had a task he needed to do once he returned that would put those tangled memories front and centre once more.

They stopped on the back terrace and took a moment to shake the detritus of their walk off their boots. Inside, he helped her with her coat, his hands resting at her shoulders while his lips pressed a kiss to the column of her neck. 'Thank you for the walk,' he whispered at her ear. He breathed her in, all fresh air and vanilla. She smelled faintly like freshly baked biscuits. It was hard to let her go. He wanted to kiss her senseless, wanted to carry her back to his bed and make love to her in the fading afternoon, to undress before her and let her look her fill as she had last night. God, how he'd loved her eyes on him last night. But no matter how her breath caught and how her pulse raced when he touched her, she needed to come to him. 'I will see you at dinner, darling wife.' He left her, wondering if she guessed what a feat that simple act was for him.

Fortis went to the study and poured himself a

brandy. He was going to need a drink for what he intended. He went to the desk and pulled out the report from Cam and settled in a chair by the fire, making himself as comfortable as possible for an uncomfortable task. The file was thick. It contained his own confused account of coming out of the forest, the surgeon's report, some other reports from other officers and Cam's account of Balaclava. He pulled out Cam's account of the battle.

We tried to retreat, but it was too late. The Russians had taken to firing indiscriminately on the troops trapped in the valley. Fortis Tresham was several yards from me. Paget was with me as we tried to gather our troops to us.

Fortis was in the thick of the fighting, on his horse Khan. His sword was raised as he tried to rally his own men. Khan reared, struck by a shot. Fortis may have been struck, too. Khan went down and Fortis with him.

I moved towards him, but the fighting was too strong, a horizontal path was not possible. It was only possible to move

*vertically. In the swell of retreat, I was
pushed forward and away from Tresham.*

*From my vantage point, I could not see
if Khan ever rose, but it seemed doubtful
that the horse would.*

Fortis took a drink, suppressing the emotions
the passage invoked. Cam had risked his life
to try to come to him. The knowledge touched
him. There was emotion, too, for the fallen
steed, for the carnage of the day. He didn't need
an imagination to envision the gore of a battlefield. His eyes went back over the last line.
The horse had been shot out from under him.
He had fallen with his horse. The horse had not
risen and neither had he.

Fortis took another swallow. He'd seen men
come off their horses in battle before. It was
imperative to get to one's feet immediately to
avoid being rolled on, struck by hooves, or simply mowed down by the enemy. The only men
who didn't get to their feet were men who were
dead or couldn't. There were two reasons a man
couldn't: he was too badly wounded or he was
trapped beneath his horse's body, crushed by
over a thousand pounds of weight. He thought
of Ferris's explanation today, that he'd fallen

free of the horse's crashing body. He'd been able to find his feet and fight on, sustaining his wounds after the fall.

Fortis stilled. The reasoning certainly explained why his nightmare didn't match what the army had told him of his accident. It wouldn't be the first time the army made a mistake. It had to be one or the other. Either he was the man trapped beneath his horse, if so he wouldn't have been crawling through a battlefield. Or, he'd rescued someone who had been trapped.

Maybe he'd been both? Maybe he'd squirmed out and freed himself and then later come across a man suffering the same fate who'd been unable to help himself. No, the first part of that didn't seem logical. A man couldn't move twelve hundred pounds of horseflesh from a prone position. He would not have been able to move his horse alone. Nor did that fit with the flashback yesterday. Someone had come and levered the horse off him. But he could have sworn in the flashback that he was the one doing the levering. Had he been the rescuer? Or was it possible, like Ferris had said, to have flashbacks in third person? Was it possible to *be* the other person? Perhaps just having so many explanations for his flashback was enough to prove he needn't worry over it. It had happened. That was all that mattered. It was a memory and it had value enough at the moment without needing to dissect it.

Fortis put his head in his hands and shut his eyes tight. He knew Avaline was right. He *had* to remember, for her sake. What kind of husband would he be to her if he could not? But just for a moment, he'd wanted to stop thinking about it—about Balaclava, about the missing year, about the missing soldier, about trying to retrieve his past—and just be a man who was falling in love with his wife.

Avaline couldn't stop thinking about her husband. Ever since he'd declared his desire to resume their marriage in its entirety, she'd been unable to escape him physically or mentally, not that she was trying very hard on either account. When he was in the room, all she could do was stare while her eyes undressed him and her imagination recalled the sight of him dripping and naked from his bath while her cheeks heated from the memory.

When he wasn't in the room, her mind managed to wander anyway. It had become impossible to read, to stitch, to write her letters without her thoughts drifting. Today was proof of it. Avaline looked down at her embroidery on a pillowcase. She'd not meant to use so much blue in the bouquet of flowers. She'd have to pull out the thread and start again, but she'd caught sight of Fortis outside in the garden with Mrs Pimm, the housekeeper, and she'd been distracted by the sight of him digging up potatoes from the hard dirt.

These days, it seemed her mind would much rather concentrate on anything Fortis-related; remembering the light touch of his hand at the small of her back when they walked, or how he would take her hand when they talked over dinner, having conversations that lasted long beyond the meal and well into a second bottle of wine, to how he'd make a habit of stealing kisses throughout the day, each kiss a promise of more, each kiss more heated than the last, as was her own response. She was growing used to this playful, passionate Fortis who loved to come up behind her and wrap her in his arms, pressing kisses to her neck, to her jaw and whisper something amusing in her ear to make her laugh. With familiarity came comfort, with him and with her own response to him.

Avaline threaded her needle and went back to work on the pillowcase, determined to concentrate on her task. Surely this fascination with her husband wouldn't last for ever. She understood the source of her obsession. Her husband's attentions were still novel and exhilarating, not only because he was home at last, but because she'd never held anyone's attention before, never had a Season. She'd been married to Fortis when she was eighteen. Except for her time at the academy, she'd never left the countryside until the Cowdens had taken her up to town.

Avaline poked the needle through the cloth, more satisfied with the stitches this time. The pillowcase set was for the Duke and Duchess and she wanted it to be perfect. They'd become her parents in the years since her own had died and Fortis had been gone. Now, it seemed Fortis was making up for all of that; a most pleasant and unexpected change. She would never have guessed he was capable of it.

'There you are!' Fortis entered the sitting room, full of energy and smelling like the wintry outdoors. 'Were you watching me out the window?' he teased, noting the position of her chair. 'I thought I caught you peeping.'

'I may have stolen a glance or two.' Avaline smiled brightly, willing away the remembrance of another Fortis, one who had wanted nothing to do with her. This Fortis was much more pleasant. 'Did Mrs Pimm get all of her potatoes?'

'Yes, we will have them for supper.' He grinned and took the chair next to her.

'You didn't used to be such a farmer.' The remark came out saltier than she intended, proof she hadn't quite shed the unpleasant remembrance.

He was undaunted. 'Is that a problem, my dear?'

'No.' Avaline was immediately contrite. She should accept the good fortune that had returned a vastly improved Fortis to her. She should not poke at it, but she couldn't seem to help herself. 'I just wish I understood what changed you. Maybe then I wouldn't be so afraid I'd lose you.'

He took her embroidery hoop and set it aside, taking her hand in what had quickly become a customary gesture. 'You are not going to lose me. Is this still about Hayworth's nonsense? Or is it something more?'

'It's everything, Fortis,' Avaline whispered.

She looked into his open, sincere gaze and her heart flipped. How could she tell this man how much he'd hurt her with his callous disregard without hurting him in turn? He'd been in earnest in all he'd pursued, including her, upon his return, that she knew telling him such a thing would devastate him. Wasn't he hurting as it was? Hadn't he endured enough? Surely he'd paid for his crimes, such as they were when it came to their marriage. Tears threatened in her eyes. 'You are so different now and I don't know why or how or if it will last.' Did she dare believe in this man only to have him disappear? She could not bear to become a recipient of his disregard again.

He played with her fingers, his brow knit. 'I might understand that feeling better than you think.' He gave her a boyish smile that caught at her heart. 'Every day I wake up here with you beside me, I see this beautiful woman, this extraordinary home and these lands. It's all mine and I don't know what I did to deserve it. Quite possibly I don't deserve any of it, not you, not this home, and I fear I might lose it all again. I, too, worry that it won't last.'

'You're the son of a duke,' Avaline broke in.

'Such things are your birthright.' The world would never be an uncertain place for him.

'Hmm.' He ran his thumb over her knuckles. 'I suppose they are. That's how the world works. But that's not what I am talking about. I almost lost you and all of this once through what can only be called my own stupidity, poor choices and different priorities. I won't let that happen again. I might not remember particulars, Avaline, and maybe I don't want to. Maybe I'm too much of a coward to face what I did or said, but I know that much. I was inexplicably cruel to you. I hope you'll give me the rest of my life to make it up to you, to earn the treasure of your love. *That's* what I'm afraid of losing. I can only hope I haven't lost it already.' He gave a small, self-deprecating chuckle. 'See, I do know a little something about what you're feeling.'

More than a little, it seemed. The tears she'd been holding back started to fall along with her flagging resistance. He'd meant to woo her. He had, with smiles, with words, and touches, kisses and confessions, things that were worth more to her than hothouse bouquets and marble mansions. Hayworth had laid out his material wealth for her and she'd found it lacking. But

Fortis had laid out his heart. She could not resist such an ardent suitor.

She leaned in, bridging the short distance between them, and took his mouth in a soft, simple kiss that he answered with a playful one of his own. His hand cradled her jaw as their mouths played, tongues teasing as the kiss took on a new intensity that moved beyond play, both of them understanding capitulation was inevitable. It was only a matter of time and it seemed that time had come. 'Fortis, why don't we go upstairs?' she whispered, before she could change her mind. 'I think it's time you took your wife to bed.'

'Are you sure?' He sucked gently on her bottom lip, his eyes half-lidded.

'Yes,' she murmured with a confidence she didn't entirely feel. But if not now, when? To put this off would make it harder to move past her reservations. This time it would be different. It would not be a hurried, obligatory half-clothed coupling. They would be naked with each other, physically, emotionally, their bodies and their hearts on display, a thought that was both beautiful and frightening.

'Then so be it.' Fortis rose and offered her his hand. She trembled as he led her upstairs.

What if she gave him everything and it still wasn't enough this time? What if she was still the naive child he thought her to be? What if she disappointed him yet again? And he, her? What if they failed at their second chance? What if these days were only an illusion? Something they could never fully have? It seemed as if the next hour would define the rest of her life. Fortis shut the bedroom door behind her, his blue eyes smoky. 'Don't be afraid, Avaline. I will make it good for you, for us. I want it too badly for it to be otherwise.'

By all the saints, she believed him in this moment when he looked at her with those eyes, when he touched her with those lips. She felt wanted beyond measure, treasured, and when his hands worked loose the laces of her gown and slipped it from her shoulders, all thought to protest, all thought to resist the pull of whatever lay between them fled in its entirety, giving up its last claim on her sensibilities. She had to let the past go if there was any chance for the future she dreamed of.

His mouth pressed kisses at the back of her neck, his hands competently intent on their work as underskirts and corset fell away to join her dress in a pile at her feet. Only her chemise remained. He drew her against him, back to chest, the heat of his groin pressed to her buttocks, his hands cupping her breasts through the thin fabric, thumbs running over the peaks of them until they strained against the chemise with a want of their own. She leaned her head back against his shoulder, her neck arched, her eyes closed, and drank in the pleasure of his touch. This was a new heaven and he'd only just begun.

His hands moved to her hips, gathering up the chemise and pulling it over her head. 'Turn around for me, my love,' he whispered, tossing away the last garment. 'I've waited for this for so long.' She turned, slowly, shyly, standing before him unclothed for the first time, far less comfortable with her nudity than he was his. But he was handsome and he was surely aware of it, whereas she was unsure of her beauty in her husband's eyes. He had not thought her lovely enough once.

'Look at me, Avaline,' he demanded in quiet tones. She raised her gaze slowly, not sure what she'd see in his face. What she saw there nearly undid her.

'Take away your hands. You needn't be shy with me and I want to see all of you.' His eyes were hot as he took her in, caressing her with their heat, giving her confidence as her hands fell to her sides and a smile spread tentatively across her face. Her husband found her beautiful.

He reached for her, kissing her full on the mouth. 'Undress me, now, Avaline, and let me give you the wedding night you should have had.'

'Only it will be a wedding afternoon,' she teased softly, still aware of how exposed she was in the daylight.

'All the better to see you, my dear.' He nipped at her ear and smiled. 'Now, will you help me with my shirt?'

And his waistcoat. She'd never undressed a man before and she savoured the details of stripping her husband, of removing the silver pin in his cravat, of carefully laying aside the pocket watch from his waistcoat pocket. There was something else in his pocket, too. She fumbled for it and pulled out the miniature. She ran her thumb over the surface of the tiny case. 'You really do carry it with you everywhere, even now.'

'I always carry you with me, Avaline. It brought me home to you.' He stole a kiss as she undid the buttons of his waistcoat and tugged his shirttails from the waistband of his trousers. He shrugged out of his shirt and she ran her hands over the expanse of his chest, all muscled smoothness with just a sprinkling of dark hair. 'I like to feel your hands on me.' He nuzzled her neck and she laughed. That made two of them. She liked to put her hands on him as well, not only because he was exquisitely made but because he made her feel welcome. This intimacy was new and uncharted, potent with potential.

'My trousers, if you don't mind?' He helped her get the trousers over his hips and down his long legs until he was entirely naked, entirely hers—hers to feast her eyes on, to touch. 'Do I please you, Avaline?' He was dancing her back to the bed, his mouth at her neck, at her jaw, at her lips and her pulse beat wildly for him, for now, for whatever came next.

He laid her back on the pillows and covered her with his length, smiling down at her, desire lighting his eyes. 'Now, you're mine to worship.' And he did, with his wicked mouth, and his gentle hands, kissing her neck, caressing her breasts, sucking at her nipples until she thought she could stand no more. She had never known such decadence existed, that such pleasure was possible. She arched beneath him, her body begging for more of whatever he offered. She opened to him and he moved between her legs, his arousal pressing against her in prelude, asking for invitation, and she gave it, cradling him between her thighs as he rose up above her, the strength of his arms taking the weight of him as he came into her. It was a slow taking, in part because there was an unspoken accord between them to savour this, and in part because he showed her every consideration their rising passion allowed.

Avaline arched, her hips pressing into his, her legs wrapping around his waist, holding him to her, in her, as she picked up the sliding rhythm of him; surge and ebb, surge and ebb, each wave bringing him closer to her core, bringing them closer to pleasure's horizon. This was exquisite and beautiful, and she was drowning in it, losing herself in it as it swept her away. All she wanted was more of it, more of him. He thrust into her deeply now, her core fully reached, and she moaned, crying out against the pleasure. She didn't want it to end, she wanted it to go on and on endlessly, the two of them twined together on ecstasy's sea, and yet her pleasure-drenched mind knew that there was more pleasure to be had if the horizon could be reached.

With each thrust, Fortis drew them nearer to that horizon. His own breathing became laboured, his muscles tight from strain. The rhythm quickened between them, anticipation of journey's end gave her pleasure a sharp edge. Until Fortis's last, claiming thrust threw them both against the horizon and shattered it and her along with it into a brilliant, scattered rainbow of pleasure. Above her, Fortis gave a final, guttural groan as he emptied himself, his body collapsing against her, his head finding rest at her shoulder. She held him there, her arm wrapped about him, her hand in his hair as she felt his body heave from his exertions and a place deep inside her knew without question this was what it should have been like that first night. Two people, together as one for as long as the moment could last. A joining in truth. The very lines that had been spoken at her own wedding so many years ago, came to her as she drifted in pleasure's wake.

'*With my body I thee worship.*'

Yes, Fortis had worshipped her well.

Chapter Ten

He dreamed of Avaline and the cave.

He was there again, with the other man. There was a small fire in the centre of the cave and pine-bough pallets laid a safe distance away from the flames. Firewood was stacked near the entrance, his Enfield rifle beside the pile. He hadn't dared to use it, not even for hunting, out of fear of who might hear the report. The last thing he needed was to bring the Russians down on them and they were well behind enemy lines. But for now, they were safe. They had food and shelter. The cave was cosy and warm. He'd lived in worse places. It was vastly improved from the first time he'd stumbled into it and so was he.

His arm and his leg didn't pain him. He was

well. He had much to be thankful for. He'd recovered from his wounds. But the man on the pallet was not recovering—it became clear that he would likely not recover. Saving him became a daily exercise in both hope and futility. He was only without pain when he lay still. The man could not risk moving. It was a miracle he'd lasted this long. But how much longer?

He refused to think about such an outcome. He could not lose this man who had become his friend over the months in this cave. More than a friend, really. They'd shared the tragedy of war together, this life in hiding together where there were only themselves to count on. To lose this man would be to lose a part of himself. This cave, this friendship, had become his world in the last four months in a manner he could not explain to an outsider. He rose from the fire, dusting his hands on his trousers. 'I'm going out to check the snares.' He hated leaving the man alone, but it was his usual custom to go in the late afternoons before the early dark of winter set in and the evening cold.

The man reached out a hand. 'Don't go, stay with me instead. We have enough food for several days.' The request gave him pause. The man he'd rescued never asked for anything. He simply stated what he wanted and assumed it would be given. It was simply his way, a habit that was much replicated by the upper classes. This was as close to a request as the man ever got and it worried him.

'I'll stay.' He sat beside his friend, taking his hand. The man was extraordinarily pale now from being indoors and from illness. 'What shall we talk about?'

They talked about numerous things over the course of the months. Talk was the only activity they had. The Treshams had come to life between them: Frederick and the incessantly pregnant Helena. Ferris and his new bride, Anne. The family nemesis Tobin Hayworth at Indigo Hall, who was forever after a neighbouring estate. Stories of a childhood with these brothers had, at some point, become their childhood together, stories of pranks and summers in the Sussex countryside peopled the cave until it was hard to tell whose life belonged to whom. He knew the man's family intimately and envied him secretly. The man he'd rescued had grown up in the privilege of friendship and love.

'Women. Today we talk about women.' Even in pain, the mention of women managed to

bring a smile to his friend's face. Ah, this was one of their favourite topics. The cave blurred, as settings often do in dreams, the world narrowing to happy voices recalling happier times. He was aware only of the steady flow of words as they talked.

'Do you have anyone at home? You've not mentioned anyone in all your stories.'

'No, I'm not like you. No family. You know that,' came a good-natured confession. From him? From the other man?

'That's not what I meant. Do you have a wife? Children? A woman waiting for you?'

'I haven't anything to offer a woman like that. I'd not wish the insecurity of being married to an enlisted man on any woman, forcing her to live on little pay and following the drum, only to be rewarded with the possibility her husband and source of income might be killed on any given day, her security ripped away without warning.' Had that burst of cynicism come from him or his friend? It hardly mattered in the dream.

'Why do you ask? Do you have anyone waiting?' came a chuckling, friendly deflection. Again, he could not tell who asked.

'Yes, matter of fact, I do. I have a wife.' It was a serious, unexpected admission.

'You must love her very much.' No one had mentioned a wife in four months of storytelling in a cave.

'Why would you think that?'

'You've not mentioned her before. A man does not parade his greatest treasures out for everyone to see. Tell me about her.'

'Her name is Avaline. We married years ago, the last time I was home on leave.' The story brought another smile to his friend's face. 'Her family owns a large estate adjacent to my father's. It made sense to ally the two families and third sons are useful that way, as alliance makers.'

'Was that all it was? An alliance? Did you love her?' It sounded like an empty marriage if that was all there was.

'I did not care for her like I should have.' The cosiness of the cave diminished a little at the admission. There was sorrow in it and regret. 'We only had three weeks together. I was young, perhaps too young to be a proper husband.' There was a pause, and then an abbreviated laugh. 'I wasn't a poor husband, not in that way, old chap. I see what you're thinking.

We consummated the marriage right enough. No, it's the other things that make a husband I wasn't any good at: thinking about her, getting to know her, the two becoming one beyond the bedroom. I was rubbish at that. I was self-ish, always out with my friends, coming home late, not shouldering the responsibility for the estate. Why should I? I was going to be gone. I hadn't wanted to invest my time in an estate that meant nothing to me. There were stewards to run it and it was her home. She knew it bet-ter than I ever could. It was irresponsible of me and I am sure I was something of a disap-pointment to her, too.'

Something was in his hand. He wasn't sure how it got there. Had he taken it out of his pocket? It was a creased letter and a locket, the kind in which miniatures were kept. Their con-versation continued in the amorphous muffling of the dream, words having no narrative ori-gin, simply existing. 'I might have disappointed her, but she didn't disappoint me. She's writ-ten every month, dutifully, all these years. This is her last letter, sent in October before Bala-clava.'

He carefully flipped the tiny catch on the locket, revealing the treasure within. Avaline's face stared back at him, long blonde hair framing a heart-shaped face that was young, sweet, yet strong with sharp brown eyes that could look into a man's soul. He passed the miniature to his friend. 'She is lovely, my friend. I would give the world to have a second chance with a woman like that...'

Fortis woke slowly. It had been another flashback in which he was seeing the conversation through the eyes of his rescuer and at times as an omniscient viewer. His mind was reluctant to leave the cave, wanting to cling to the pleasantness of the memories for fear that the morning could not possibly match the fantasies spun in the cave, fantasies of Avaline and second chances, only to find that Avaline was not a dream. She was real and warm and beside him in his bed. Fortis opened his eyes, releasing the remnants of his dream in favour of the morning, in favour of the woman lying tucked into him, his body wrapped around her, protective and possessive. She was his. His waking body thrummed with the knowledge of it and the wanting of it. Of course he'd wanted her. That was a given. He'd spoken of her in the cave. Thoughts of her had sustained him.

'Avaline,' he whispered at her ear, rousing her tenderly as his arousal grew. 'Are you awake?' He nibbled at her earlobe.

She gave a soft sigh in response, her body shifting against him in sleepy invitation. 'If I'm not, I think I will be very soon.'

His body could not wait. He sheathed himself in from behind, holding her close, her breasts filling his hands, her mewls of newly discovered delight filling his ears. But once seated, his body was in no hurry to rush. He moved in her slowly, savouring the slow burn of morning desire and the little purrs of pleasure it brought his wife. *His wife*. He had his second chance and, by God, he was going to make good on it, every day and every night of his life. He moved faster now, his body drawing taut in anticipation of climax, urged there by her cries, no longer soft mewls but begging gasps as he spent himself deep inside her. *This* was perfection.

'This is what I came home for.' He held her close long afterwards, not willing yet to be parted from her. His chin rested on her shoulder, the faint rosewater scent of her hair tickling his nostrils with its sweetness. 'To make love to you, to repent of my sins and be a good husband.' One night couldn't wash away the past, but it was a start. 'I dreamed last night, Avaline, of the cave and you. We were talking about you, the man I rescued and myself. I had your miniature even then. How wonderful it was to wake and find that you were real.'

'I'm glad you're dreaming good dreams, at last.' Avaline rolled over to face him and snuggle against his chest. 'Perhaps the worst is over, Fortis, and you're able to put it behind you.'

'Hmm. Maybe so.' He played with the long strands of her hair, letting them slip between his fingers like slippery corn silk as he told her, 'I am lucky. I walked out of that cave and came home to you. My friend didn't. He died in there.' Ferris was wrong about that. The man hadn't left him. There had been two of them in the cave for a long time, but only he'd walked out. What had happened to the other man?

'And you feel guilty because you lived?' Avaline asked quietly.

'I suppose so. I tried to save him, but I wasn't enough. He couldn't be moved. I couldn't get him past Russian lines or to the British surgeon, but it may not have mattered. Broken ribs can be deadly in any case.' He angled his neck to look down at her. 'It's not all guilt, though. There's more. It's difficult to explain. I feel as though I lost a best friend, a part of myself even when he died. It doesn't make sense because I didn't know him. He was not a man under my command. I had no prior interaction with him except for that rescue and yet I felt so close to him, like a brother. Losing him tore a hole in me I don't know how to fill.'

She looked up at him with a smile that nearly made him weep. 'You will, in time, because it's what he would have wanted for you if the two of you were as close as you say.' She stroked his chest. 'Did he have a name? I don't think you've ever told me. Perhaps you could contact his family?'

'I wish I could. He had no family. He told me he was entirely alone in the world. His mother had died and he never knew his father.' How did he know that about the man's father? It hadn't been in the dream. It hadn't been in any of his flashbacks, but he knew it was a truth he could wager on. Maybe that was good sign. Maybe Avaline was right and he was getting better, his memories returning.

But he wasn't cured. His memories had not returned in their entirety. If they had, he'd be able to answer her question, be able to make sense of it all, that dratted missing year. It was difficult to admit and even more difficult to share this one shaming secret. 'I don't remember it. I remember him, I remember the cave, I remember the details of our daily routine, how I'd go out and check the snares in the afternoon, but I don't remember his name. It kills me, Avaline. If I could just remember the name of a man I thought of as a brother…' His voice broke.

'But you remember him in more important ways,' Avaline soothed, fierce in her assurance. 'The rest will come, it's already coming. You're remembering more each day. Let it be enough for now that you're alive and safe.'

'And I've come home to the woman I love,' Fortis added, holding her close, noting how her hand stilled on his chest at the words. She'd want to protest, to be cautious and say it was too soon for any declarations. He was aware part of her still wanted to hold herself in reserve, to protect herself from hurt once more despite having shared his bed and her body with him. 'Shh…' he hushed her. 'Don't say anything, just let me say the words.' He had so few truths he could hold on to at the moment, those truths had become precious gems to him and this was one of them. He loved Avaline. He'd been born for it. He knew it in his bones as cer-

tainly as he'd known the man in the cave had
been alone in the world. Perhaps Avaline was
right. It was enough for now to simply know
these truths. There would be time later to dissect them.

The truth was a slippery creature and Tobin
Hayworth had come to London to catch it. He
prided himself on being able to catch it better than most. Often times, that catching was
done best with pound notes and the right connections. Those connections had brought him
to the cramped basement offices of the War
Office thanks to an ambitious gentleman eager
for shares in Hayworth's Bengal indigo planta-
tion. In exchange for those shares, the gentleman had willingly given up the name of a Mr
Marbury, who was one of the hordes of under-
secretaries for the War Office and known discreetly as someone willing to sell information
for a price.

Marbury was a greedy man with a sharp
mind and beady eyes and a soft stomach that
stood as proof to his greed. The man liked his
luxuries and Hayworth was happy to provide
a few luxuries in return for some information.
'The Crimea has been an organisational disas-

ter from start to finish.' Marbury steepled his hands over his stomach. 'From information to supplies, it's been the devil's own work to get anything where it needs to go.'

Hayworth recognised Marbury's opening salvo for what it was—a negotiation ploy. 'Apparently so. The army managed to lose a duke's son for nearly a year,' Hayworth reminded him. 'I can't imagine the Duke of Cowden would care to hear that his son was missing as a result of mismanagement. The family has suffered enough, thinking he was dead, then found, but not found. The army couldn't make up their mind as to who was Fortis Tresham. I'm here to ensure that this time they got it right.'

The mention of the Duke made Marbury nervous. 'Did the Duke of Cowden send you? I was unaware he was making enquiries.'

'He should be. Since he's not, I am doing so on his behalf as a devoted neighbour.' Hayworth feigned concern. 'I would not want to see him swindled and since the army's record for accuracy in this particular war has been a poor one, I am doubly concerned.' He leaned across the desk conspiratorially. 'I am told promotions were handed out to those who assisted in Tresham's recovery. With those kind of rewards on the line, I am sure many people were eager to secure Fortis Tresham's return.'

Marbury's beady eyes narrowed. 'What are you suggesting, sir?'

'Nothing you can't already guess yourself.' Hayworth gave a cold grin. 'Certain officers may have conspired to pass this man off as Fortis Tresham in order to gain rewards for themselves.' He shook his head. 'But I am not asking you to verify that. All I am asking you for is a copy of the file containing the information on Fortis Tresham's return and what happened in camp before Major Lithgow arrived.' He slid a few pound notes across the desk. Marbury's eyes lit up.

'I would also like a list of names of other men who were reported missing in action.'

Marbury eyed the pound notes and made a decision. He put the notes in his pocket and rose. 'Just a moment, I think I might have the material you're looking for.'

Hayworth smiled and sat back to wait, planning his next move. He would give the list to a Bow Street Runner. They would be far more effective than waiting for the army to bungle through the list and track the others down. The army might take years. He didn't have years.

Time was of the essence. The longer this man got to be Fortis Tresham, the less leverage Hayworth would have. Tresham would be accepted and Hayworth's claims would look like the ravings of a jealous man who'd lost as opposed to the other way around. Right now, Hayworth was the one who was 'established' and Tresham was the 'outsider'. Society was still trying to wrap its collective mind around his miraculous return which meant there was still room to sow doubt. But if Cowden didn't question his son's return, society would soon cease to speculate. Hayworth couldn't lose that edge. The longer he waited, too, the more likely it became Tresham's memories would return and that would be another edge he'd lose. It would undoubtedly be far easier to confuse and discredit a man who wasn't entirely sure of himself. Every day he delayed, Tresham grew stronger.

Chapter Eleven

Her husband loved her. It was a realisation that grew stronger by the day and Avaline didn't know what to do with it. It was as if she'd been granted a gift after wishing for it for so long only to be overwhelmed in the receiving of it. She'd wanted to be loved and now she was. She'd wanted a husband who was eager to build a life together and Fortis was all that and more. He woke her with kisses and she fell asleep each night in his arms. They faced the challenges of the days together, sometimes meeting with Benning to discuss crop rotation for the upcoming year or to discuss how best to handle the estate's lingering debt. They were not out of the woods where money was concerned. Other times, the day required they pursue separate courses: Fortis to help with repairs on stone fences and she to assist with projects at the village church. And some days the challenges were private ones instead of public. Fortis struggled with his memories and she struggled alongside him, determined that he not fight this battle alone.

She knew it bothered him, a torture not all that different from the trials of Tantalus. His memory would show him enough to be tempting and then shut him out just when he was on the brink of clarity. That was the new struggle: the fight to make sense of it all. She knew his mind chased around two questions hour after hour: What was the name of the man he'd rescued? How had he died? If he knew, he could contact the man's family and give them peace. He made a habit of poring over the reports that had accompanied him home in both the hope and fear the papers would trigger memories. These were the questions and quests that haunted him and, as she watched him fight, it broke her heart knowing that at some point she was unable to help him.

The lack of remembering took a toll on him. Some days she'd come home from her meetings and find him curled in a ball under the desk in the estate office, asleep. He'd awake, confused, thinking he was back in the cave. Then he'd see her, his vision would clear, he would remember he was home and he was safe. But there were good days, too, when the elusive past didn't haunt him and they'd spend the afternoons making love before the fire in the estate office, too hungry for one another to make it upstairs. She'd lie in his arms afterwards, letting the flames warm her naked body and his words warm her heart. He would kiss her softly and whisper, 'I love you.' He was patient and he did not press her to say the words in return, nor did he understand that, while he lay beside her in these rare moments of contentment, those words brought her both supreme satisfaction and roused suspicions against her will.

This ardent lover was so unlike the husband she'd known, this warm pleasure so unlike the callous coldness Fortis had shown her, that it overwhelmed her. If Fortis's devotion was a river, it was a raging river barely contained by its banks, sweeping away everything in its path. *She* was in its path, clinging to a branch while the flood of his regard rushed past her, tempting her to let go and join the deluge, yet she resisted for all the very same reasons she should have accepted it.

Fortis loved her.

It was too good to be true. So, followed the perverse conclusion, if it was indeed too good to be true, then it probably wasn't. The seeds of Hayworth's claims took slow root and the beginnings of doubt coupled with her own fears threatened in the form of another wicked syllogism.

Fortis Tresham did not love her. This man loved her. This man was not Fortis Tresham.

No. She would not go down that road. War changed a man. War brought new perspectives on life. She clung to that belief. She would not give Hayworth's jealous claims validity. But no matter how forcefully she fought back against Hayworth's doubts and her own worries, they found their way back.

'What are you thinking, my love?' Fortis drew a blanket about them as they lay before the fire, the afternoon sun fading from the long windows of the estate office. He was warm and drowsy, his movements languid as he settled the blanket over them. They would not stay that way for long.

'I was thinking how much I'd like to stay this way, for ever. Just you and me before the fire with the world locked outside the door.' She ran her fingernail over the flat of his nipple, feeling it pebble as he sighed his pleasure. If they could stay in this room, Hayworth's doubts, her worries and Fortis's inability to remember would cease to matter. Those issues would no longer define their days.

He chuckled, low and intimate. Would she ever get used to that wondrous voice? Still rough on the edges, lacking the ducal crispness of the upper classes. She hoped not. He rolled her beneath him and kissed her. 'We might get hungry. But up until then, that sounds like a lovely idea.' His pelvis moved against her hips, a slow inviting gyration. She opened to him, her body welcoming him, wrapping around him until it was impossible to tell where one began and the other ended. She let the pleasure push away the fear that paradise could be snatched from her. She would be happy. She would revel in the moment and the future be damned.

'You seem happier today.' Helena smiled over her sewing. It was just the two of them this afternoon in the cosy sitting room at Bramble. Anne was out making medical calls with Ferris on his father's tenants and the Duchess had pled weariness and opted for a nap. Avaline didn't believe that for a moment. The Duchess was indefatigable, which only meant one thing. The Duchess had wanted Helena to speak with her alone.

'I am happier,' Avaline assured her.

'May we attribute that happiness to Fortis? Are things going better for you?' Helena asked with embarrassing frankness. By 'things', Avaline knew perfectly well what Helena referred to.

Avaline tied off a piece of thread. 'Is this why the Duchess is taking a nap? So you can ask me if I've got my husband into bed?'

Helena laughed, not put off by her bluntness. 'That seemed to be a point of concern last time we talked.' Her eyes sparkled with well-intended mischief. 'It's been two weeks. That can seem like a lifetime when love is on the line. I know it did when Frederick and I were courting. Every day seemed to bring some new development.'

'It does feel a bit like we're courting,' Avaline confessed. She felt Helena's gaze on her, soft and compassionate.

Helena reached out a hand and took hers. 'I'm glad. You deserved more of that the first time. Fortis did not make it easy for you. Now he's making up for it and succeeding from the look on your face.' She squeezed Avaline's hand. 'You needn't be shy about it. We've been sisters for a long time.' Not blood sisters, of course, but sisters of experience. They'd been together at Mrs Finlay's Academy for Excellent Girls, although Avaline had been younger. Now they were sisters-in-law.

'But you're the legend,' Avaline said. 'You married a duke's heir and promptly made a habit of having sons.' Whereas she had married a third son and after seven years still had an empty cradle. There was no legacy in that, not that anyone would ever be jealous of Helena. She was too kind for jealousy and she'd had her own battles.

'Well, if Fortis is anything like his brother, you'll have a babe within the year.' Helena's words were meant to be reassuring, she could not have known the secret worries they represented to Avaline. A baby would be the best and worst thing right now. 'I am happy for you.' Helena paused, far too perceptive for Avaline's tastes. 'What is it? There's something else bothering you. Aren't you happy, too?'

'Too happy,' Avaline confessed. She set down her stitching, her worry rising to the surface against her will. She hated thinking about it, hated the doubt that tinged the happiness she and Fortis had so recently carved out for themselves. That happiness was so fragile that any doubt assailed it. But if there was anyone she could tell, it was Helena. 'I am afraid this much happiness can't last. There's simply too much of it. How can something this wonderful sustain itself? It can't and I don't know what I'll do if I lose him again.' She swallowed hard, her voice cracking as she whispered the last. 'Helena, he said he loved me.' Those words had come to mean the world to her. They defined who she was now: someone beloved.

'Oh, my,' Helena responded quietly, her sharp mind taking in the exquisite agony of such a revelation. 'Have his memories returned?'

'Many. Every day it seems more and more. He shares them with me now.' There was exquisite agony in that, too. She had the openness she'd craved and a place at his side as he walked through his journey of recovery. But the more he remembered, the more she feared their happiness would end. 'Helena, am I a terrible person? Sometimes I don't want him to remember. I just want things to stay the way they are.'

'Is that what you're worried about, my dear?

That he'll remember the past and not love you any more? War changes a man and it's definitely changed Fortis, for the better.' Helena leaned forward and took her hand once more. 'You need to trust the change in him.'

Avaline shook her head. That was not it. She did believe the man in bed with her loved her and she thought she loved him. 'It's the change I'm worried about, Helena. Fortis did not love me. Fortis wanted nothing to do with our marriage and he made no secret of that when he left. War didn't change him. He'd had years of war during which he did not write, he did not seek to make any reparations for his neglect right up to Balaclava. Suddenly he is lost for several months, returns to camp confused and disoriented and can't even remember his name. Then he comes home as the most devoted husband a woman could want. It doesn't make sense.' She held Helena's gaze, willing her to see.

'Then whatever happened in the woods changed him,' Helena argued doggedly, her blue eyes turning flinty with determination, but Avaline was just as determined.

'I've seen him naked and I've listened to his dreams. He has scars. One on his thigh and one on his arm from a blade or a bayonet. They're not the kind of scars one gets from a horse falling on them. A horse would crush someone, not stab them.'

Helena was quick to respond. 'Balaclava was not the only battle he fought in. He could have picked them up at any point, assuming he didn't have them already and you simply didn't notice?' Helena probed delicately, but they both knew there'd been no real intimacy between she and Fortis prior.

'No, he says they're from Balaclava. In his dreams, he's wounded. He's told me that much. He talks about crawling through the dirt on his belly, his arm and leg on fire.' Avaline put a hand to her mouth as if she could hold her rising panic inside. Saying the words out loud to Helena made her worries seem so much more real than when they simply existed in her head.

'What are you saying?' Helena's tone was suitably horrified as realisation began to dawn.

Avaline gathered her courage to name the fear that ate away at her and threatened her happiness. 'What if this man isn't Fortis?'

'Do not let Tobin Hayworth's ravings sway you,' Helena said fiercely. 'He's up in London and hopefully he'll stay there and stop bothering us. You needn't fear him any more.'

'No, not as long as Fortis is home,' Avaline was quick to answer. 'But what if he's not? I have to think about that. Can you imagine what happens if my husband is not my husband?'

'No, I cannot. I will not imagine it and neither should you. Hayworth would love to exploit that if he knew he'd got to you. Don't be his weapon,' Helena said sharply, levelling her rebuttal. 'How could he *not* be Fortis? He had your miniature in his pocket and your last letter when he walked into camp. He knew you on sight when he returned. He knew Hayworth. He called both of you by name without hesitation. Major Lithgow, his best friend, brought him home. He *is* Fortis. The physical resemblance alone confirms it. He looks like Fortis— furthermore, he looks like his brothers, with slight variations, of course.'

'Yes, of course.' Avaline breathed out a sigh. 'It helps when you put it that way.' Indeed, Helena's defence made her concerns seem ridiculous in the extreme. Perhaps Helena was right and she was taking Hayworth's threat too seriously.

'There's something else.' Helena's tone softened. 'The family is known for their romantic marriages. If Fortis loves you, it's proof he's following the family tradition. At last. He was a little slow out of the start, but he's catching up nicely.' A smile teased at Helena's mouth in encouragement. Avaline returned her smile with a tremulous one of her own. Oh, how she wanted Helena's confident belief!

'I know you've suffered these past years. Your marriage, the deaths of your parents, keeping the estate together. It's been a lot in a short time. That kind of tragedy marks a person, changes them as assuredly as going to war. But it's over now. There are good days ahead for you.' Helena patted her hand. 'Avaline, accept the good news. Your husband has returned penitent and physically whole. He wants a second chance. Give it to him. Give it to yourself. Give yourself permission to be happy and let go of the ghosts.' Helena's gaze pierced her with a strong warning. 'Besides, what choice do you have to do otherwise?' Helena smiled. 'I know just the thing—come with us to the Romani tonight. They've arrived and set up winter camp on the edge of the property where Bramble joins Blandford. There will be dancing and music.'

The annual arrival of the Romani was something Avaline had looked forward to ever since she was girl. To her, it signalled the official arrival of winter and the holiday season. 'Perhaps we will.' Avaline smiled in return. A visit to the camp might be just the thing to help her set aside her worries. Parties always put one in a good mood. That gave her another idea. Fortis's birthday was coming up. Perhaps she would give him a party, too. After all, as Helena said, what choice did she have?

Avaline thought about that choice all the way home. To pursue her doubts served no purpose except to feed the fervour of a man she despised, a man who'd tried to coerce her. She would do nothing to abet him, even unintentionally. *Even if it meant harbouring an impostor?* The unbidden thought would not be put down, not even with the force of Helena's rebuttal still lingering in her mind.

She pushed the thought away. She did not want to think it. Perhaps Helena was right and she was merely making trouble for herself where none existed. Perhaps she hadn't been happy for so long, she'd forgotten how. She couldn't remember a time when she simply hadn't just moved from crisis to crisis. Had she lived that way so long she didn't know how to live any other way? Well, if so, she would learn. She would have to if she and Fortis were to have a chance at happiness. The refrain came again: What other choice did she have?

Chapter Twelve

Fortis knelt before his campaign chest in his dressing room, hands resting on the brass clamps that held it shut. He had no choice. He had to open it. He'd not opened it since he'd been home. He hadn't needed to nor had he wanted to. He knew what was in it. He'd used it daily when he'd returned to camp and had awaited Cam's arrival. The top portion held extra clothing. The first drawer, dining utensils and toiletries. It was the second drawer he feared. Avaline's letters were in there.

He'd read the letters, of course, while he'd waited in camp. Those letters had been a source of comfort to him. He'd hungered for the images of home and domestic comfort she'd painted with her words and stories. They'd helped settle his mind when the whole world around him was chaos. But that was before he understood the tragedy of those letters. They were unanswered. He'd never answered any of them. How could that be? How was it that he'd not written a single line? What sort of man did not pay attention to his wife? He'd not gone back to reread the letters since, perhaps not wanting to know the answer to that. But now, he had to know. He had to face the truth, whatever it was for the sake of the future.

The trunk beckoned from the corner of his dressing room like a Pandora's box. He feared if he opened the letters, memories would fly out. There was temptation in that. Perhaps those memories would be the last pieces of what he needed to put the past in order. But in order to claim those valuable pieces, he would have to contend with the pain. Fortis bowed his head. He didn't want to know any more of the ways he'd hurt Avaline with his neglect. It was difficult enough simply knowing he had. He'd been a selfish, arrogant husband. Although not claiming those memories might also mean he'd never know why he'd been such a husband, just as not remembering the cave meant sacrificing knowing the name of his friend who had died.

No. He was not a man who shied away from

truth. He was going to open the trunk. Whatever memories were in there he would confront them. He was a soldier. He was supposed to be courageous. Only a coward would hide by living in the present. He had to remember that hope was in Pandora's box, too. There might be some of that for him inside his trunk as well and he'd never know if he didn't look.

Fortis drew a deep breath and pulled open the second drawer. The letters sat there, neatly wrapped in a blue ribbon. That was an addition he'd made when he'd returned to camp. The letters had been strewn about the drawer haphazardly when he'd found them. He'd read them, sorted them by date and tied them with a ribbon, only to untie them and read them again and again. All seventy-two of them. Six years of letters. One letter written a month, including the one that he'd carried in his pocket the day of Balaclava. He must have cared at least a little. Why hadn't he written back? Ever? Avaline hadn't pressed him for an answer since that first day in the garden, but she must wonder why he hadn't written, as did he.

Fortis slipped the blue ribbon off the packet and selected a letter at random. He unfolded it and scanned the date with a smile. This was one of his favourites, the one where she'd described Christmas at Bramble. The food, the candles, the gifts. He could almost smell the goose...

'There you are!' Avaline swept into the little dressing room, her cheeks rosy from the ride from Bramble. 'I've been looking for you. I have something to tell you.' She hadn't been looking for too long, though, since she was still in her coat. The proof that she'd come straight to him was warming.

She drew off her gloves and began to work her buttons. 'What are you doing?'

He held up the letter in his hand. 'Reading. I thought it might help me remember something, anything.'

Her fingers stilled on her buttons and some of the rose faded from her cheeks. 'Those silly letters? I am surprised you even still have them. What might you remember from them?'

He reached for her hand and drew her down to the floor with him. 'First of all, they are not silly. I read these when I returned to camp. They gave me peace. They calmed my mind. I was determined to get home, get back to you when I read them.' He sighed, understanding how incongruous the response was to reality.

'I thought I might remember why I never answered them. I opened them, you know. They'd all been opened when I returned to camp, so I know I'd read them before which begs the question—why wouldn't I answer? Perhaps I could understand not answering every one of them. War keeps a man busy and it's not always the best news to put in a letter. But six years of no answer? I don't understand it of myself and I want to.'

'Did looking through them help?' Avaline's face was concerned, anxious. He wished he had better news for her.

He shook his head. Reading the letters had been a pleasant exercise in futility. They'd not restored any memories. 'I was only reminded of how much comfort they gave me when I returned to the British lines. When I came back, I didn't recognise anything in my tent, or my trunks. Everything about me was all confusion. But I knew you. I had your miniature in my pocket and your letters in my campaign chest. When I read the letters, I felt as though I was home again. I knew the people you wrote about. I knew Blandford. I even knew Hayworth. Those letters were a lifeline, which is why I can't imagine not having written back.'

He reached for Avaline's hand. 'But you know why, don't you? Will you tell me? Was I such a poor husband? I think you've been shielding me from the hard truths of our marriage.' He blew out a breath. He didn't want to think of what he might have done. It was bad enough he'd obviously not given her pleasure in bed in the early days. What else had he done? Had he cheated on her? Flaunted a mistress? Gambled? Drank? Whored? It was unfortunate a gentleman had so many vices available.

She pulled her hand away, her face pale. Dear Lord, she didn't want to tell him. That only made it worse. What was she hiding? What was so awful that she was afraid to speak it? Had he hit her? Had he beaten her? Was she worried how he would respond? That perhaps he would have a relapse? 'I can handle it, Avaline. Whatever it is. You don't need to protect me,' Fortis protested, hoping to encourage her.

She shook her head. 'We've managed to avoid the subject for a month, perhaps that was proof enough that we don't need to revisit the past. It can't be changed and we're happy enough in the present.'

Ah. He'd been wrong. It wasn't him she was protecting. It was herself. There was something she feared for herself in the telling. 'Avaline, I won't be mad. I promise. I give you my word. Please tell me. There should be no secrets between us.'

Avaline looked up, worry and sadness etched across her features. There was resignation in her eyes, an acknowledgement that she had to tell him. 'Fortis, you didn't write because you didn't love me.' He felt the weight of her gaze on him as she let him consider her words. 'You did not want me.' He heard the hurt that still lingered after seven years. Part of him knew relief. He'd not physically hurt her or socially shamed her with flagrant behaviour. But part of him could see the pain in her eyes as she remembered what must have been awful words spoken by him. Words hurt as much as fists. He wasn't sure how he knew that, but he knew it was true.

'I cannot believe that. I *don't* want to believe that.' Fortis rose and began to pace the small space of the dressing room. 'Why didn't I love you?' He scrubbed a hand over his face trying to imagine not loving Avaline. It needn't have been a grand passion. Love took many forms, some milder than what he'd experienced with her since his return. 'Surely I had some modicum of affection for you?' He was desperate to believe that. Perhaps she had misunderstood? Perhaps he had not clearly communicated his affections?

'Fortis, it was a marriage of convenience arranged by our parents to protect the estate and me from Hayworth. You know he's always been greedy for this land because it was unentailed and wouldn't go to my cousin, my father's heir. Owning Blandford would give him the largest estate in Sussex once it joined with Indigo Hall, larger even than Bramble. He's forever putting himself in competition with your father,' Avaline explained, but she was still being delicate about it, shielding him.

'A lot of men of my station have arranged marriages. I can't have been surprised by it,' Fortis argued, hoping his arguments would prompt her to offer more detail.

'You felt I was a child. I was eighteen. I hadn't been to London or had a Season. But you were home, briefly, my father had been ill most of the winter, his health was beginning to decline, our crops had failed for the third year and Hayworth was starting to press more ardently. Our parents decided to move quickly. There was no room to wait for an engagement period. Who knew when you'd be home again and war is always a dicey business.' Her eyes slid away from him and fixed on her hands folded tightly in her lap. There was more she wasn't telling him.

'Did you also resent the match?' Fortis asked quietly. A thousand emotions were running through him, most of them akin to self-loathing. He'd been upset about the marriage and he'd taken it out on her.

She shook her head but she would not meet his eyes. 'No, I was nervous, of course. I had just finished my last term at the academy. But, I was naive. I thought there was a fairy-tale quality to the wedding. I went straight from the schoolroom to being married to a duke's handsome son. What could go wrong? Surely, my husband would come to love me and we would live happily ever after.' The slight sarcasm beneath her words cut at him. He'd given her cause to regret her assumptions.

'I was a child you felt forced to wed. You made your feelings on the subject plain, Fortis.' And so had she. While he'd been busy railing against his circumstances, she'd been in love with him, willing to make an effort at the marriage. He'd cast aside her affection and her efforts with careless disregard.

Yes, he'd known the framework of their past before now. He'd known he'd been cruel, that he'd not cared for her as he should have, but it was the details that cut him today. To hear her put the specifics into words forced him to face his sin in a more direct manner. Now he knew exactly what he had done.

'Why didn't you want to tell me? Is there something more you'd protect me from?' He hoped not. These were hard truths to face about himself, but he had to face them if he stood a chance of recovering who he was. Recovery wasn't only about remembering the good, but also the bad.

Avaline rose and shook out her skirts. He recognised it as a dismissal tactic. She wanted this conversation to be over. She would not get away with it. 'Tell me,' Fortis insisted, casually moving to block the doorway, his gaze stern.

Avaline's chin set in a defiant jut, but she relented. 'I didn't want to tell you because I'm selfish. I didn't want you to remember how much you didn't like me. Satisfied?' She moved towards the door, but he didn't budge.

'Not quite.' Fortis smiled softly at his wife,

her admission filling him with tenderness. 'Why didn't you want me to remember that?' He suspected he knew, but he wanted to hear her say it. Now he was the one being selfish.

'Maybe I like the man who came home to me just as he is.' She bit her lip, but not quickly enough. Fortis caught the tremble before she could quell it. Her bravado was fading. He saw the line of her jaw tighten and her throat work madly against rising emotion. 'Maybe I liked my husband falling in love with me.'

He folded her into his arms and pressed a kiss to the top of her head. 'Maybe I like it, too.' He saw her more clearly now. She'd been afraid of losing him, of losing the way he was now. There was hope in that. She feared because she loved him, too, even if she wouldn't say the words. He felt her arms wrap around his waist, her head against his chest. He was a lucky man even if he didn't always like or understand who that man was.

'Fortis?' Avaline whispered, tilting her head up to look at him. 'Would you do something for me?' Her hips moved slightly against him, the tiniest of motions causing him to quicken.

'Yes, anything.' His voice was husky with fast-mounting desire. 'You know I would.' Especially in moments like this when his body was rousing to her and she had him in her thrall.

She turned and gave him her back. 'Help me with my laces.'

Chapter Thirteen

Avaline wanted to be naked, wanted to shed her cares with the same certainty she shed her gown. Urgency drove her now as she stepped out of the gown pooled at her feet and she wanted Fortis to be naked, too, skin to skin, as if that physical closeness would drive away the mental ghosts that hovered on the periphery of her happiness, waiting to destroy it with their doubts. She tugged at his shirt, pulling it hastily from the waistband of his trousers, her fingers fumbling in their haste with his buttons. She'd come home from Bramble with every intention of seizing her happiness as Helena had suggested. She'd had every intention of shutting the past away and focusing on the present, ready to accept that obsessing about the past might be prohibiting her ability to live fully in the present. But there'd been no escaping the past, not when it was spread out in letters on the dressing-room floor before him. When he'd looked at her, his blue eyes full of questions, the ghosts had come swarming, for him as well as for her.

She pushed his shirt from his shoulders, her mouth catching his in hard, frantic kisses while her hands moved on to his trousers. Fortis's questions were not dissimilar to her questions. He, too, was riddled with doubt about who he was. He merely asked the question differently. Where she asked, 'Why did he love her now?', he asked, 'Why hadn't he loved her *then*?' Two different ends of the same equation, with no answer in the vague middle. Neither of them knew what had changed him. She had not wanted to speak the words today. She had not wanted to hurt him *and* she had not wanted to expose herself—how much she'd come to care for him, almost against her will, and how much she feared losing him.

She knelt before him, tugging his trousers down over lean hips and long legs, until he was revealed to her in his entirety, her body and soul hungry for him, desperate for him, in fact. In bed, they could banish their doubts. She made to rise, only to feel the firm pressure of his hand at her shoulder. 'Stay, Avaline. Would you do something for me?' His voice was deliciously low as he borrowed her words.

'You know I would do anything for you.' She looked up at him, from the intimacy of her knees, giving him back his words wrapped in the husk of her own seduction. She was as aroused as he. His Adam's apple worked as he swallowed hard.

'Give me your mouth, Avaline, on me.'

His phallus, already primed, seemed to jump at the words, her own pulse quickening at his request, the words erotic in their explicitness. On him, on the most intimate part of his maleness. This was new territory, men and women asking for their pleasure, naming it. 'Yes,' she whispered, feathering him with the light warmth of her sigh and closing her lips around the tip of him. This was decadent pleasure indeed, to lick at his length, to suck and taste him on her tongue, to hear him moan in desperate response with wanting and know that he desired her, that he desired what she did to him. She felt his hands clench in the depths of her hair. He was all salt and strength in her mouth as she coaxed him towards completion. His body tightened, the sounds of his pleasure coming faster in staccato repetition as he reached his limits. 'Avaline,' he warned hoarsely in a final gasp. She slipped her mouth from him and took him in her hand as he spent. It was miraculous and new to behold pleasure in this manner and it awed her.

'Here.' Fortis reached for his discarded clothing and found a handkerchief. His voice was shaky as he slid down beside her. 'I'll show you some proper pleasure once I recover.' He smiled at her, his blue eyes crinkling at the corners and the ghosts were banished, just like that. Nothing mattered except that they were together. As long as there was that, they could overcome anything, even their past. Fortis stretched out on the floor, his head propped in his hand as he studied her. 'Thank you. That was divine. Did you mind?'

'Did I mind? No, not at all. Should I have?' Avaline worried her lip, suddenly concerned. The next moment she let out a shriek as Fortis grabbed her and drew her alongside him, his hand at her hip, his body warm against her.

'No, I don't think so at any rate. There are some women who might tell you otherwise, that it's not proper. But that's not true.' He lavished her with soft kisses at her brow, her jaw, her nose, her mouth. 'Our bodies were made to be enjoyed by ourselves and by the ones we love. I do love yours, Avaline.' He bent his lips to the column of her throat. 'Your neck is so slim, so elegant.' He whispered endearments as his mouth journeyed down her body. 'Your breasts are like vanilla fairy cakes with a raspberry on top,' he murmured as he sucked at her nipples and kissed the sides of her breasts. 'Yes, little cakes indeed.' He kissed her navel. 'Shall I go on?' he whispered wickedly. 'Although I need champagne to worship this delicacy correctly.'

'Why is that?' She hardly dared to breathe, his words, his images as intoxicating as any wine.

'Because this, my darling, is a chalice.' He blew against her belly. 'From which only the finest champagne should be drunk, sip by sensual sip.' He paused, his gaze travelling up her length, two burning blue coals. 'Shall I sip from you as you did from me? Shall I attempt to drive you mad as you drove me?'

'Is that possible?' The prospect piqued her curiosity and she levered on her elbows.

'Yes.' His eyes danced, wicked, playful flames. 'But you must give me something in exchange. Information. Why were you looking for me today when you came home?'

'Who says I had anything to share?' she teased.

'I do.' Fortis moved over her, straddling her on all fours. 'You had news. You were flushed and you hadn't bothered to take off your coat. You came looking for me straight away and we got distracted.'

Avaline lay back, revelling in how well he could read her. He was kissing her again, blowing little puffs in her navel. 'I did have news. Helena says the Romani have arrived. The family is going down to welcome them tonight. She thought we'd like to come along.'

'Then we should definitely go.' Fortis smiled, but it was a polite smile. It did not mirror her own enthusiasm for the outing.

Her mind registered the reason. *He doesn't know. He didn't remember the Romani.* The horrible scope of all that had been taken from him hit her hard in that moment. He'd lost integral memories, joyful memories. The Romani had camped on Panshawe-Tresham land for over two decades. The Tresham boys had grown up with them.

Avaline said nothing, not wanting to embarrass him over something else he could not re-call. Instead, she vowed to herself they would have a grand time tonight, she would see to it. She would try to give him back a little of the joy he'd lost. 'There's something else, too,' she murmured, enjoying his ministrations. 'I've decided to give you a birthday party.'

Fortis looked up from his kisses, an odd, touching expression in his eyes, and for a moment he seemed vulnerable. 'Really? You want to give me a party?'

Avaline smiled, enjoying that the idea pleased him so much. 'Yes, now carry on.' She laughed. 'You have to make good on your end of the deal.' One would think he'd never had a party before from the way he was looking at her. 'I decided it on the way home from Bramble. It's the perfect way to celebrate your return. The neighbours have kept their distance this past month out of courtesy for us, but they're bound to be curious. We don't want to hole up here like hermits,'—or as if they had something to hide, she thought to herself. 'Everyone will want to welcome you home.' She gave a short, sharp gasp as Fortis slipped a hand between her thighs and birthday parties became suddenly less important.

'Ah, I see. It's to be a *re*-birthday party.' Fortis's hand pressed on the little nub hidden in her folds, sending an exquisite burst of desire through her. 'Will there be fairy cakes? Vanilla ones?' he dared wickedly.

'If you'd like.' She shifted beneath his hand, trying to claim more pleasure.

'And when is this gala to be?'

'December twelfth, on your actual birthday. Two weeks from today. There's just enough time to plan it if I send the invitations out tomorrow.' But not right now. Oh, Lord, not right now. She could hardly think straight when he touched her like that.

'Will there be presents?' he asked with a boyish charm that nearly undid her as much as his hand. 'I already know what I want you to get me.'

'Mmm-hmm.' She stretched, enjoying this new aspect of pleasure far too much to think about birthday parties. She arched her hips up to meet him, 'Whatever you want, Fortis.'

'Whatever I want? I like the sound of that.'

There were other sounds Fortis liked, too: Avaline's mewls as he built the pleasure within her, her desperate gasps as climax neared, her cries when she achieved it and he knew he'd been the one, the only one, who'd brought her to such an end. Perhaps it was male arrogance on his part to take pride in giving his wife such pleasure, but it pleased him no end to see her lose herself in his touch. To see it from the intimate cradle of her thighs, his gaze travelling up over the perfect hills of her breasts, along the elegant arch of her neck as she took her pleasure, was another pleasure entirely. He'd given her this—might it make up for whatever he'd not given her before.

'Avaline, let me carry you to bed.' He probably should have taken her there when all this play had started, but she'd been frantic in her need and the idea of taking her here in the dressing room had carried a certain decadence to it. He'd been frantic, too, wanting to push away the things she'd told him, wanting to prove he was a better man than the one who'd ridden away. There'd been no time for a bed. But there was time now, all the time in the world. He lifted her in his arms, letting her hair fall over his arm in a golden spill. A rebirthday party it would be. He'd come home a new man, a man Avaline could be proud of. It was time to start enjoying his life *en totale*, embracing who he was without a shadow of a doubt. Today had been a start by facing those letters and the truths that Avaline had shared. Tonight, he would continue stepping into the future as Fortis Tresham, as himself; the third son of a duke, a man who had everything. It was time he stopped letting the past weigh him down and started enjoying the present.

It was a frosty night, the very best of winter evenings when the stars were out, shining like diamond brilliants in a dark velvet sky, and the air was crisp—a perfect night for a carriage parade through the starlit darkness. Avaline laughed when he whispered his fanciful notion to her in the carriage they shared with Anne and Ferris, top down, fur lap robes tucked about them.

'A parade, is it?' Avaline squeezed his gloved hand beneath the lap robes, a private reminder of the greater intimacies they shared just hours ago. 'That sounds rather grand.'

'Are we not "rather grand"?' Fortis argued good-naturedly, gesturing to the carriage ahead of them and the one behind them followed by a wagon. They were indeed a procession. His parents rode ahead in their own carriage and behind them came Frederick and Helena with the five boys, sans nursemaids, piled into their own vehicle. Frederick had insisted he and Helena could manage their own children without help on the outing. 'And if that fails,' Frederick had said with a wink as they'd all piled in, 'there are grandparents and uncles to lend a hand.'

Fortis admired that about his brother. Frederick meant to be a real father to his brood, a father in more than name only. It was the kind of father he wished to be if ever given the chance. If he and Avaline kept at it as they had this afternoon, he just might have that chance. The thought brought a quiet smile to his lips as Avaline slid him a covert look of question, but he kept his secret to himself. 'We are grand indeed. It takes a cavalcade of carriages to mobilise the Tresham clan,' he exclaimed.

Ferris and Anne laughed with them. 'That's very alliterative, Brother. A cavalcade of carriages, indeed.' Ferris grinned and broke into a little song that was soon taken up by the other carriages, the boys joining in with enthusiasm from Frederick's. They made a merry party, singing gaily as their carriages rolled along the night trail, lanterns sending bobbing streams of light ahead that soon met with lanterns coming from the other direction. The scene touched something deep inside him. He wanted to remember these moments, to capture them in mental pictures that could never be erased. His soul was hungry for such moments of belonging, of peace, of being part of a family.

'Look! Everyone has come out to meet us.' Avaline clutched his arm excitedly, her own enthusiasm infectious as lanterns flanked the carriages and Romani voices took up the tune, joining the song as the carriages continued into the camp. 'Vano will want to greet your father and properly thank him for his hospitality.' She nudged him with her elbow. 'Vano will want to greet you, Fortis, now that you're home. He's on your land, too.' Fortis supposed that was true, although it hadn't occurred to him until now that he might be required to formally act the lord of the manor. Three carriages had come out to greet their guests and a wagon laden with foodstuffs and blankets of alpaca wool sent over by Viscount Taunton, a friend of the family who owned a mill in Somerset.

He and Ferris helped the ladies down and then they were surrounded, everyone exchanging hugs and greetings, old friends who hadn't seen each other for a year. 'This is a much happier end to your year this time, isn't it?' A young woman with dark hair hugged Avaline and then hugged him. 'Your handsome husband is home.'

Avaline laughed. 'Fortis, this is Selina. She tells our fortunes. Last year, she told me I would find happiness.'

Selina tossed glossy black curls over her shoulder. 'She did not believe me, milord. But see, I was right!' She grabbed his hand and dragged him towards the centre of the reunion. 'Come meet Vano and the men. Then, we'll dance and eat and tell more fortunes.'

No sooner had Selina dragged him away than Fortis was engulfed in the festive whirlwind. He shook hands with the other men, only to be grabbed into swift, tight hugs and kissed soundly on the cheeks as person after person exclaimed over his return. Always, Frederick and Ferris and his father were nearby, someone always at his shoulder. When had he ever been so loved? The welcome was nearly overwhelming and he wished—oh, how he wished—that he remembered these people and could return their hospitality. Next year, he promised himself as he took a seat at the campfire, Avaline to his right, Ferris at his left. Next year, he *would* remember them and they would talk about this night together. Someone pressed a bowl of hot stew into his hands and across the fire someone made a toast to the Duke of Cowden and Lord Fortis Tresham's generosity.

'They should be toasting you,' he whispered to Avaline. 'It's your land.'

'It's ours,' she corrected. 'I don't mind, truly.' She snuggled against him. 'You're happy. I knew you would be if you came.'

'I was already happy, Avaline. I'm with you.' Fortis smiled at her, his heart filling with a new sense of contentment. They'd conquered the obstacle of the letters today. It made him optimistic that they would conquer whatever else lay between them as well.

Selina came to sit beside them, taking Avaline's hand. 'Grandmother will tell stories soon. But first, this.' She turned Avaline's hand over and traced her palm with a finger. But instead of saying anything, she was silent and studied Avaline.

'What is it that you see in my wife's palm?' Fortis prompted, unnerved by her silence.

Selina gave him an enigmatic smile. 'I don't know. Something that wasn't there last year. It's very unusual.' She turned her attention to Avaline. 'It suggests your husband has returned, but that you will have two great loves.'

Avaline laughed, unbothered. 'That's not so unusual. I love my husband and perhaps the second love is a child. Perhaps I should be a fortune teller?' Selina laughed with her, but there was a shadow in her eyes that suggested she disagreed with Avaline's interpretation.

Around them the fire circle grew quiet as Selina's old grandmother took to the centre and began stories, one about a lovely witch who fell in love with a mortal. The story soothed him—the sound of her voice, the rise and fall of words, the hypnotic dance of flames from the fire. It drew his mind back to other stories, other voices, other fires, another time not so long ago when there'd been nothing but stories to entertain himself with, a time when his friend had been alive and the world had existed of a cave deep in a forest...

Chapter Fourteen

*H*e brought tea in their single tin cup and a bite of hard tack to the wounded man. 'At least the tea is warm. I wish I had something more to give you for the pain.'

'You can give me conversation. Would you tell me about yourself? That I might know my rescuer? It would take my mind off my own injuries.' The wounded man sipped cautiously at the tea.

He shrugged and settled beside the man. 'There's not much to tell. I joined the military eight years ago. Or rather, I was "encouraged" to do so in order to avoid gaol, but in hindsight I don't regret it. It's been a good opportunity for a wild young man to learn some discipline and respect and some skills. I've got to see the world and I've not had to worry about my next meal.'

'What were you going to gaol for?' the man asked, interested.

'Stealing. Theft.' He wouldn't mince words to impress the patient. The man seemed intent on making him out to be a hero. He wasn't. 'I was caught red-handed, as it were, with my fingers on a duchess's ruby tiara. I'd have got away with it if the maid hadn't come in. I'd been halfway to the window before the maid had screamed.

'Red handed, ruby tiara, ha, ha.' Tresham's laugh turned into a cough, then a gasp and a sob. Aidan propped him up until the coughing passed. 'God, it hurts.'

'I'm sorry, no more humour.' Aidan smiled in commiseration. 'Your ribs will feel better in a few days.' If they were bruised. If they were something more, well, he'd worry about that if it came to it.

'Tell me,' Tresham asked once the pain had ebbed, 'how was it that you came to be in close proximity to a duchess's jewel box.'

'Oh, that's a very good tale.' Aidan chuckled, getting as comfortable as he could with his leg. 'Much more suitable for soldiers by the camp-fire than swapping histories. The Duchess was in bed asleep. I knew because I'd been in bed

*with her just minutes before and was respon-
sible for that very sound sleep.'*

*The man fought the urge not to laugh. 'That's
a very good story. But, thief or not, you saved
me. I owe you a great debt.'*

*'You do not. We are comrades in arms. Any-
one else would have done the same. What's
your name?' he asked, steering the conversation away from talk of debts and owing. But his
patient would not be swayed.*

*'My name is Major Lord Fortis Tresham of
the Fourth Queen's Own Hussars.' The man
reached for his arm, gripping it with surpris-
ing strength. 'Listen to me, I am the third son
of the Duke of Cowden. We have a home on
Portland Square in London. You are to go there
and tell them...'*

*He covered the hand on his sleeve with his
own. This was desperation talking, he'd seen it
before with frightened men, men who thought
they might die. 'You can go there yourself, or
we can go together if it means that much to
you,' he soothed. He would see to it. This man
had people in the world who cared for him.
Those people were probably desperately awaiting word right now of his fate.*

'What's your name?' the man asked.

'I'm Aidan Roswell, infantry, enlisted. Not nearly as glamorous.'

Granny's story was ending, he could tell from the cadence of her voice, but damn it if he could recall how it had gone. His own mind was reeling from its own recollection and its own revelations. It had been like all his other flashbacks to date, like a visual story unfolding in his mind, one that he watched outside his body, through the eyes of another. But this time, it had been clearer. There was no confusion over whom the voices belonged to. This time, he had come away with a name and he clung to it with all the mental tenacity he could muster lest it elude him again. He rose from the circle, half-staggering, stumbling, towards the quiet of the darkness beyond the flame. In the darkness he could think without distraction. What had he learned? What did it mean?

In the dark, elation and fear swamped him in turns. He had the long-coveted name he'd searched his memories for! Aidan Roswell. A sense of relief settled on him, as if a circle had come full. He had wanted that name so badly. He'd believed if he had that name, it would solve everything. He had not imagined the second man. His mind had not doctored his memories. He had a quest now. He could leverage all his familial resources and find Aidan Roswell. He could discover what had happened to him. If the man could be found alive, Hayworth's ability to sow doubt could be put to rest for good.

Fortis had to halt his thoughts there. He was putting the cart before the horse by miles. The reality was that if he found Aidan Roswell, it would probably be in a grave. As Ferris had pointed out weeks ago, the man was likely dead. Still, he'd like to know. The man had rescued him, made it possible for him to come home. For the first time since he'd come home, pieces were starting to fall into place. So, why the fear? It was there, pulsing beneath the elation too strongly to ignore. What was in the flashback that he feared? In the other flashbacks, the fear had been generated by something external: discovery in the cave, discovery by the scavengers on the battlefield. But tonight's fear was different. It came from something inside him.

The name. He feared the name. It came to him in a moment of blinding insight. He sat down hard on a bench as he let the realisation take him. He loathed the name as much as he loved it, the one thing that he thought would free him, that would bring closure and completeness. His fear told him he was wrong. The name did not bring completeness. It brought questions, questions he should have been asking all along. Only one man had walked out of the forest. Why? What had happened to Aidan Roswell? Why did he see his time in the cave through Roswell's eyes? Why did he have Roswell's scars?

He knew Ferris's answers to all that. Even before there'd been a name, Ferris had explained it was simply how the mind might choose to work. Flashbacks might carry their own fictions within them as the mind mashed up memories and joined them with others. That might be true. There was no reason to believe it wasn't. But there was another explanation, too, one that he'd not dwelled on, and why should he have? There'd been so much to dwell on: saving his marriage, falling in love with his wife, reconnecting to his life, to his family, learning what it meant to be a duke's son. Amidst all of that, he'd accepted the premise he'd been given by the army, by Cam Lithgow, a premise reinforced by his parents, his brothers, his wife—that he was Lord Fortis Tresham. From the beginning, he should have asked the most important question of all: What if the man who came out of the woods wasn't Fortis Tresham, what if that man only thought he was?

He began to shake. It would be the cruellest of tricks for a mind to play, to persuade oneself that he was someone else. What if Tobin Hayworth was right? What if Hayworth wasn't the villain all along? What if the villain was himself and Hayworth the hero? Fortis clutched at his head, trying to soothe himself, soothe his mind. He sought reason. This newest explanation was no more true or false than Ferris's explanations. He need not give this any credence. He need not let fear rule him. He had a choice.

'Fortis? Are you all right?' Avaline's voice came through the darkness, a soft whisper. He felt her on the bench beside him. 'You've remembered something, I can tell. I wanted to give you time, but when you didn't come back I got worried. Do you need me to get Ferris?'

'No, I don't want Ferris.' The words came out too harshly. They'd stunned Avaline in their sharpness. He drew a deep breath. 'I just need you.' It was true. He already felt better simply having her beside him, her patience endless in the silence while she waited for him to gather his thoughts.

'Was it awful?' she asked after a bit. Beyond them, by the fire, dancing had started.

'Only what I made of it.' He could see that now, in retrospect. He need not be afraid of the memory. He had merely raced to dangerous conclusions.

'And what was that, Fortis?'

But fear was not so easily defeated. The simplest of questions poked it awake and it drowsily got to its feet. He wouldn't have long to subdue it before it was in full force again. 'That perhaps I was not Fortis Tresham. That I was the other man in the cave.' The horrible words tumbled out. He would be brave and own them with Avaline. His thoughts affected her. She had a right to them, a right to know what went on his shattered mind.

She hesitated a moment before responding, much as she had that first day in the garden when he'd asked her if she was happy he'd come home. That hesitation worried him now as it had worried him then. She would give him an answer he might not like. 'Why would you think that?'

'Because I remembered the other man's name.'

He felt Avaline smile in the darkness, felt her joy for him. 'That's wonderful. It's what you've wanted.'

'Except now I wonder if that's the reason I see the flashbacks through his eyes, why my scars don't match Cam's report of being pulled from under a horse. That would have bruised or broken my ribs, not scarred me.'

'But one of the men had broken ribs,' Avaline reminded him.

'Was that man me? Why don't I remember the cave through the eyes of the man who lay on the pallet?'

'Ferris has told you why,' she argued with him in quiet determination. 'Do you no longer accept your brother's explanations?'

Did he? That was one of the bigger questions looming tonight. 'I don't know,' Fortis admitted. 'What if I am not who I thought I was?'

'What if you are and you insist on torturing yourself with a lie you can't prove? What if you insist on marring your—*our*—happiness with that lie?' Avaline slid to the ground before him, on her knees as she grasped his hands tightly. There was a fierceness in her tone that hadn't been there before. 'Look at me, Fortis. You have a choice. You can spend your life wondering about your identity, waiting for your memories of the battle and the cave to come back, or you can start, right now, living like a whole man, living like Lord Fortis Tresham.'

'Avaline, what if…?' She didn't let him finish.

'There are no what ifs. There is no room for them. This is what Hayworth wants. He would be so pleased to know his doubts had taken root in you, the very fellow he wants to bring down. We cannot let him win. The stakes are far too high.'

His gentle wife had become a termagant. No, not a termagant. A general, marshalling her troops for a fight that mattered greatly to her, and he understood in those moments that she was on her knees, fighting for *him*. For them. Because, even though she hadn't said the words, she loved him and her courage overwhelmed him. He had not been the only one fighting battles. She'd had her own war to wage upon his return. She'd been thwarted in love before by him. To trust him again was an act of bravery on her part. She'd decided he was worth it. He hoped he was.

Was Hayworth playing with his mind or was his mind playing its own tricks, and in all this where was the truth? Could he even assume there was any truth at all? Or were his memories just another casualty of war, something that would never quite be restored? Never work again like they used to? Some men went to war and lost limbs. Avaline was right. Perhaps he'd gone to war and lost his mind. Like lost arms and legs and eyes, he might not get it back. How much longer was he willing to mentally put his life on hold and let his fear paralyse them both? She was right, too, that the stakes were enormous. To not be Fortis Tresham would ruin them both and the family. He was not willing to risk people who loved him with his doubts. He had to set those doubts aside as Avaline had set aside her doubts about loving him and embrace the happiness he was given.

'You are Fortis Tresham, my husband,' Avaline said fiercely. 'Now and for ever, that is the only truth I know, the only truth I *need* to know.'

It was the only truth that could save them. He would accept it. He would push aside the doubts that had come upon him tonight and he would not think about them again. They were the products of a broken mind, nothing more. It was time to start living. He had a choice. Why would he choose fear when he could choose so much more? Fortis rose and raised Avaline to her feet. He smiled down at her, 'Come dance with me, Wife.' He felt her gaze settle on him like a benediction. The past had finished and gone. Everything had become fresh and new. Tonight, with Avaline beside him, he had found himself.

Aidan Roswell had been found. Revenge had a name at last, and a history—a rather unsavoury one. Everything was finally coming together and just in time. Over the past two weeks Tobin Hayworth had spent in London, word had reached him of Avaline's efforts to throw a birthday for her errant husband. The news he'd just received would make quite the birthday present. Hayworth eyed the folder on his desk with a certain amount of glee. Happiness was not an emotion he was familiar with, but the satisfaction he felt at this moment was close enough. Thanks to a bribe at the War Office he had a name and now thanks to the footwork of Bow Street, he had more than a name. He had a history and a rather unsavoury one at that.

He smiled coldly at the Runner who stood before his polished mahogany desk awaiting further instruction. Bow Street had been very clear this name had emerged by default. Everyone else on the list of the missing after Balaclava had been accounted for in some way or another. Some had died, some had been found, some didn't meet the physical appearance, some had come home. The one thing they all had in common was that someone, somewhere, knew them: a parent, a sibling, a wife, a relative. No one had known the name Aidan Roswell. There wasn't a wife, sister, brother or mother who was awaiting word about what had become of him. Men who weren't missed didn't come from good families. They came from poor families who were hardly families at all: single mothers, whores, poor widows with too many children to raise on too little money.

Hayworth was a practical man. No one appeared out of thin air. Some men were just better about hiding themselves, but in the end, everyone had a past, even Aidan Roswell. He'd sent Bow Street to the prison records, gaming hells and whorehouses, and Bow Street had done their job admirably. Of course, it helped that people were predictable after all, no matter who they were. His hunches had been right.

Hayworth thumbed through the folder while the Runner waited. Roswell had been found on the gaol rosters for jewel theft, apparently, caught for stealing a duchess's tiara. That particular duchess, the Duchess of Chichester, was still alive and well. That could be useful for him and embarrassing for Cowden. The very man masquerading as his son had also stolen from a fellow peer. This was just getting better and better. 'Looks as though he commuted his sentence in exchange for time in the army,' Hayworth mused out loud. The act probably saved his neck, too. The man could have hanged for his crime. Roswell might still hang after he was done with him.

He shut the folder. 'You were discreet? No one must know you're enquiring for me.' It would look badly if certain people thought he'd actively hunted for evidence against Fortis Tresham. No one would hand out a knighthood to a man who attempted to destroy his neighbours. But they would applaud him if he was right. Then he'd be the saviour of the aristocracy, the defender of the gates of the peerage so that its generations of privilege were not tarnished by the infiltration of an impostor who passed himself off as something more.

'Always,' the Runner assured him.

'Then your work here is done.' Hayworth dismissed the man and rubbed at his jaw. It still pained him when he took too big of a bite. He allowed his mind to run free. What compelled a man to take the risk Roswell had taken? Surely he knew if he were caught there would be no surviving it? Surely he knew he would lose everything, including the support of the family he'd recently gained? The Cowdens would be devastated. Avaline would be shattered. *If* he could make the connection stick. Tobin was well aware he'd found a man, but that was no assurance the man was actually posturing as Tresham.

Maybe in the end it didn't matter if the man was an impostor. It only mattered if people believed it. Belief would be enough to send Fortis Tresham to the gallows, real or not, and Tobin would be there to pick up the pieces. This time, Avaline wouldn't refuse him. She couldn't, not if she wanted to escape scandal and keep her home intact. He doubted anyone would look favourably upon a woman holding so much land when she'd demonstrated such a lack of discernment that she couldn't tell her own husband from a fraud. He would have Avaline on her knees in all ways. He shifted in his chair, hard from just thinking of it. Soon, he told himself. All that remained now was to pack and leave for Sussex in order to make it in time for a certain birthday party to which he was not invited. He chuckled at the thought. It was all quite quid pro quo. It seemed invitations didn't mean what they used to. They didn't stop Tresham from crashing his harvest ball and they wouldn't stop him from crashing Tresham's birthday party. He knew just how he'd do it and it would be perfect.

Chapter Fifteen

❦

His birthday had been perfect so far and was only bound to get better, Fortis reflected as his valet shaved him for the evening festivities. His birthday supper and his birthday ball were still to come, the final two events of his birthday gala planned with loving attention given to every detail by his wife. Avaline had outdone herself with help from Anne and Helena. Fortis smiled, remembering how the day had begun—in bed with Avaline who'd awakened with him kisses. With luck, the day would end that way, too.

'Hold still, milord,' his valet scolded in exasperation. 'We can't have you going to supper with a nicked face. Milady would never forgive me. She's instructed that you be turned out to your finest.'

Fortis wiped the smile off his face and tried to remain stoic long enough for his valet to finish his work. But it was hard not to smile when he thought about his day. He'd been fêted from one end of it to the other. His brothers had arrived for an early ride through frost-tipped woods and a brisk gallop through the meadow. His parents and the rest of the Treshams, nephews included, joined them for a magnificent breakfast set in the Blandford dining room.

Fortis knew without question he would always remember the sight of the long table neatly filled with thirteen Tresham faces from oldest, his father nearing seventy, to the youngest, a chubby-cheeked one-and-a-half-year-old toddler, who bounced in his highchair and threw crackers on the floor to the amusement of all. With luck, some day he and Avaline would have their own children at the table, maybe as many as Frederick and Helena, maybe more. They'd not discussed it. There were so many things that had taken precedent upon his return. Still, he had hopes they might not have to wait too long. Avaline had said nothing yet, but he'd been counting. A large family was just the thing, even if it was as noisy, unruly and sometimes unpredictable as Frederick and Helena's boys proved.

If his nephews had eventually slipped down from the table and played a wild game of tag while the adults lingered over coffee and tea, or if it was occasionally difficult to carry on a continuous conversation without being interrupted, Fortis didn't mind. He was surrounded by family. Even after being home for almost two months, he had not grown tired of his brothers riding over, sometimes—well, most of the time—unannounced, or riding to Bramble to spend afternoons with his father and talk over improvements for Blandford while his mother sat with them, stitching.

Breakfast had been followed with a 'frost fair' on the front lawn for Blandford's tenants. He and Avaline had joined them to stroll among the booths with their sweets and trinkets, and he'd been filled with the sense of what it meant to be Fortis Tresham, son of the Duke of Cowden, to stroll the parklands of his own estate, dressed against the elements in warm winter wool, with his wife on his arm, his pockets filled with coins to spoil his wife with pretty trifles: a red silk ribbon for her hair, a hot meat pasty for her lips, a mug of warm mulled wine to chase the chill from her fingers as she cupped it. He was young and healthy, and beloved, a man who was complete in himself, who had the world at his feet.

In the afternoon there'd been games and races with prizes. He managed to win the marksmanship competition and Avaline had blushed when he claimed a kiss in front of everyone. That, too, had filled him with elation. He had never felt more himself than when Avaline was in his arms, looking up at him with love. He was safe. The war was over. He was home, physically, mentally. A more complete 're-birthday' he could not imagine.

Now, there was a brief respite between the fair and the formal evening for the surrounding 'citizens of standing'. Truthfully, Fortis would rather have built a bonfire, tapped a keg of the tavern's best ale and danced under the cold stars on a plank-wood dance floor with the tenants than send them home. They were his friends. He knew them. He'd worked side by side with them. It had meant the world to him to have John's birthday congratulations.

His valet patted his face with a towel. 'There, milord, I am finished. Shall we dress? I have your evening clothes laid out. Your trousers are pressed, your shoes are polished.' New clothes had been ordered for the occasion. His others, which had looked perfectly fine to him, had been declared out of fashion, although he couldn't tell the difference. A black suit was a black suit. But Avaline had insisted, so he'd been measured and a tailor in London put to work. Robert had been in alt when the box had arrived two days ago.

Fortis stood patiently, letting Robert have his moment dressing his lord in evening finery. He was halfway dressed when there was a knock at the connecting door and Avaline entered, radiant in an evening gown of mazarine silk trimmed in silver lace. Pearls set in silver hung at her ears, a matching pendant at her throat, her hair up to expose the exquisite length of her neck. In her hands, she held a small, elegantly wrapped box. He was so struck by her loveliness he could do nothing but stare.

'Leave us, Robert, I'll help him finish dressing.' Avaline smiled her dismissal. 'Has he been difficult, Robert?'

'No, milady, just a touch squirmy while shaving.' Robert bowed.

Fortis laughed at the teasing. 'I'm hardly a

tot to be managed. I dare say I can dress myself without any help from either of you.'

'I don't think tonight's the night to test that hypothesis, dear.' Avaline set aside the small box and began working his buttons as Robert made his exit. He could smell the soft rosewater scent of her hair and the delicate perfume at her neck. She smelled like winter, warm vanilla mixed with a hint of sharp pine.

'Did it take long to get into that dress?' Fortis murmured at her ear.

'Not terribly. Why do you ask?' She finished the last button and reached for his collar.

'I'm wondering if I have time to take it off you before we go down.' He wouldn't want to go down at all at this rate. He wanted to lie down with Avaline, skin to skin, and breathe her in.

She fastened his collar in teasing but definitive refusal. 'We cannot keep the guests waiting and I fear there's a great risk of that. I know you. Once we get started, there's no telling where we might end up or when.' *She knew him.* What a glorious concept and one that had been hard won since his return.

He sought her mouth with his, his hands at her waist. 'Let me have a kiss, at least, pretty lady, or I shall not last the night.' He moved his hips against her, making her aware of his arousal. 'I would scandalise the ladies if I were to go downstairs in my current state.'

'Fortis!' Avaline laughed. 'You're scandalising me!' She placed her hands on his chest. 'This is not what I came in here for.' She smiled. 'I came because I wanted to give you my birthday present before you went down.'

The warm scolding in her eyes warned him to stop playing. It was a cue she wanted to be serious. He sat down on the bed. 'I can't imagine what more there is to give,' Fortis said with quiet sincerity. 'You've given me a most perfect day, all any man could want, even if I have to go downstairs and put myself on display for the local gentry when I'd rather be in bed with my wife.' Even ale with the tenants paled beside the prospect of bedding Avaline.

She knelt before him, reaching for the small box. 'There is one thing that might make your day more complete, at least I hope so.' Her hands trembled when she handed him the box. He had not realised she was nervous until now.

'What is this, Avaline?' The small box was heavier than he would have thought. He carefully unwrapped it and opened the lid. A crystal-cut cube in the shape of a child's block lay inside, surrounded by blue silk. The cube was pretty, catching the light when he held it up to the lamp, the detail exquisite; the crystal edges were carved to resemble the ruching of a ruffled blanket hem and each panel held a letter carved into the surface. He studied each of the letters. B-A-B... He nearly dropped the cube when he saw the last letter. Y. *Baby.* Oh, sweet Lord, he was going to be a father!

His eyes searched Avaline's face; her tremulous smile, the anxiousness in her gaze. 'Is this true? You're with child? When?' His questions rushed out and he was incoherent in his joy. He set the block aside and fell to his knees beside her. He gathered her to him, hair and dress be damned. He wanted to hold her, to touch her, to tell her what this meant to him, but his words were failing. After all the war, after all the wandering, he was home, at peace. He was whole with her in a way he'd never been whole before, no matter what had happened in the past. That past seemed to matter very little at the moment. All that mattered was the future he and Avaline would build together with this child, the first of many, God willing.

Avaline was laughing and crying against

his shoulder. 'You're happy? It's not too soon for you? I was so worried it would be…' She was babbling as much as he was. He silenced her with a kiss, her beautiful face between his hands.

'I am happy, happier than I've ever been,' he whispered between kisses.

'Happy enough to go downstairs and be civil to the guests?'

Fortis laughed. 'Yes. I know it's important to you.' It was even more important now, when he thought about the child. Blandford would be its home. These neighbours and their children would be his child's playmates and contemporaries. He needed to make a good second impression with these neighbours in case the first one years ago had failed to impress. He wanted them to see him as a landowner, a fellow citizen of this part of the world, a man who would be a good neighbour, a good friend. Most of all, he wanted everyone to see how much he adored his wife. Whatever anyone might have thought of their marriage in the years before, he wanted to put those suspicions to rest.

Avaline helped him finish dressing and they headed downstairs together, hand in hand. At the top of the stairs, Fortis paused, his gaze taking in the decorations; all blue and silver. If the Blandford entrance hall glittered like a winter wonderland, he could only imagine the magic that awaited in the ballroom. He leaned close to Avaline. 'May I tell my brothers our news? Discreetly, of course.'

She smiled, eyes twinkling mischievously. 'Yes. You may tell them they'll be uncles this summer. But not the rest of our guests. Let's keep them guessing as to what has put that smile on your face tonight.'

A guest might guess many things had put that smile on his face, Fortis concluded at the end of supper. He had so many reasons for it: the delicious food, the rich wine, the genteel company, the thought of opening the ball with his lovely wife, or maybe even the sheer delight of cutting into the extraordinary cake that stood in pride of place in the centre of the refreshment table, flanked by two enormous carved ice swans. The cake rose eight articulating layers high, each layer smaller than the last and each layer alternating in colour, white, mazarine, white, until it reached the top. A strand of pearls circled the base of each tier and carefully crafted flowers of hand-blown sugar decorated the rising tiers.

'What flavour is the cake?' Fortis couldn't help but ask as he led Avaline on to the floor for the first dance.

'Depends on the layer. There's chocolate, there's lemon.' She laughed up at him. 'You're giddy, like a school lad. I love that it pleases you so much.'

'Tell me there's vanilla.' He nipped at her ear, not caring who saw. Tonight, he was wholly, completely in love with his wife.

'Yes, you naughty man, there's vanilla.' She blushed furiously and he knew she was thinking of a set of very different vanilla fairy cakes.

The orchestra struck up the first chords. The opening dance would be a waltz because it was what the guest of honour had ordered. Fortis swung Avaline into the opening steps, holding her too close for decency's sake. 'Do you know what the best part of being married is? I get to dance with you all night and no one can say a thing about it.'

'Do you like your party?' Avaline whispered.

'Yes, absolutely. Everything is perfect.' He smiled, revelling in the word. His party was perfect, his wife was perfect. His life was perfect. No man had ever had more. He would not allow himself to ruin that perfection tonight with the thought that when everything was perfect it was usually right before the bottom fell out of all that perfection.

Chapter Sixteen

It was the ideal setting for the little play he was about to enact. Drury Lane could not have set the stage any better. Tobin Hayworth handed his evening cape and top hat to the footman and gave Blandford an assessing once-over. Not bad. The entrance hall wasn't as big as Indigo's or as lavish, having been built centuries earlier and not refurbished. He strode towards the ballroom, taking a glass of chilled champagne from a passing footman. He sipped. Good champagne. Apparently, no expense was to be spared. Rightly so. It wasn't every day a duke's son rose from the dead.

Hayworth nodded to people he knew as he wove through the crowd. This wasn't the afternoon's village rabble. This was a collection of people who mattered. Fortis Tresham would need their approval. A man jostled his arm accidentally and swiftly apologised as champagne sloshed. 'It's no problem, it's a crush in here,' Hayworth said easily, hoping to engage the man in conversation. 'It will probably happen again before the night's out. Everyone for miles must be here.' Just what he'd hoped for. No time like the present to start sowing his doubts.

'Not much else to do around these parts this time of year. Might as well come to a party.' The young man laughed and held out his hand. 'I'm Elias Paul. My father's one of the magistrates. I'm just home from Oxford. Did you see the cake?'

'Ah, yes. Extraordinary, isn't it? The Treshams haven't spared the expense. Why should they? It is quite the miracle.' His words had the desired effect. Elias Paul, who'd been tucked away at university, hadn't known the significance of this party. This was no ordinary birthday.

'Miracle? I don't rightly understand.'

One question from Paul and Hayworth filled in the details of his suspicions to a rapt audience. 'Of course, I want them to be happy,' Hayworth concluded. 'But I don't want my neighbour taken advantage of.' He shook his head for effect. 'I am not sure I would have celebrated so soon. I think there are questions that should be asked. It's all a bit too pat for my tastes. A good impostor could pull it off, when you think about it. Too much coincidence for me,' Hayworth surmised. 'A duke's son goes missing in action for nearly a year, a grieving family wanting desperately to have their son back, practically begging for news, a young widow deprived of a titled, wealthy husband in his prime? They're all susceptible. They would believe anything.'

'Do you think there's a chance it's not him?' Elias Paul knitted his brow in contemplation.

Hayworth shrugged. 'I don't know. I just think the family is vulnerable and when things sound too good to be true, they invariably are. It bears investigating at the least.' Fortis and Avaline swung past on the dance floor, eyes only for each other. 'Just look at them. He has her entirely in his thrall. I fear for her.'

'They seem happy together,' Elias Paul commented. 'What sort of woman doesn't recognise her own husband?' The wheels were turning of their own accord now. Hayworth hadn't even needed to plant that seed.

'A very desperate one, I suppose.' Hayworth smiled ruefully. Damn her for looking happy with Fortis Tresham. Damn Fortis Tresham for winning her attentions. All this would be easier if he could have turned Avaline's head with doubt. Avaline would want to protect her husband. In general, she was reluctant to believe evil of anyone—except him, it seemed. For her to suspect someone she loved of evil would take an act of God. To turn her loyalty from them would take another. But when he was done with Fortis, she might not have a choice if she wanted to save him.

Hayworth excused himself from Elias Paul and circulated throughout the room, spreading much the same message from person to person—how lucky and how coincidental young Tresham's return was—especially those who'd come to gape at the war hero and knew little of the details behind his return. Then he waited. He waited for the rumour to percolate and he waited for the Tresham men to come looking for him. He would make it easy for them. He had no intention to hide. He wanted to be found, wanted to be hauled before Cowden and make his deal while the Duke felt the pressure of a crowd nearby. He had started the rumours and he could end them for a price, or he could feed them.

The bastard, Hayworth, was eating his food and spreading nasty rumours. The sight of the man's arrogance made Fortis's blood boil from across the room. He had no right to be here, making a nuisance of himself and trying to ruin Avaline's party. If Fortis didn't feel the need to behave for his wife's sake, he'd haul the man out of the ballroom by his heels. 'Easy, Brother.' Frederick put a steadying hand on his arm. 'We don't want to make a scene. It will only make matters worse. Let him be the one to look bad.'

'He is spreading lies about me. I cannot let this go unchecked.' Fortis grimaced. The nasty gossip had come to his attention ten minutes ago. In his opinion, he'd already waited nine minutes too long to confront Hayworth for many reasons, not the least being what the rumour was doing to his mental state. The cloud of perfection and confidence he'd been floating on earlier had collapsed at the merest poke from Hayworth, which didn't say much about the state of that confidence. He'd vastly overrated it.

His mind was a riot of what ifs. All the worries he'd thought he'd set aside and conquered since the night in the Romani camp had come flooding back, charging through the gates of his confidence as if it had never existed, led by one single question: What if he wasn't Fortis Tresham? What if he'd misunderstood the flashbacks? Would he never be free of that one doubt? He thought he'd conquered it, but here it was again, rearing its ugly head. No. He simply could not let Hayworth play him like a puppet on strings any time he wanted to. If he let Hayworth get away with this treachery now, the situation would only escalate. He looked about the room for Avaline. Had she heard the rumours, too? They'd fought through so much to get to a place where they could be together as themselves and they'd only just arrived there. It would be so easy to fall from that pinnacle of happiness. The slightest push… He would not give Hayworth the chance. It was what Hayworth wanted.

'I've sent Anne and Helena to her,' Ferris said, low voiced, reading his thoughts. 'If she's heard, they'll be a comfort to her. If she hasn't, then it's best to hear the nastiness from them. They will keep it all in perspective.'

Fortis nodded. 'It would be best if she didn't have to hear it at all. I think Tobin Hayworth has eaten enough of my food. Shall we evict the party crasher?'

'Just be careful,' Frederick warned, his brother's grip on his arm tightening with his seriousness. 'You're right, we do have to respond. But he knows that. He's counting on it. He wants us to approach. He's ready for us. Chances are, he's got more surprises to spring. We have to think with our heads, not our fists, Fortis.'

'Understood.' He split his gaze between his two brothers. It was good to know his brothers had his back. 'Now, shall we? Before he eats any more of those cream puffs?'

They crossed the room politely, stopping here and there to make conversation long enough to show the room that the Tresham brothers were united and gave no heed to Hayworth's thoughtless rumours except to address his considerably poor taste in spreading them at a birthday party. But the damage was already done, in Fortis's opinion. Even as they stopped to talk there was a new tension in the air as they conversed. Guests looked at him with speculation.

They reached the dessert table and Hayworth met them, looking too smug for Fortis's taste.

'You were not invited,' Fortis said without preamble. He didn't have to brawl with the man, but neither did he have to feign ignorance of what Hayworth had done.

'You crashed my party. Now I will crash yours. Tit for tat.' Hayworth reached for another cream puff with insulting nonchalance. Fortis reached out at lightning speed, his hand manacling Hayworth's wrist before it reached the tray.

'*I* did not eat your food or slander your character,' Fortis growled, standing between Hayworth and the refreshments. 'I claimed only what was mine. There's nothing here that belongs to you, so I suggest you stop by the cloakroom, gathering your things and be off.'

'You suggest it, do you?' Hayworth sneered. 'My, you've grown a fine set of manners. Goes right along with your fine clothes. You could almost pass for a duke's son. That's what you're hoping for, isn't it?'

'I *am* a duke's son.' Fortis bristled. So, this was the surprise Hayworth had prepared—an attack on his identity. He would not let Hayworth see the doubt his words created.

'You don't know that.' Hayworth's voice was a low growl as the two men began to circle one another, two wolves wanting to prove their dominance.

'Are you suggesting I am not who I say I am?' Fortis studied his opponent. If it came to blows, he wanted to be sure he won. He'd had the advantage last time. Hayworth was a large man, not poorly built or without some athletic grace. He probably boxed well for a civilian, Fortis thought. But he was not a military man.

'I am suggesting you are nothing. *You* don't even know who you are. You are a broken man who came out of the Crimean forest with nothing, not even a name until the army gave you one. Even now, your mind is not even your own.' Hayworth was relentless with his slander and Fortis's temper heated even as his old doubts rattled the bars of their cages. Isn't this exactly what he'd thought in those dark moments at the Romani camp? That somehow he'd only thought he was Fortis? He could not give in to those fears. He could not be Hayworth's plaything.

'If you have accusations to make, you should make them at a more appropriate time than a birthday party. I don't think my wife will thank you for causing a scene with your lies,' Fortis cautioned. He caught sight of Avaline moving towards them, Helena and Anne behind her. She was pale, concern on her face, and he hated himself for having put it there. She should not worry over anything tonight. This evening was for celebration.

'She might thank me, if I kept a scoundrel out of her bed,' Hayworth drawled. 'Or is it too late for that? Have you already made a whore out of her? If you're not Fortis Tresham, she's committed adultery.' Restless eyes slid about the room, whispers beginning to rise in tone.

'Enough of this talk, Hayworth,' Frederick intervened. 'Step outside with us and let us settle our business privately.' His eyes glinted like hard sapphires.

Tobin laughed. 'Three to one? Is that how you settle business? That's hardly sporting. I say we settle your business right here where I have witnesses.' He paused. 'Unless it's something you can't settle in public?'

'You know very well what we want.' Ferris glared. 'We want you to leave and take your rumours with you. You came to this party to gossip and spread falsehoods.'

'Are you sure they're falsehoods?' Hayworth smirked. 'Are you sure he hasn't hoodwinked the lot of you?' His eyes locked on Fortis, deadly intent evident. 'I know all about you. Shall I tell them who you really are, Aidan Roswell, jewel thief?'

No. He was *not* Aidan Roswell. Not a thief. That man had died in the cave. Doubt surged around the barriers of his mental restraints, seeping into the cracks of his surety.

You could be and you know the reasons why, his mind whispered its fractured cruelty one more time. *It would explain the orientation of the flashbacks, why you sometimes weren't sure who was speaking or whose story belonged to whom. It would explain why it's been so hard to accept that you never wrote to Avaline and why you didn't love her once upon a time. Because it hadn't been you.*

No. He would not listen to those reasons. There were other explanations and he clung to them, repeating them like a litany of truth in his mind. He *was* Lord Fortis Tresham, the son of the Duke of Cowden, brother to Frederick and Ferris, uncle to five little boys, husband to Avaline, master of Blandford Hall. He *knew* who he was. But there was no challenging Hayworth. The man would just spew more lies. There was only one way to silence the man and redeem his honour. He'd played the gentleman tonight long enough.

'I *am* Fortis Tresham and you will get the hell out of my house!' Fortis swung at him. Even ready for it, Tobin wasn't fast enough. Fortis's fist found his jaw and sent him staggering into the dessert table and straight into an ice swan. Off balance, Hayworth grabbed for the swan to steady himself, but the ice was slippery. There was no purchase. He went down, the swan and two hundred serving plates with him in a shattering cascade of ice and china that brought the ballroom to utter silence. In that silence came a desperate cry. 'Fortis, no!'

His head swung around, his eyes looking for the voice. He couldn't find it. Couldn't find her. Surely, the voice was Avaline's. But where was she? The ballroom was fading, the walls giving way to the forest, to the cave. Fortis squeezed his eyes shut, willing the ballroom to come back. He would fight this. He would not give in, not now when he would embarrass Avaline. But when he opened his eyes the ballroom was gone entirely.

Chapter Seventeen

*A*idan scratched a line on the cave wall with a charred stick, adding a mark to a long line of hash marks. 'What month is it?' Fortis asked from his pine-bough pallet near the fire. He was paler, weaker.

'February.' They'd been in the cave for three months and there'd been no progress. Saving his comrade had become an exercise in both hope and futility. Reality told him hope was useless. The ribs were not healing. Fortis was only without pain when he lay still. The man could not risk moving, let alone walking to wherever the British army was camped now.

'February? Even as short a month as it is, I won't see the end of it.' There was a pause. 'You're free to go, you know. I've kept you here long enough and for no reason. I will die *whether you stay or not. Build up the fire one last time so I might have some light and heat by which to face my end and when it dies, I will die. I will just move and it will be over. Or you can leave a shot.'*

'I will not hear such gruesome talk. I am staying with you and you will get better. You've made it this long.' He took his friend's hand and smiled in reassurance, but he feared the reassurance was a lie. Yesterday, Fortis had begun to cough up blood, the last piece of proof both of them needed to confirm the worst: Fortis had a broken rib and finally that rib had punctured something vital. It wouldn't, couldn't be long now. The knowledge of it tore at Aidan. He could not lose Fortis. Fortis had become his friend. Aidan could count on one hand how many people in his twenty-eight years could lay claim to the title of friend.

Fortis returned his smile weakly. 'You're a good friend, Aidan. You've given me months I wouldn't have had, time in which to make peace with myself. I am nearly ready to go, there's just one more thing that needs doing. Do you remember I told you about my wife? Would you get her miniature out for me?'

Aidan fumbled in Fortis's coat pocket for the

miniature and opened it for him. 'She's still beautiful. You are a lucky man.' He kept up the pretence of a future.

'I am not lucky. I will not see her again, I will not have a second chance with her. I need to ask you one more time, Aidan. Do you have a wife? A woman waiting for you? Someone who compels your heart?'

'No, you know that I don't.' Aidan pressed a hand to Fortis's forehead, worried his friend was delirious. They had discussed this before.

'I need you to do something for me, you must promise.' Fortis gripped his wrist to stall any protest. 'We have to stop pretending I'm going to get up and walk out of here. I will be dead very soon, tonight or tomorrow. I've asked so much of you, but I want to ask one more thing.'

'Anything, you know that,' Aidan promised desperately as if promises could keep his friend alive.

Fortis nodded. 'I want you to go to her after I'm gone.'

'Fortis, this is nonsense.' But it wasn't. Very soon Fortis would be gone. Already, he seemed to fade before Aidan's eyes. To pretend otherwise would be to lie, to waste what time was indeed left. 'I will. I'll go to her and tell her

everything, how much you wanted to try again, how much you regret not being there in person.'

Fortis shook his head. 'No, not like that. She married me to protect herself and her land from Tobin Hayworth. She needs my name. She needs me. I am no good to her dead.' He coughed, winded from the anxious speed of his words, blood staining the rag Aidan held to his lips. It was a long while before he was able to continue, panic rising in his eyes as he realised time was truly running out and his plans were not set. 'I want to give you my life, Aidan. Listen to me, carefully. We are of similar height and bearing, dark hair with blue eyes. Blue eyes are rare and to have the same shade, it's almost as if this was meant to be, Aidan. I've told you of my family, who they are, where to find them. I've told you stories of my childhood with my brothers. You can use them as proof. Who else would know the three of us locked our Latin tutor in his room one afternoon to escape lessons? And you know other stories besides. Whatever you don't remember, claim battle trauma, say your memory has been affected.'

This plan of his was crazy in its thorough-

ness. *'How long have you been plotting this?'* Aidan asked quietly.

'Since I was sure this was the end for me,' Fortis answered honestly. *'My family will want me back so badly they'll want to believe you.'*

'And Avaline? Will your wife welcome back her husband?'

'If she does not, convince her otherwise. You're a handsome man, I am sure you can be quite charming. No doubt you'll be a better husband than I was. I'm counting on it, Aidan. Avaline is sweet and kind, but she has backbone. She wanted a family, she had such dreams for us and I did not value them. I had only dreams for me: glory and battlefield promotions. She was just an ornament on my arm, sometimes a shackle, albeit a pretty one, that came with land my father had acquired for me, when I bothered to notice her at all. I regret I will not be able to make it up to her in person. I would have liked to try again.'

'Impersonation is a crime,' Aidan hedged. The request was as enormous as it was tempting. *'What makes you think I'll do any better as a husband? I'm a former thief.'*

Fortis chuckled and paid for it with a racking, bloody cough. *'You're the most noble thief I've ever known, nobler than most men I've known. You've taken care of me all these months, you put your safety aside for mine when you pulled me out from under Khan. You've kept us both alive on next to nothing when you could have left. You might be alone in the world, but you know what love is.'* Fortis coughed again, unable to catch his breath, gasping and choking. Aidan held him up, murmuring nonsense about things being fine. 'Things' were worse than ever.

The cough subsided at last, leaving Fortis exhausted. His eyes were closed as Aidan eased him back down, but Fortis's grip was as tight as ever on his wrist. 'Promise me, Aidan, you will go to her. There are more letters in my trunk at camp. Promise me, when I am gone, you will go to the British lines and tell them you're Fortis Tresham, that you've been wandering in the wilderness, sick and alone, and disoriented. You have the scars to prove it. Tell them to send you home. There is no one to gainsay you. In one fell swoop, you can have all you've ever wanted.' Temptation roared loud now. It could be done.

'Don't work yourself up, Fortis. Save your strength.'

'For what?' Fortis's eyes opened, blue and steady. 'I am waiting only for your promise and even then I don't know how much longer I can wait.' His breath rattled in his chest. A death rattle, some surgeons called it. Speech was hard now, his lungs filling fast for the last time.

'Fortis.' Aidan couldn't keep the emotion from his voice. It couldn't end like this. Was there something he should have done? Something that would have saved him? It was all happening so fast now. He wasn't ready to let Fortis go.

'Promise me, Aidan. I give you my life. I give you Avaline. No one will ever know. Promise?' The man who asked for nothing had just posed a question. The end times most certainly.

Aidan took his dear friend's hand and held his gaze, holding his own mad grief at bay. There would, unfortunately, be time for that. 'I promise.' He did not look away, did not let go, until the last spark of life faded from Fortis Tresham's eyes. The first tear fell and Aidan let the madness come. Fortis Tresham was dead. Long live Fortis Tresham.

He was *not* Fortis Tresham. Fortis Tresham was dead. He'd died in the cave. It was all coming back to him in vivid, startling, reality-shattering clarity and the realisation was devastating. Aidan began to shake violently, his body trembling from the intensity of the flashback and the realisation that accompanied it. Someone was there, wrapping him in a blanket and soothing him with reassuring words. He guessed it was Ferris. His brother. His mind stopped him. Corrected him. No. Not his brother. He didn't have a brother, or nephews or a father, certainly not a father who was a duke. Aidan Roswell had no one.

'Fortis, open your eyes. I am here. You are safe.' That voice belonged to Avaline. His wife, the mother of his unborn child. He had to correct himself once more. No. *Not* his wife. Fortis's wife. But the mother of his child. Oh, God, the baby! An illegitimate bastard. Tainted, the poor thing, and it wasn't even born yet. He groaned against the agony of the realisation. The facts and consequences of what he now knew were overwhelming.

How did he open his eyes? How did he go on from here? How did he tell Avaline? What would happen to them? To him? The flood threatened to wash him away. No. He had to be strong. Avaline was going to need him. He needed to protect her. He'd promised Fortis. He pushed the realisations back one by one and locked them in their cages. He would cope with this latest crisis the way he coped with battle-fields: one step, one hurdle, one enemy at a time. He would focus on what was in front of him.

Aidan opened his eyes, slowly letting his senses take in the details of his surroundings. Ferris and Avaline knelt beside him on the floor of a small sitting room, the room Avaline used as her office. His shoulders lifted under the weight of the blanket. Avaline's fingers laced through his in a reassuring touch. 'Fortis.' A soft smile played on her face. He should not let her call him that, but he couldn't bring himself to disabuse of her that particular truth just yet. Not when there were other truths to acknowl-edge, too. And selfishly, he wanted to enjoy looking at her face when it shone with love for him. He would lose that when she knew the truth very soon. Surely, no one would begrudge him a few minutes more of that smile.

'I've ruined your party.' He managed to get the words out. Speaking seemed difficult, a monumental task to translate the rampaging thoughts in his head into simple words.

'Don't be silly. Our party will be the talk of the county for weeks.' Avaline laughed. 'I don't care, Fortis. Truly. Hayworth provoked you. He came here to make trouble. He tried to sow seeds of doubt where none even existed. No one but him ever questioned who you were.' Except himself. He'd questioned who he was at the Romani camp. Turned out, he'd been right to do so.

'Did he succeed?' Aidan held her gaze. Was there doubt now? Was the word of a duke all that was holding those doubts at bay? In truth, he cared less about what a room full of strangers thought than what Avaline thought. What did *she* think? Did she believe anything Hayworth had said? She had fought so hard for him that night at the camp, down on her knees, holding his hands and now her fight had been betrayed. She'd fought for the wrong man although she didn't know it yet.

'He's in with your father and Frederick right now. Between your father's ducal rage and your fist, he'll be sorry he showed up at all,' Avaline tried to reassure him. But there was nothing she could say that would soothe him. He knew better. He'd hit a man for speaking the truth. He wasn't Fortis Tresham. Of course, the man spouting the truth could have been more delicate about it if he'd truly cared. Hayworth's intentions had been malicious, but no less true because of his malice. It was a bitter pill to swallow.

'And the guests?' His nerves were starting to calm.

'Helena and Anne have seen them off. No need to worry.' Avaline swallowed. 'What happened, Fortis? What did you remember?'

'I don't know. I remember something shattered.'

'Yes, the swan, the dishes,' Avaline supplied, eyes bright and anxious.

'Suddenly, I was back in the cave.' He winced. Only in his mind, though. In reality, he'd never left the ballroom. Oh, Lord, what had he done? New fear swept him. 'What did I do? Was anyone hurt? Was it awful?' How might he have embarrassed her?

It was Ferris who answered. 'Frederick and I pulled you off Hayworth and got you away. I don't think anyone suspected it was more than just an angry temper.' Aidan breathed a little easier, thankful for that small piece of mercy. Avaline would have to live among these people later, after…obstacles and issues rattled the bars of their cages. He shook his head to tamp them down. He couldn't think about them now. Those were obstacles much further down the road.

'Fortis, what did you remember about the cave?' Avaline prompted, no doubt wondering what was left to remember.

He would have to tell her. It served no one except himself to delay the news that his memory was fully returned and, with it, certain key pieces of information. He glanced at Ferris and the man rose, understanding immediately his silent request.

'I'll let you talk in private. I'll just be outside the door if you need anything.' Ferris nodded to Avaline. Aidan knew what that meant, too. Ferris would be on hand in case he broke down again.

Aidan waited until Ferris had shut the door behind him. He gathered his thoughts in the moments that remained. How did he tell her he was a lie? That what she thought was true was all a fiction? Yet, if she gave him a chance, the one thing that mattered most was still true. 'Avaline, I need to tell you some difficult things. You will not want to hear them any more than I want to say them. They will change many things, but not the most important thing. I love you. I love the child we made and I will fight for both of you with all that I have.' Perhaps if she could hold on to that one truth it would help her hear the other truths. 'After I have told you, we can decide what is best to do.'

'Fortis, you're frightening me. I'm afraid.'

His hands tightened around hers, wanting to give them both strength but he would not give her a lie, not another one. 'You should be.'

'Fortis, tell me. Let us face the cave together.'

'Don't call me that,' he snapped. 'I remembered everything tonight, Avaline. Most importantly, I remembered who I was. Unequivocally.' That was the difference. Time seemed to suspend as he uttered the words, 'I am not Fortis Tresham.'

'How can that be? Of course you're Fortis. You have my letters, my miniature, his uniform. His trunks. Your memories are jumbled, but you know why. You know you are mistaken, my love.'

My love. He savoured the words. It might be the last time she'd ever call him that. But even as he cherished the words, he heard the defeat in them. Her arguments were pro forma. He could see in her devastated eyes that even she didn't believe them any more or perhaps she never fully had. Perhaps, like him, she, too, had had her doubts and bravely thrust them away for the sake of the new marriage they might make between them. They could hide from those truths no longer.

'No, you must listen to me, Avaline. I am Aidan Roswell. The reason all my flashbacks were through his eyes was because that was me, it was no mind trick. Ferris was wrong. *I* pulled Fortis out from under his horse. *I* dragged him to safety.' Just as he'd thought. The story poured out, the words coming fast as he made his case. She listened enrapt to the fantastical tale of their lives in the cave, how he—how *Aidan*—had kept Fortis alive.

'He was sorry, Avaline, for the marriage. He regretted his behaviour. He wanted a second chance and when he knew he wouldn't live, he asked me to come in his place. He knew you needed protection against Hayworth, that if he were dead he could not give you that protection.' How did he make her understand he hadn't wanted to deceive her? That this was what Fortis had wanted for her? To give her this last gift? An apology of sorts? 'Please, Avaline, listen to me.' Oh, God, what if she didn't? He couldn't lose her. He could lose all else, but not her. Not his anchor, the one thing that had kept him sane, yet he felt her hands tug inside his grip and, because he could deny her nothing, he let her go.

Chapter Eighteen

Avaline ran from the room, tearing through the house in a mad race to her room, not caring who saw her. Let the servants see, let the guests gape. She had no time for them. She barely had time for herself. All she wanted was to reach the safety of her room before she broke. She was holding on to her sanity by a thread and she did not let go of the last thread until the door of her room was shut firmly behind her and she was alone. Only then did she let her emotions swamp her.

She threw herself on her bed and sobbed. Her mind was a maelstrom of thoughts and she grabbed at them, trying to catch them like hats in a windstorm. Her mind closed around one, maybe the only one that mattered. Her husband was not her husband. It couldn't be true, because if it was it meant she'd been duped in love twice now. She'd loved a man who hadn't loved her and now she'd fallen in love with a lie. There was no fairy tale. Fortis hadn't fallen in love with her at last. This time, it was worse than the first. A stranger had taken her husband's place and *pretended* to love her in order to…what? Get his hands on her land? Weasel his way into the good life? Take advantage of her? Sobs welled up again, uncontrollable and racking. She'd known her husband so little that she'd been an easy dupe. What must he think of her? A woman who'd so readily accepted him in the most intimate of ways? He would think she was a fool and maybe he was right. She'd been so desperate she'd grabbed at the first illusion of a lifeline. The man she thought she loved was a liar in that love. At least Fortis had been truthful in his dislike.

She'd certainly been taken advantage of and she couldn't even lay the blame for it entirely at his feet. She'd been the one to fall. If she had resisted, if she hadn't allowed herself to be charmed by him, perhaps she would have seen the ruse. Perhaps she wouldn't be pregnant.

The baby! That thought brought on another bout of weeping, another bout of unanswerable questions. Where did they go from here? Where could they go? Where did she want them to go? Was there even a 'them'? Did she want a 'them'? Did she have a choice? She thought of the arguments she'd made that there was no choice but to be Fortis Tresham. There was still no choice, she supposed. The only choice was how they lived with it; together or apart. It would have to be the latter. She could not live with a liar. She could not live day to day in the presence of someone who had duped her and pretend everything was all right. Perhaps the Treshams would give him funds to live far away, out of sight, where he couldn't hurt them any more. But that was a consideration for another time when she could think more clearly. Right now, she was too wrapped in her own sorrow to contemplate theirs.

Sorrow. Not anger, not pure anger anyway. Avaline lay on her pillow, listless, her tears drying as she stared at the ceiling. Time passed. How much time she wasn't sure. Hours ticked away and still there was only sorrow, a deep grieving sorrow that cleaves a soul in two. She had lost so much to his lie: happiness, love, completion. She had liked the world that existed inside that lie. For two months, she'd had perfection, the fairy tale—slightly tarnished to be sure, but a fairy tale none the less. And now it had all been torn away, none of it real. She'd known how to go on when Fortis had left. She'd survived for years going through the motions because she'd had some misguided sense of hope. She did not know how to go on from this. She did not know how to survive it. Her world would never be the same. There was no hope left.

Shortly before dawn, a soft knock sounded on her door. She did not answer. She did not want her maid, she did not want any of them.

'Avaline, let me in. Let me explain.'

It wasn't the maid. It was him. Fortis. Aidan. The liar. The man she loved. She'd thought she wanted to see him least of all, yet she found herself dragging her legs over the side of the bed, stumbling, exhausted from hours of sobbing, to the door and unlocking it. He looked terrible; shirttails untucked, cravat undone, hair dishevelled, eyes bloodshot from lack of sleep and tears. He might be her mirror image and yet she was not ready to offer pity or forgiveness. She might never be.

'You lied!' She hurled the accusation at him.

She would have the first word, dammit. 'All this time it was a lie. You were playing at being Fortis, you made me believe you loved me!' She shut the door behind him, shutting out anyone who might intrude on their private exchange.

'Not a liar, Avaline, not how you think. If you would allow me to explain?' he pleaded fiercely, his voice hoarse and cracking. and she found she could not deny him his plea any more than she'd denied him the door.

'Tell me, then, how you have not lied to me, how all this isn't a lie, how we aren't facing a nightmare in consequences for your little game,' she spat out, flopping down on the bed. How many more lies would he be willing to spin? Did he even realise what he'd done not just to himself, but to her? Did he even care? How she could protect herself against him, against Hayworth, against the accusations that would follow? She was betrayed and exposed on all fronts.

He leaned against the bedpost, weary and defeated, and still managed to look devastatingly handsome. 'When Fortis died, I was overwhelmed. I don't know how to explain it, or how to make someone understand what those months were like. My world shrank to the cave, to that one man. Every day, my most important chore was to gather food, water and firewood and to nurse Fortis. Every night when I lay down to sleep my one prayer was thanksgiving for having had one more day and a plea that we be granted another. That was the sum of my world. We had no entertainments except ourselves. Talk bound us together. We spent the days telling the stories of our lives. I fell in love with his family, with his life. Maybe I was even jealous of it. I had nothing like it, no one who cared, and he had everything.'

He paused here, the emotion too strong to go on, and she saw the pain in his eyes. He cleared his throat and found a way. 'Soldiers tell stories around campfires in the hopes of being remembered. We do it all the time the night before battle, out of fear that we might fall and no one would have known us. It's a bid for a minute piece of immortality. All those months in the cave, while I was hoping for a miracle, that he might somehow recover, he was making his bid for immortality. He was telling me his story. I see that now.' His eyes were on her, perhaps willing her to believe him, perhaps gauging the story's effect. She wish she knew. Which man could she trust? A liar? Certainly not. But the man she thought she'd come to know? Perhaps. If that man truly existed at all.

'And when he died?' she prompted, curiosity getting the better of her.

'He took the world with him. Saving Fortis had been my only mission for months and I lost him. A broken rib finally punctured his lung, as I suppose he knew it eventually would. He'd planned it all so carefully, Avaline. I argued against it, of course. His plan was madness. But even hurt and dying, he was quite compelling. His men must have loved serving under him. I'd seen your miniature. I'd heard the tales. He was offering me a life I'd only dreamed of. It was a hard offer to resist and he was dying. I was already half in love with you. He asked for nothing, only that you be taken care of. But I didn't impersonate him, I didn't mislead you, Avaline. Until tonight, I truly thought I was Fortis Tresham. You know this.'

Avaline got up from the bed and paced before the long window. She pulled back the curtains and studied the greying dawn. Everything hinged on that, didn't it? That he truly hadn't known who he was. If that was true, it changed everything. It gave her back hope. It gave *them* hope. Did she believe him? She did not doubt the sincerity of what he'd told her at the Romani camp. It was the very first time he'd doubted who he was. A man who was deliberately defrauding someone didn't try so hard to deny his identity. That seemed counter-intuitive, yet Fortis had been desperately adamant about that revelation at the camp. Why? It didn't serve him other than providing him with truth.

'Do you believe me, Avaline?' Fortis—no, Aidan asked quietly from the bed. How should she refer to him?

Avaline turned from the window. Her answer would determine what happened next and how it happened. Tears welled in her eyes as she looked at him. It wasn't just the proof of his reaction at the Romani camp that swayed her. It was all the other things. How many times in the past two months had she seen that selflessness exhibited for her benefit? And she knew in her heart, as the sun rose behind her, that his name didn't matter. This was a good man. She was moved beyond measure at the selflessness of this man who had tried to bring her husband home, how he'd suffered the loss of Fortis, perhaps been driven mad by it. She had never loved Fortis Tresham. She'd only ever loved Aidan Roswell, a man who was loyal and good. Who defended those he loved. She gave him the words he sought. 'Yes, I believe you.'

She believed him. Aidan nearly sagged with relief. He might have collapsed if he hadn't had the bedpost to steady himself. 'Thank you, Avaline. You have no idea how much that means.' The one person who mattered had not lost faith in him. Had anyone ever had the faith in him that Avaline was exhibiting right now? He knew the answer to that. Yes. And that person was Fortis Tresham. Fortis was counting on him to see this through. He could not fail now.

Avaline remained by the window and his heart ached to take her in his arms, to kiss her senseless with his joy. If they were as they'd been earlier this evening, he might have. But they were different now. No longer Avaline and Fortis, people who thought they were married to each other. They were Avaline and Aidan and, while he knew her, she did not know him. Some might call it splitting hairs. But he understood too well this was not a fine line between them, but a chasm. He was a street rat and she was a baron's daughter, the wife of a duke's son. She was so far above him it was laughable to think that, had circumstances been otherwise,

he would have ever stood a chance with her. It
was only Fortis's deception that had provided
that chance now. Once she realised that, she
might believe him about his honest confusion,
but she might not want him. She was meant for
finer men. So, he did not invite her to sit beside
him on the bed. He did not go to her at the window, but gave her the space she needed to ask
her questions and hear his answers.

'Why did you decide to do it? You said you
argued against it. What changed your mind?'
Avaline asked.

'I don't know that I did ever consciously decide to do it. I didn't leave the cave right away
when he died. I couldn't bring myself to leave.
I had nothing to dig a grave with and I was not
ready to leave my friend, perhaps even the best
friend I'd ever had, alone in the dark, prey for
whatever wild beast might find its way in. I
couldn't give him a decent burial, but I *could*
mourn him and I did. I don't know how long.
I lay on the floor of that cave with him in my
arms and I cried. It had all been for naught. I'd
tried my best and he died anyway. Why should
he have died? He had everything to live for.
Why not me? Why hadn't I died? I had noth-

ing and no one. My life was expendable, but he mattered. He had worth.'

'You are not worthless, Aidan,' Avaline interrupted. He looked up to meet her gaze, the words warming him. It was the first time she'd used his name, his real name. But she was just being kind. He was worthless. She just didn't know it yet. He ignored the comment and carried on.

'Finally, I could stay no longer. I was out of food and water and I had no reason to stay. Grief had undone me completely. I gave him the best tribute I could. I put on his uniform. I gathered his valuables and I walled up the cave with stones to offer him some protection. Then I found my way out of the forest, feverish from lack of nourishment and undone by grief, unsure of who I was, of where I was going, of what I was to do except that I needed to get back to you. You know the rest and now you also know I am not who you thought I was. It changes everything.'

'It changes many things,' Avaline corrected. 'Not everything. Not the one thing that matters most. You said so yourself. You love me. You love our child and I love *you*. I love Aidan Roswell. In your own way you gave your life for Fortis. There is no greater sacrifice one can make for another.'

He shook his head, unwilling to accept them. 'You don't know me, Avaline. I am not worthy of your love. I see that now. If you knew what else I had done, what my life was like before the army, you would think differently. You wouldn't want anything to do with me.' He was well aware that they were, in a way, back at the beginning where they had started with each other in October, two strangers standing alone in the Blandford hall, wondering, 'What next?'

'I will know all that, too, in time and in time we'll overcome it.' Avaline was pacing, her mind working. 'I think we have enough to deal with at the moment and not much time to do it. There's Hayworth and his rumours to quell.'

Aidan could not restrain himself any longer. He left the bed and went to her, taking her hands, forcing her to stop her pacing, to look at him. 'Those are important, but not as important as our marriage. Before all else, we have to decide what we want for our marriage, for our child. Where do we go from here? It should be your choice. You are the wronged party here, whether by intention or accident.' He'd thought long and hard about his decision as he'd sat on the floor of her little sitting-room office, his head hung in despair. He knew what he should do. He should let her go. He should confess all to Cowden and throw himself on the Duke's mercy in the hopes of walking away with his life. 'I will let you go if that's what you want,' he said quietly, sparing her the pain of asking for it.

She shook her head. 'I was afraid you would say that. It is just the sort of thing a selfless man would say, thinking of others first. But what of your child? Will he or she grow up without a father, always wondering? What should I tell them?'

It was a good argument. He had no ready answer for it. 'Tell them I died. Tell them I was a soldier.'

'I won't tell my child a lie and I don't need to. We have other choices.' Avaline began to plot. 'We can keep this to ourselves. No one else need know what you told me. Cowden will defend you to the teeth as Fortis, especially against Hayworth. Hayworth doesn't know the half of what he's unleashed by going against a duke's word. He doesn't truly understand the power the aristocracy has. We can spare Cowden the grief of losing his son all over again.'

Aidan studied his beautiful wife. Even in despair and grief, she was lovely and she was nearly his, his for ever, if he would just agree to one more lie. The idea was appealing in theory. Yes, there were a lot of reasons to keep this between them. They could do it. Then it occurred to him what existed between the lines. 'You want to keep me? A man you don't know, as a husband? You will not be able to unseat me, Avaline, should you change your mind.'

'I know enough. I nearly lost you tonight. I didn't think I'd survive it. I don't know what I would have done if you hadn't knocked on my door,' she said quietly. He recognised what an enormous leap of faith this was, especially for her—a woman who had lost in love once and had nearly been betrayed a second time. Yet, she was willing to risk it again. For him. 'You will not betray me. True love doesn't lie.' Which was why it was proving difficult to agree to tell one last lie to the Treshams, to the Duke of Cowden.

'I would become Fortis Tresham for ever.' He would never be himself again. 'We would both be living a lie.' He didn't want that for Avaline, didn't want her dirtied with a secret. 'But I would be giving up my true identity. Aidan Roswell would have died in the cave.'

'Perhaps it is too much to ask.' Avaline dropped her gaze. 'I hadn't thought of it that way, for essentially asking you to die for me.'

'No, it's not that. It's asking you to live a lie for me. I don't want you dirtied. You are all that is good and pure in my world and I want you to stay that way.' Aidan was silent for a long time. 'I would gladly die for you time and again.'

'Aidan, I'd rather you lived for me.' She was shy suddenly.

'Then I think we have our answer. I cannot deceive the Treshams. I think we must take them into our confidence. Fortis's brothers, his parents, all deserve to know how he lived his last days and his last wishes.'

'But what if they cast you out?' Panic rose in her eyes.

'I can't lie to them. I am an honest man now, Avaline. I owe them that courtesy.'

'Even if it costs you your life? What about me? Our child?' Avaline drew in a shaky breath. He pressed a finger to her lips.

'Shh, say nothing. I understand the position it puts you in, but we cannot live with ourselves any other way.' If Cowden didn't countenance the lie, Avaline would have to choose between him and the protection of a duke. She would be choosing for two: herself and their child. He hoped it wouldn't come to that. He hoped he had not misjudged Cowden and that the truth would hold some weight with him. 'Let's go and tell them. I believe they're still downstairs. Mrs Pimm was plying them with coffee when I last checked. We'll be brave, together.' If Avaline was beside him, he could brave even the fires of hell.

Chapter Nineteen

'Fortis died bravely. His last thoughts and concerns were for his family and for his wife.' Aidan swallowed against the lump in his throat. Reliving the reality of the cave for the third time in rapid succession, was taking an inevitable toll on him—first the flashback, then the agony of telling Avaline and watching her world crumple, and now going through it again with all the Treshams in attendance. He was no longer the prodigal returned, but merely a messenger, and he was exhausted, but he couldn't give in to that exhaustion. Not yet. There was too much still to settle, there was Avaline to protect and his child. He could not sleep until he knew they were safe from whatever consequences his truths held. He would fight for them and he would make whatever sacrifices needed making for their sakes.

His tale was met with abject silence. Every face around him was filled with awe and with grief as they each grappled with their own understanding of this new reality and in some ways reliving the loss of Fortis for the second time. Fortis wasn't coming home. Frederick and Ferris no longer had a brother. They were no longer expectant uncles. The Duke and Duchess had lost a son. They would not be grandparents for the sixth time in the summer.

It was the last that hit Aidan the hardest. He had no connection to this family. Outside the bonds of marriage to Fortis, Avaline had no connection either. Their child would not be related to anyone in this room. What had been joy earlier this evening was now a great source of sorrow. The truth had cost his child so much. Aidan Roswell had nothing to offer a child or a wife while Fortis Tresham had everything to give: a home, a family, the practical protections of wealth and power.

Cowden spoke first, his eyes thoughtful as he weighed each word. 'You did not have to tell us. Some might argue that you'd be saving us from great hurt by not telling us. Why not let us go on believing Fortis was returned to us? You could have had everything and we could have been spared the grief.'

Aidan tensed. Did the Duke mean to dispossess him, after all? He should expect no less. He knew how the aristocracy worked from an outsider's perspective. He'd seen the rich men his mother had entertained. They cared for no one but themselves in the end. They'd had no time for an ageing prostitute once her beauty was gone and even less time for her son, not even when he'd gone to them to beg for medicines for her. He did not expect Cowden to be any different, yet he'd felt compelled to tell the truth any way, a truth that might cost him everything, as Cowden had pointed out. 'If we don't have truth, we have nothing,' Aidan answered evenly. 'I am sorry I couldn't save him.' He wanted them to know how much losing Fortis had meant to him, that he knew quite intimately the pain they felt now in their own sense of loss.

'How could you have saved him?' Ferris consoled. 'There are no guarantees with broken ribs even with a physician in attendance.'

'It takes a brave man to speak the truth when his own gains might be the price of that truth.'

Cowden nodded. 'Thank you.' Cowden's gaze swept the group, resting on his wife, who cried softly into a handkerchief, and his sons whose faces registered stoic shock. 'The question is what to do now. We have a baby coming and Hayworth on the loose with his interpretation of the truth.'

'Which is what?' Aidan asked carefully.

Shall I tell them who you really are? Hayworth had threatened. If Hayworth had known his real name, what else did he know? Or was there a chance Hayworth was only bluffing?

Cowden slid a folder towards him. 'It's not very pretty. Hayworth says Aidan Roswell is the son of a prostitute, a street rat turned seducer who managed to cultivate the affections of a few notorious ladies of the *ton* from whom he stole jewels. The last time he tried, he was caught.' The damn ruby tiara. Yes, he knew. The ruby tiara had been the start of all of this.

Aidan hazarded a look at Avaline. How was she taking this latest revelation? Her evening had been as eventful as his. She'd not only learned her husband wasn't her husband, but that he was a former jewel thief. 'Avaline?' She'd made her decision in the sitting room without this information. If it changed her mind, if distancing herself from him seemed a better option now, he had to be prepared to let her do that. His child would have a better chance living in the shelter of Cowden's protection without a father than growing up with a jewel thief for a parent.

'Yes, we should ask Avaline.' Cowden took the cue from him. 'Daughter, what would you prefer? It seems to me that you are the one that is perhaps most wronged in this affair. Two husbands have been forced on you, neither of them ideal.'

Aidan knit his brows. Perhaps he should make the decision for her? Perhaps it was wrong to expect her to decide? Was Cowden putting too much pressure on her? Even if she wanted distance, wanted to forget him, would she have the strength to say it? She'd been put through so much tonight. Maybe this was how he had to fight for her, by giving her up. 'Avaline, if you want to let me go, you mustn't be afraid. I will go as quietly as possible. I would never harm you or our child.'

'Go quietly?' Avaline gave him a smile of disbelief that warmed him and made him want to laugh despite the circumstances. 'Do you think there's any chance of Hayworth allowing that? You will not be permitted to go quietly, not by Hayworth or by me, although we have our very different reasons.' For a moment her gaze and her words were for him alone. 'I believe we've already discussed this. It's you I want, as Aidan, as Fortis, whoever you may be.'

Aidan wanted to weep with relief even as he worried she would regret her decision. But not here. He could not break down here. Maybe later. When she was safe, when they were safe. They were a long way from safe, though.

Cowden's gaze split between the two of them, mirroring caution. 'He cannot be Aidan, Avaline. He can never be Aidan. Aidan Roswell can be thrown in gaol, put on trial as an impostor and for crimes committed years ago and he may very well be found guilty.' Cowden was in deadly earnest. 'Aidan Roswell has a date with the gallows and Tobin Hayworth will see that he keeps it.'

So this was what it would come down to. Cowden's insinuation was no different than Avaline's more blatant argument. Aidan Roswell had to die. There was no future for that man. But there was still a future for Fortis Tresham. Cowden looked at each member of his family, waiting for their approval as Aidan held his breath. 'Frederick?'

'I think Hayworth has made a grave error in mistaking my brother for a thief.' Frederick grinned at Aidan. 'Avaline has never been happier. I would not take that from her. Blandford village has never looked better, the villagers' morale is restored. For the first time since her father's death, the estate has hope of standing on its own feet once more. I would not take Avaline's happiness or her home from her.'

Spoken like a true heir. Aidan had not even thought of Blandford beyond it being Avaline's home. He saw now the limits to his thinking. Blandford might be Avaline's home but all that a wife had passed to her husband upon marriage. Putting Blandford in Fortis's protection had been the whole purpose of their alliance in the beginning. Blandford was Avaline's by heritage, but Fortis's by law. If Fortis were dead, Avaline might lose Blandford.

Cowden nodded at his heir's wisdom. 'Ferris? What do you think?'

Ferris glanced at Aidan. 'I think a remarkable man walked out of the Crimean forest and I am proud to call him my brother. He put another's life above his own. That kind of man will make a spectacular husband in a way Fortis never could.' He gave the group a rueful smile. 'We all loved Fortis, but it needs to be said he was imperfect. He had an officer's arrogance and an aristocrat's selfishness, a man who was blind to the privilege he was born to. But, he was honourable. He did his duty to Avaline. However, it was never more than a duty. As a couple who shared each other's lives, they were not well suited. Their marriage suited Blandford only. It is to Fortis's credit that he sought to fulfil his duty and that he felt regret for his selfishness. He sent this man in his stead. We would not want his sacrifice to be in vain.' Ferris's words were the words of a physician, a man sworn to protect the lives of others, a man whose very occupation shunned the concept of selfishness. That he thought of Aidan in such a light touched him deeply.

'Thank you, Ferris.' Aidan swallowed against the emotion.

'My wife? What is your will?' Cowden asked at last.

The Duchess gave a soft smile through her tears. 'I think Fortis has come back to us in a way most unexpected, but no less glorious.' She rose and crossed the room to him. 'Welcome home, my son.' The Duchess of Cowden wrapped him in her arms and gave him a mother's hug.

The dam broke then for all of them. He was swarmed. Frederick and Ferris embracing him in turn, the women kissing his cheek. There was laughter and tears of joy, the early morning suddenly turning back on itself to the happiness the previous day had begun with. He had his arm around Avaline, determined to never let her go, savouring the joy in her eyes, the relief. Some of the pressure and the pain of the last hours had been resolved. Frederick poured drinks for everyone and passed around the glasses, raising his own in a toast when everyone had been served. 'Long live Fortis Tresham!'

They answered in him a loud, rousing chorus. 'To Fortis!' And they drank, all together, eyes glistening, mourning and merriment mixing. Aidan understood. In affirming him, they were celebrating Fortis's life. He'd never been more moved in his life than he was right now. Not the grief he felt at his mother's death, or Fortis's death, could match the elation he felt. The family he never had surrounded him, the wife he thought he could never have, stood beside him, his child in her belly, the beginning of the family they would make together.

He took a final swallow of his brandy and whispered his own tribute. 'Thank you, Fortis. Thank you for everything.'

Cowden let them celebrate until glasses were empty before calling them to order once more. 'I need everyone to understand what we've committed to. This choice is not just about thwarting Hayworth. It is about thwarting society. For ever. The point of no return has been reached. We cannot retreat from this.' He gestured towards Aidan. 'You cannot retreat from this.'

Aidan nodded. He understood fully what each of their commitments meant and he understood his. To be Fortis Tresham would be to deny his former life, to disavow twenty-eight years—or was it thirty-three? Fortis had been older than himself. He supposed he'd lost five years in becoming Fortis. But that was the least of what he'd lost and the least of what he'd gained. If he had a new birthday and a new age, then so be it. He'd gained so much more.

'We may have to take others into our confidence,' Cowden warned. 'Major Lithgow, perhaps even Viscount Taunton, and Sutton

Keynes.' His friends. Aidan had not met the latter two. What would Lithgow say? 'We all need to recognise that it may get worse before it gets better.'

Frederick nodded and picked up the conversation. 'Hayworth may not let this go. We stalled him tonight, but he was not pleased. His accusations were also threats. He accused us of willingly harbouring an impostor in order to deter him.' And now Hayworth would be right.

'What can he do, though? It's his word against a duke's,' Ferris put in.

Cowden returned to the conversation. 'He can have Fortis arrested on charges of playing the impostor. If he can prove it, he can have Fortis-cum-Aidan tried for theft and then it's a very short trip to the gallows. He will try to implicate us, but he does not understand how powerful a duke is. The concept of true power eludes him. The aristocracy is not dead yet and it will certainly rally against the likes of him. But it may be messy, there will certainly be some scandal while we put him off.' He nodded in Avaline's direction. 'You will bear the brunt of his attack, my dear. If it comes, there will be no escaping it.'

'I will protect her,' Aidan said resolutely.

'You will have to. You will be the only one who can.' Cowden's reply was serious. 'You cannot break from your façade for a moment. Her only hope and your child's only hope is to defeat Hayworth and prove beyond a shadow of a doubt that you are Fortis Tresham and no other. If you fail to do that, the Treshams will survive intact, but Avaline will not.'

'I understand.' He tightened his hold on Avaline, feeling her sway against him. 'I will not fail.' Like any battle, it was a zero-sum game. 'It's been a long night. I know there is more to discuss, but I would like to take my wife to bed. You are welcome to stay. There are plenty of rooms and we can talk again when we're all rested. I can send word to Bramble and my servants will see that your driver is taken care of.' The words came easily to him. He wondered if a year ago he would have spoken the commands so naturally? It occurred to him that in that moment the mantle of master of Blandford settled comfortably and permanently on his shoulders. Perhaps now the transition from Aidan Roswell to Fortis Tresham was truly complete.

Helena came forward and squeezed his hand. 'Yes, take Avaline to bed, dear Brother, the early months can be so tiring.' She kissed them both on the cheek and another mantle, far more precious to Aidan than that of master of the house, settled on his shoulders as well—the mantle of belonging. He was part of a family. They'd pledged to give their all for him and he would do the same. They would not be sorry. He would defend Avaline and the Treshams with all he had.

Aidan Roswell's position was indefensible. Tobin Hayworth marshalled the multiple steps of his attack in his mind from behind his desk. He would have to win the civil trial first in the Court of Common Pleas. Then, there'd be a second, criminal trial at the Queen's Bench—the one that would decide if the impostor would hang. Tobin Hayworth sat back in the comfort of his leather chair, digesting the strategy laid out for him by his barrister, one Clarence Montgomery, a conservative, distinguished fellow with just the right tone for the delicate task.

Tobin had picked him especially. Montgomery was in his early forties and had a successful career behind him. He dressed in sombre blacks and greys, was clean-shaven and wore his hair close-cropped, a look that would appeal to the upper classes, the very audience

Tobin needed to win. This case had to be presented as an attempt to protect the aristocracy against unwanted infiltration, not as a strike against it, which in truth it was. They'd denied his nabob money for too long. They would have to deal with him now either as a saviour or as an enemy.

'It shouldn't be hard to win. We have the truth on our side.' Tobin gestured to the folder that lay open between them on the desk. 'The man's a jewel thief. He's seduced well-born ladies before. It should not be difficult to prove that Avaline Tresham is just another in a long line of susceptible women and his act against her is just another crime in an equally long string of crimes.' Really, Tobin thought, Aidan Roswell could not have made it any easier. People were predictable, Roswell was no different. He was repeating his pattern: wealthy women, wealthy crimes. Only this time, he'd reached far above himself. Had he really thought he could impersonate a duke's son for the rest of his life?

'Easy?' Montgomery raised a sceptical eyebrow. 'You think this will be easy? You are asking a duke to denounce his son, something he seems unlikely to do. He's already told you he does not believe there's any doubt about his son's identity.'

'I have witnesses who say otherwise. The Duchess of Chichester, from whom he stole the ruby tiara,' Hayworth replied confidently.

Montgomery gave a hard laugh. 'The Duchess of Chichester? As a witness? Be prepared for her to decline. I doubt she will testify there was a man in her bedroom that night, it's tantamount to confessing adultery. If she says he was merely a burglar who broke into her bedroom unannounced, she risks perjury if Roswell turns on her.' Montgomery gave a sigh that bordered on patronising. 'This is where it gets hard, Mr Hayworth. I do not doubt there are witnesses. But I do doubt their ability and willingness to testify.'

'Throw money at them. I find that usually works,' Hayworth said crossly. Good Lord, did he have to do all the thinking? 'She's not the only witness. There are others and they are less well bred and less likely to care about the personal repercussions of their testimony as long as they have some jingle in their pocket.' That was the problem of dealing with prigs like Montgomery. They carried their ethics with them like a calling card.

Montgomery shut his leather writing case. 'Very good, Mr Hayworth. I will get the necessary items in order and prepare our case to go to trial in the new year. Meanwhile, enjoy the approaching holidays.'

'Ah, the holidays.' Tobin tapped his fingers on his desk in thought. 'I want him arrested the moment the accusation is drawn up. After spending the holidays in Newgate, our fake Fortis might be his own worst enemy.' Most men were. Tobin smiled coldly. The game was shaping up very nicely in his favour. In fact, he didn't see how Cowden or Roswell could succeed. He had them in check.

Chapter Twenty

'Checkmate.' Avaline beamed as her bishop claimed victory. Aidan conceded his king with a laugh. He had won the first game and now their set was split at a game apiece.

'How is it that you're so very good at chess? I didn't think ladies played the game much.'

'You can blame Mrs Finlay's Academy for that. Mrs Finlay believed a woman should refine her mind as well as her body so that a man might find pleasure in both when used in the right ways at the right time.' Avaline set the pieces up—a third game seemed a foregone conclusion now, although she hadn't been so sure a half-hour ago. Aidan had proven to be a determined opponent.

'We all went there. Well, almost all of us. Elidh didn't attend. Did you know that? It's something your friends' wives have in common. We weren't all there at the same time, but it's an interesting coincidence. Helena is the school's legend because she married a duke's heir. But Sofia, Conall, Viscount Taunton's wife, was there with Helena. Then, later, Pavia, Cam's wife, attended, and of course I went.'

'I know who Taunton is. I know Fortis's friends,' Aidan said quietly and she grimaced, hating herself for the slip. She hadn't meant to do that—to fill in the facts for him with little explanations.

'I'm sorry.' She'd been doing it ever since the night it had all come out that he wasn't Fortis. She was sorry, she knew the habit bothered him, but Aidan had to be protected and the only way to do that was with information. Now that they'd all committed to the ruse, there was no room to slip. She'd probably do it again. He was welcome to hate her for it as long he was safe, yet the habit was creating distance between them. Not an enormous chasm, but enough distance to notice.

Ever since the decision had been made, Aidan had withdrawn in little ways, becoming quieter, more reticent with the family as if he wanted to make himself an outsider. She supposed it was only natural. It would take time for him to feel that he truly belonged now that he knew he didn't. She could only imagine the blow it must have been to think he had a family and then learn he did not. But what she hated the most was how he withdrew from her. Even when he'd been struggling with his memories, he'd shared the struggle with her. Now, he shared nothing. Prying stories from him about his real past was like taking gold from a miser. He would politely resist with phrases like, 'you don't want to hear about that', or 'it's not important'. It was important to her. She wanted to know him. She knew why he did it. He thought he had no value. He still saw himself as a street rat. He needed to let go of that past as much as he'd needed to let go of the cave.

Avaline finished setting up chess pieces. Outside, rain came down in hard sheets interspersed with icy hail. But they were safe and warm inside, playing chess before the fire, the perfect way to spend a dark, winter evening. She didn't mind if it rained liked this for weeks. No one would think of travelling out in such weather. That, too, meant Aidan was safe. Even Tobin Hayworth would think twice before venturing abroad in such conditions.

'Don't be sorry, Avaline. I shouldn't have snapped. I know you mean well. I just don't want you to worry. It's not good for the baby or for yourself. I don't want to be a cause of concern to you.' Aidan smiled at her and that smile melted the tension that was so often present between them these days as they all readjusted to the reality that Fortis was dead. It was an awkward time of mourning the past mixed with celebrating the future and worrying over what that future might be. Was Hayworth bluffing? Would he strike? When? They'd been waiting nearly two weeks since the party and there'd been no word. She was grateful for that and she was terrified.

Avaline reached across the board and took his hand. 'How is it that *you're* such a fine chess player?'

'A soldier in my regiment taught me. He had a travelling chess set. He was a minor gentleman's son. We played almost every night.' Aidan's smile faded. 'He was killed at Alma, a month before Balaclava. The set is in my trunk, wherever that is now. He'd been joking the night before the battle that the set was mine if he was killed.' He shrugged. 'It's a morbid sense of humour, but it gets a soldier through, helps them to say difficult things. I didn't really think he'd die. He was one of those people who seemed charmed.'

'Like Fortis.' Avaline couldn't help herself.

'Yes.' Aidan pursed his lips in a tight line she'd come to note as a means of holding back emotion. 'I had nothing to live for, no mother or father waiting for me. But I lived. I don't know why. His family needed him, but he died. It doesn't make sense.'

'It makes perfect sense. I need you. Fortis needed you.' Avaline smiled, wanting to do so much more to ease his pain and not knowing what that might be.

Aidan said nothing, choosing to give his attention to the newly set board. 'Queen's pawn to D-Four.'

'Queen's pawn openings are not *comme il faut*.'

'It suits me. I am not very fashionable,' Aidan challenged.

Avaline cocked her head to survey the board. 'Are you setting up for the Queen's gambit?' She moved her black pawn to E-Six, a deceptively passive move.

'Ah, minx, you're waiting for me to commit.' Aidan chuckled. The firelight caught his profile, limning all its angles and planes to perfection, turning him devastatingly handsome. It was easy to see how he'd charmed those ladies mentioned in Hayworth's report.

'I expect there have been a lot of women waiting for you to commit.' The roguish nature of his past revealed in Hayworth's document had not repulsed her. Instead it had heightened her fascination with him, but he remained frustratingly reluctant to share that piece of his life with her. Even now when it was out in the open between them, it remained a steadfastly closed box. 'Have you had many women, Aidan?'

His hand stilled on a piece. 'Are you asking if Hayworth's report is true? You already know it is.'

'*Everything* in the report is true? Or is some of it greatly exaggerated by Hayworth?' Avaline pressed.

'Enough. You don't want to know. You don't need to know,' Aidan said tersely, committing to the Queen's Gambit with his next move.

She moved to accept. 'I do want to know. I want to know everything about you. The good and the awful. You don't need to hide it from me. I won't break.'

'I know you won't. But the past is of no consequence, now, Avaline. Knowing anything of it can only hurt you. If Hayworth presses his claims and if he proves them, the only thing that will save you is your ignorance. You have to claim you knew nothing of my identity, that I misled you. It will be your only chance. You will have to cut yourself free of me. Promise me you will.'

The game between them was forgotten. She left her chair and came to him, sitting on his lap. She had her worries and he had his. 'Please, don't talk like that.' She knew he wasn't sleeping. She'd wake at night and see him standing by the window, sometimes for hours. When she'd wake in the morning, he'd still be standing there, watching the sunrise. He spent his days doing little tasks about the hall, going over ledgers, never sitting still. She knew what he was doing. Last things. In case the worst happened. He was making preparations, trying to see that she was taken care of. It was sweet and all the more reason to love him. She hated what Hayworth was doing to him, to them. The waiting was slowly destroying them, the worry over *what-ifs* eating them alive.

'Are you afraid, Aidan?' she asked softly. He was always so strong for her, from the moment he'd swept her up in his arms at the Harvest ball, yet always so worried he wasn't strong enough. How could there be any doubt?

'A good soldier is always afraid. It's what keeps him sharp, it's what keeps him alive.' He held her gaze with those beautiful blue eyes. 'It's what keeps the people he loves safe.' His fingers tangled in her hair, his mouth slanting over hers. 'Distract me, Avaline. For a few minutes, I don't want to be afraid.'

These were the moments she lived for, the moments when they could push aside the threat Hayworth posed to their lives. She shifted, straddling him in his chair, her mouth returning his kiss, her hands working his trousers open. She felt his hands beneath her skirts, pushing them up, her thighs exposed. His hand cupped her at the juncture of her thighs. 'I adore you like this,' he murmured between kisses, his voice hoarse. 'So wet, so ready, for me alone.'

'I like you this way, too.' Avaline sighed, rising up just enough to tease the tip of his phallus with the wetness at her entrance. 'All hard, hot male. For me alone.' There might have been lovers in his past, but she was his last, his only from here on, of that she had no doubt. She slid down his length, taking him inside herself in a long, languid ride, delighting in the way she could make him moan. Then she began to move against him, a deliberate, tantalising motion that drove them both into the slow burn of ecstasy's flame. His hands gripped her hips, her own hands digging into the muscles of his shoulders until, at last, they slipped to the floor before the fire, pleasure achieved in chorus of gasping cries.

'You wreck me.' Avaline sighed. 'Every time, even when I'm in charge. How do you manage it?'

Aidan's chest rose and fell, still rapid against her cheek, his arm about her, hugging her close. 'You wreck me, too.' His eyes closed. 'Tell me about Christmas at Bramble. Tell me what it will be like.'

She gave a soft laugh. 'If I didn't know better, I'd think you were a child with all this excitement for the holiday.' Avaline drew tiny circles around his nipples. She'd told him this story before. In the weeks since his birthday party, it had become something of a favourite topic with him. 'Didn't you have Christmas growing up?' Surely he'd had a small celebration.

'None, my dear. Christmas is a surprisingly

busy time for prostitutes. It was always a bustling evening at the brothel, at any rate. People looking to not be alone, I suppose. At any rate, no one wanted a little boy underfoot.'

Avaline rose up. 'But Christmas is for children. The sweets, the toys. Children are what makes it so much fun.'

'Children remind gentlemen of the duties they're neglecting at home,' Aidan countered. 'I spent Christmas on the streets, waiting for my mother's gentlemen to leave. It was good earnings on Christmas, though. Gentlemen feel guilty and pay an urchin well to hold their horses and watch their carriages while they're frolicking inside. One Christmas I earned enough to buy us oranges. Two whole oranges. It was a fortune.'

Two oranges. She could not imagine the level of that poverty. How many Christmases had she eaten oranges without a thought? They'd had bowls of them at Blandford even for the servants. She reached up and smoothed back his hair. His story broke her heart, although she dared not say it for fear he would never tell her another thing. She would treat this story as the rare treasure it was. He had shown her so much in that simple story: how he'd lived, how he'd been selfless even under the worst of circumstances.

'You will never be on the streets again. Christmas at Bramble is a wonder. There are greens up everywhere, a giant log in the fireplace, there's a huge feast for everyone, and church at midnight in the chapel. In the morning, there's an enormous breakfast and presents at our places. All the wives make their husbands something homemade.' This year she was looking forward to that tradition. This year she wouldn't be left out. She had a husband.

Aidan's hand slid over the flat of her belly. 'You've already made me something.' He laughed.

'Yes, well, I made you something else, too.'

'What is it?'

'You will have to wait and see. Just two days now. You can manage that.' He tickled her then, trying to tease the secret out of her. She laughed and squealed as he pulled her beneath him.

She was in mid-squeal when the sound came. Startled, they both froze. 'It's the rain,' Avaline said.

'No, it stopped a while ago.' Aidan eased off her as the sound came again. 'Someone's at the door.' He rose, doing up his trousers. All fun and good humour faded from the room. The tension was back. He held her gaze, a thousand words passing in that glance.

'No one would be out this time of night in this weather.' Avaline rose, too, straightening her skirts as voices sounded in the entrance hall. Men, several of them.

The butler entered the room, but these men, led by Tobin Hayworth, preferred to announce themselves. Hayworth, greatcoat drenched from the rain, strode forward, pushing the butler aside. 'I am here with a warrant for your arrest.'

'No, you can't.' Avaline rushed forward, but Aidan stepped in front of her, his broad shoulders shielding her.

'On what grounds?' Aidan asked coolly.

'On grounds of impersonating a duke's son and wrongfully claiming the identity of Fortis Tresham. I have compelling evidence and testimony that you are a dangerous criminal who has likely duped this woman and the Tresham family. Those are grounds under which you will be taken to Newgate where you will await trial.'

'No!' Avaline pushed around Aidan, tearing away from him when he reached for her, determined to stand between him and what-

ever disaster came next. She was frantic with
fear. 'You are doing this out of spite and jealousy for perceived wrongs. You cannot take
him. It's nearly Christmas.' What sort of man
arrested someone two days before Christmas?
She cast about in her mind for the right arguments. 'He'll give parole, we'll post bail.' Were
those the right words? She'd tried to listen carefully when the Treshams had plotted against
this. Had she accepted too much by asking for
those things? By asking, had she implied that
there was some guilt to defend against? Had
she given up the high ground? She didn't know.
She wished fervently that Frederick was here.
He would know what to do, how to make Hayworth leave, what to say and when to say it. She
was a poor champion for Aidan.

'I must ask you to stand aside.' Hayworth's
gaze met her own, cool and steely, devoid of
emotion. 'Resistance can gain you nothing,
ma'am. We will be taking him into custody
whether you approve or not. I would prefer not
to take you with him. Newgate is not a hos-
pitable place for ladies, but I will do it if you
persist in obstructing justice by attempting to
prevent his arrest.'

'You're taking him to London?' Avaline's

hand went to her stomach, steadying herself, the words like a physical blow. Not only to London, but to Newgate, a veritable hell on earth. 'He's done nothing wrong, what about being innocent until proven guilty?' The world was reeling…she couldn't think fast enough.

'There is substantial and likely reason to think him guilty of fraud and theft. That makes him dangerous enough to await trial in prison and that is all of the legal system I am going to waste my time explaining to you, Avaline. You've expended what patience I have.'

She could feel Aidan bristling behind her at the casual address. It was an insult to her. Still, Aidan should have let it pass. There were more serious concerns to think on now. But he didn't. 'You will address her at Lady Fortis Tresham,' Aidan growled. 'She is a titled lady and you will show her the respect she deserves.' It was a sharp reminder to Hayworth about who held the power even if it wasn't in clear evidence at this precise moment. 'You think you have power right now because you can physically enforce your will, but that's a bully's power, Hayworth.'

'I have more than that, Roswell,' Hayworth sneered. 'I have the law.'

'That is Lord Fortis Tresham to you,' Aidan shot back.

'That remains to be seen.' Hayworth gestured to the men he'd brought. 'Take him now by whatever force necessary. The roads are bad enough as it is without having to travel half the night.'

'Then come back in the morning,' Avaline argued desperately, but already the men were closing in on them, intent on their purpose. Irons dangled from one man's hand. Horror rose anew for her. They would not take Aidan out of this house like a common prisoner. He'd done nothing wrong. He'd only tried to fulfil a dying man's wish.

She did not move, although Aidan begged quietly at her ear, 'Avaline, I think I must go with them.'

'No.' She didn't want to cry. She wanted to be strong. She didn't want Aidan to worry. But the tears came anyway. 'We were supposed to have Christmas. You were supposed to unwrap my gift and sing carols in the church and walk under the midnight sky together. I've waited so long to...' To have someone to love, to have someone who loved *her*, and now she was going to lose him. God only knew what would happen to him behind Newgate's walls. Would he even make it to trial? Did Hayworth want the publicity of a trial or did he just want Aidan dead? That would certainly expedite things even if it didn't come with a public dose of revenge against Cowden.

Aidan dead.

The thought of it broke her completely. 'You can't leave this house, you can't.' She broke down completely, sobs overwhelmed her. Aidan's arms were about her, turning her to him, muffling her cries against his shoulders. She clung to his shirt, her fingers curled into fists inside its folds. The shirt smelled like him. She buried her nose in the fabric and shut her eyes, holding on to every piece of him in every way for dear life.

'Avaline, don't cry, don't give Hayworth the satisfaction.' Aidan made no attempt to lower his voice. 'Pain gives him pleasure, my dear, and we will not feed his monster. We are Treshams and we are too proud for the likes of him.' He should not have said it. The brave words would cost him. She felt the tenor of his comfort change, his arms tensed a fraction of a moment before she was dragged away by brutal hands, the other man clapping Aidan into shackles while her captor mauled her.

'Avaline!' Aidan's hoarse cry ripped through the hall as she struggled. 'You will take your hands off my wife!' The hall erupted into brawling chaos. Shackled or not, Aidan was her champion. Aidan lunged for the man nearest him, proving shackles were a mistake. He got the length of chain around the man's neck, choking him into unconsciousness with quick efficiency and charged for the man holding her. But Hayworth was faster.

He stepped in front of Avaline, knife drawn. 'Once a street rat, always a street rat. You even fight like a scrapper. My man has an appetite for pretty women like your wife. You come quietly now and she'll be safe. You make trouble, then I won't stop my man from having his way.'

'She is pregnant,' Aidan growled. 'You're despicable. My father was right. You haven't a shred of decency in your body.'

'Your father?' Hayworth laughed. 'You don't even know who your father is and neither will that brat she's carrying once I get done destroying you. But that's for later. Will you come?'

Her captor squeezed a breast with hard, cruel fingers. Avaline bit back a cry. It's what Hayworth wanted—to use her to provoke Aidan. Perhaps Hayworth would find it efficient to kill Aidan here behind the thin guise of self-defence.

'I'll come, let me say goodbye.' Aidan was cool steel.

Hayworth stepped aside and sheathed his knife, a victorious smile twisting his mouth. 'You do not set conditions.' He made a sweeping gesture towards the door.

'He needs a coat,' Avaline exclaimed, wrestling free of her captor. Aidan wasn't prepared to go out into the night, the cold, the hail.

'I will be fine, Avaline.' Aidan's voice was terse and full of warning. 'Take care of our child. I will be home soon and this nonsense will be behind us.' Hayworth pushed him towards the door. He stumbled and caught the door jamb to steady himself. Hayworth punched him in the kidney and Avaline screamed as he buckled. Hayworth and her captor grabbed him between them and dragged him towards the carriage. Even in pain, Aidan called instructions to her, playing his part to the hilt. 'Go to Bramble, tell my father. He will not stand for this! Take care of yourself, Avaline. Do not risk our child on needless worry!'

'I will, Fortis. We will be in London before you know it. All of us,' she cried as the driver pushed past her, dragging his unconscious comrade out to the coach. There was nothing she could do. She watched helplessly as the coach door swung shut behind Aidan and drove off into the night taking the man she loved with it to a very uncertain future. Never had she felt so powerless. She began to shake. No, she would not give in to weakness again, no matter how powerless she felt.

She called for the butler. 'Ready the carriage, I must leave for Bramble at once.' Giving orders helped calm her, helped her find a sense of control. 'Tell the maids to pack my things, have the valet pack a trunk for Lord Fortis. I want trunks ready before I leave.' She drew a deep breath, calling up the reserves of her strength. She would focus on the next step, and then the next. Each little step would take her closer to Aidan.

Chapter Twenty-One

Each mile took him further from Avaline, further from the Tresham stronghold. He was in the clutches of his enemy, a man who would see him debunked and dead. Aidan wedged his shoulder against the side of the carriage to keep his balance over the rutted road, a reminder that, here in the coach, he was on his own. No title would protect him. He had only his wits and his fists, such as they were in irons. He was entirely on his own as he had been for much of his life. It should not seem strange. Being among the Treshams was the anomaly, not the norm, yet his mind struggled to remember that. When had it happened that this feeling of being surrounded by family had become the norm? When had it supplanted the expectation that he must manage alone?

It hardly mattered. It was gone now. The skills of his past had come flooding back, a testament perhaps to the reality that no matter what his name, a part of him would always be Aidan Roswell, street rat. How many times had he had to fight on the streets as he had tonight, with any weapon available? Bottles broken into sharp, jagged blades, sticks wielded like deadly clubs, chains, boards with rusty nails discarded as rubbish in an alley. His child's imagination had been very good at converting the ordinary into weapons. It had to be when survival was on the line.

Even now, in the dark interior of the coach, his mind was seeking a weapon. He had his chains. In the close confines, it would be possible to get his chains around one man's neck. He'd have to disarm Hayworth first, though. Hayworth had not done himself any favours by drawing that blade back at Blandford. It exposed Hayworth's hand. Now, Aidan knew exactly what the man carried. That didn't change the fact that the blade would be deadly trouble. Aidan was astute enough to recognise Hayworth might not be wedded to the idea of keeping him alive. For Avaline's sake, he had to make sure Hayworth did.

God, he didn't want to think about Avaline now. This evening had destroyed her. When she'd collapsed in his arms, he'd been ready to do murder to the men who'd brought her to it. It would have been so easy to finish off the one man. But that was murder, that was resisting arrest. He couldn't see that any good would come of it, only bad, and there was enough of that already. It wouldn't help his case. But he'd been thankful for the moments he'd had to hold her, to feel the feminine warmth of her one last time, the one last chance to give her comfort. It would have to stand them awhile. He would think instead of what she was doing now. She would be at Bramble by now, sounding the alarm, raising the troops. Frederick and Cowden would be underway at sunrise, maybe Ferris, too, if they thought he might need a physician. Aidan hoped Cowden would persuade the women to stay behind.

He had more than a passing acquaintance with Newgate. He'd been there for a week over the ruby-tiara incident before he'd signed with the army. It was not an experience he was looking forward to repeating, but he would handle it. He did not want Avaline to have to handle it as well. Hayworth was right about one thing. It was no place for a lady. All manner of depravity took place there. He would not think about that now. It would only create despair and he needed his wits sharp, not dragged down by hopelessness. He would survive Newgate. Avaline and his child were waiting for him. This time, he had everything to live for. It was hard to believe that just a few hours ago, he'd been making love to his wife. His mind sought that memory; of Avaline warm and willing astride him, taking him deep inside her, but he denied it. He forced himself to push those memories away. They were not for public consumption. He refused to think of making love to Avaline in front of Hayworth.

Hayworth shifted on the seat across from him. 'You should sleep. You'll get precious little of it where you're going. Sleep in Newgate, you end up with your throat slit.'

'Would that disappoint you?' Feeling out Hayworth's commitment to keeping him alive would be a useful way to spend the time. Perhaps Hayworth didn't want to dirty his own hands. It would be easy enough to pay someone on the inside to kill him. There would be no trial. Hayworth only needed the pretence of a trial, an excuse to lock him up and then let the nature of Newgate have its way. No one would be able to prove his death had been anything but another Newgate casualty. 'Seems that killing me now would expedite your claims, put you back to where you were in October,' Aidan mused out loud. 'Avaline a widow, unprotected by a husband's name.' He didn't like thinking of such a thing. He would have failed Fortis if that came to pass.

'And me without my revenge,' Hayworth put in with a decided sangfroid that would have chilled a more squeamish man. But Aidan had seen the corruption of the streets and the violence of battle, he knew just how cheaply life was held by men like Hayworth. 'It's worth it to me to keep you alive long enough to stand trial and raise a scandal that will discredit Cowden if he continues to stand with you.'

Aidan scoffed, 'He will always stand with his son, scandal or not. I think you've forgotten the truth of the situation. You're the liar and now everyone will know.'

'You've got balls, I'll give you that.' Hayworth chuckled. 'But it's early days yet. We'll see what shape your balls are in after a few weeks in Newgate. You'll have time to cool your heels, can't get you to trial until the twenty-first of January.'

'Do you think I'll live that long?' Three weeks in hell. He didn't dare let Hayworth see how the thought affected him. 'Newgate might finish me off with or without your permission. A duke's son is easy pickings.'

'You are not a duke's son. You're a survivor.' Hayworth eyed him. 'You'll do what it takes to make it through.'

'Perhaps I'll do it myself just to cheat you out of your revenge. Avaline will never marry you.'

'I can always blackmail her with the truth of her child's father's identity.' Hayworth was unfazed. 'She can't claim it's Fortis's child if he's been dead for a year already and you aren't him. That child would be branded a bastard faster than she could blink. But that's all hypothetical chess. You won't do it. You have too much to live for these days. The only way forward for either of us is through it. We both need you to stand trial. One of us will walk away exonerated, the other disgraced.'

There was an unfortunate truth in that.

Newgate was as he remembered it: damp, dirty, dark and dangerous. There were other D words he could add to the list of Newgate's alliterative deficiencies: depraved, decrepit, debilitating. This was a place where people came to die. There was no hope here, only desperation. Another D for the list.

Aidan could feel the last vestiges of his own hope leach away as Hayworth's coach passed through its gates, echoes of the past rumbling in his bones, rousing him from slumber. Newgate was wasting no time trying to change him. He would not let it. He was a soldier in Her Majesty's army, who'd comported himself with honour in battle, a man who knew discipline and strength of mind as well as body. Whether the world saw him as Tresham or Roswell, that was who he was. He was *not* a street rat any longer. It was the one piece of his identity he could claim as his own. He would not let Newgate drag him down. He would not let Newgate define him. Hayworth was watching him, guessing perhaps the weight such an arrival might carry with him, the exquisite torture this journey held. 'Does this bring back memories?'

'Why should it?' Aidan schooled his features. 'I've never been here before.' A blatant lie for Aidan Roswell, but an absolute truth for Fortis Tresham. He had to remember who he was in the present, had to play that role to the hilt. Any crack in the façade and Hayworth would have all the justification he needed.

The gates shut behind the carriage, sealing them in, and sealing out the bustling world of the London streets. It was still early morning, but London was alive with vendors, street carts, milkmaids and bakers. He knew the rhythm of the streets, the pulse of the day, as if it was still part of him. Maybe it was. Perhaps he would never fully moult that skin. Perhaps a man never truly escaped his destiny no matter how hard he tried or how far he ran. After ten years of trying, he was back where he'd started.

No. Aidan tamped down on the thoughts. He could not afford to think like that, for his sake and for Avaline's. The driver set the steps and Hayworth exited. The other two men followed, reaching back in to drag him out. They gripped him unceremoniously by the forearms and shoved him down the steps, according him no courtesy, treating him like a common criminal. It would be the first of the humiliations he would suffer today. He would weather it and all the others to follow. He concentrated on a final look at the sky, at daylight. Those things would be luxuries soon. He simply had to get through it.

He had to survive. For Avaline. With luck, he only need to endure it for a few hours, maybe a day, until Frederick came. It was the latter he thought of as the gaolers searched him for weapons and then again for any personal effects that would be taken from him. Finding none, the gaoler punched him in the stomach, furious. But even doubled over with pain, Aidan felt a sense of pride in outsmarting them. He'd prepared against this. The day after the party, he'd stopped carrying anything of value in his pockets: no pocket watch, no fobs attached, wearing no stickpins in his cravat. The miniature of Avaline was home safe at Blandford on his bureau. If he hadn't been taken at night after playing chess with Avaline, the gaolers might have had his onyx cufflinks. But he'd even robbed the gaolers of that since he played chess with his shirtsleeves rolled up. Those onyx beauties were probably still sitting next to the chessboard where he'd left them.

By the time the gaolers marched him back to Hayworth and the warden in a far more dishevelled condition than when he'd left, Hayworth had convinced the warden he was dangerous.

'Tell your gaolers to be careful around him. He got his chains around the neck of one of my guards when we went to take him.'

'I was defending my wife,' Aidan ground out, acutely aware of the lie. Avaline was not his wife, not in legal truth nor perhaps even in the eyes of God. He could never marry her in church or at the Register. As Fortis Tresham there was no need. As Aidan Roswell, he could never attempt it, nor would he. Aidan Roswell had as little to offer a wife today as he had ten years ago.

'Insolent, too.' Hayworth made a show of adjusting his pristine shirt cuffs where they peeped out just the precise distance from his wool jacket.

'I am a duke's son and this treatment is intolerable,' Aidan argued with all the command he could summon.

'He's crazy is more like it.' The warden eyed him. 'We see chaps all the time who think they're someone else.'

Hayworth didn't like that. 'No, I assure you he is not delusional. He is posturing as Lord Fortis Tresham quite deliberately with the intent of stealing land and fortune from Tresham's widow and the family.' Hayworth slid the requisite payment and more across the desk. A insane man couldn't hang. He wanted the gallows for Roswell, not an asylum.

The warden shrugged and pocketed the money. Ultimately, he didn't care what the prisoner was here for. He cared only for what he could make. How anyone thought justice was served by a prison system that required prisoners to pay to get in was beyond Aidan. In this case, Hayworth was all too glad to pay. 'Then come along, Lord Fortis Tresham,' the warden mocked, nodding to one of the gaolers to take him away. 'Let's see what the rabble makes of you. You might not be lordly for long.'

The gaoler led him down a slick cobblestone maze, past cramped cells filled to irreverent capacity. Newgate was no respecter of station or crime. Murderers and felons lived cheek by jowl with debtors and petty thieves caught only stealing a loaf of bread. At a cell at the end of the maze, the gaoler stopped and took a ring of keys from his belt. He fitted one into the lock. He shoved Aidan forward, the door clanging shut behind him. 'This chap here claims to be Lord Fortis Tresham, son of a duke.' The sneer was evident in his words. The cellmates laughed. 'I suppose we'll see about that. How long do you think your father, the Duke, will let you languish in here before you get a proper chamber? Just in case your father is delayed, Jimmy here is King of this particular castle.' The gaoler laughed at his own wit as he sauntered off, the last of Aidan's freedom jangling at his waist.

Aidan surveyed the motley crew before him, sizing each man up in turn as he knew they were sizing up him. King Jimmy was a hulking brute who occupied the single bench in the cell as if it were indeed his throne. The rest of the men gathered about him, giving a twisted appearance of being his royal court. Aidan understood that. Prison politics hadn't changed in ten years. Money and influence bought favours and protection in here as it always had.

'What do we make of him, lads?' King Jimmy asked with a belch.

'He sure is pretty. He's so tall and so *clean*. Makes me want to mess him up, get him dirty,' a lean, emaciated fellow hissed from King Jimmy's right shoulder. Aidan knew the type. This was Jimmy's sycophant. The nuance of Newgate slid over Aidan whether he liked it or not. He would kill this man first if it came to it.

A tall, bearded man built like a bear stepped

from the shadows at the edge of Jimmy's court. 'He's too big for you, Sligo. He'd sooner kill you than look at you.' Ah, so King Jimmy had competition for his throne. Aidan nodded in the man's direction and sidled over to stand with him. He'd have an ally if he needed it. He hoped he wouldn't. He hoped Frederick was on his way. Already, despite his best efforts, he felt Newgate trying to reclaim him, its tentacles wrapping about him, drawing him towards its gaping maw. Aidan slid to the ground, his back to the wall, the best defensive position he would have in here. He wrapped his arms around his knees, hugging what little body heat he had to himself, and thought about Avaline.

He'd not wanted to think of her in this place, but she was his best weapon for holding the darkness inside him at bay—Avaline with her light, her laughter, her trust. He had a thousand pictures of her in his mind: Avaline at the workers' picnic, setting out baskets of apples; Avaline sneaking glances at him as he roofed when she thought he wouldn't notice; Avaline in his bed, soothing his nightmares; Avaline dressed in silver, dancing in his arms at his birthday party, her face shining with love. What a night that had been! Right up until Hayworth had destroyed it. Hayworth and Newgate were darkness. Avaline and Blandford were light. God and Cowden willing, he'd see them again.

By mid-morning, the gaoler was back, gruff and out of sorts as he unlocked the door. 'You…' he pointed at Aidan '…have cost me five quid. Get up. Seems you have friends in high places after all.'

'*You* shouldn't have bet against me,' Aidan couldn't resist saying as he followed the man out. Relief filled him. Frederick was here. The man had made beastly good time. He must have left before sunrise. The thought cheered him as they went back through the maze and up towards the light. Up another flight of stairs, they reached a small chamber. The cot, the rickety table and the single chair crowded the space. There was no window, no light, but it was private. Already, those little blessings seemed like luxuries.

There was a thump and a commotion in the hall and Ferris appeared in the doorway, directing a man with a trunk. 'There you are, Brother! This place is ghastly.' Ferris swept him into an ungainly embrace and then drew back with a grimace. 'Gaoler! Lord Brixton explicitly instructed you to have these shackles removed!' A look passed between Ferris and Aidan as he held out his wrists for the key. He might have laughed if the situation weren't so dire. So, Frederick was here, too, and throwing his ducal family's weight around. Brixton was his honorary title, one of Cowden's subsidiaries. The shackles fell to the floor and Ferris wasted no time imperiously dismissing the gaoler. 'How dare they treat you like this.' Ferris hugged him again. 'Frederick is working his magic with the warden right now.'

Aidan sat at the edge of the cot and rubbed his wrists. 'How is Avaline? The men roughed her up when they came, I tried to fight…' He never wanted to be helpless to defend her again. Never wanted to see another man touch her in anger. All talk of strategies could wait. Avaline was more important.

Ferris came and sat beside him. 'She is fine. She came straight to us. She has your trunk.' He nodded to the monstrosity filling the room.

Aidan gave a short laugh. 'A trunk for Newgate? This is not the Grand Tour.' He knew, of course, that people paid for the right to have clothing, to have good food. Inside Newgate, someone with money could have nearly any luxury if they paid enough for it.

'Avaline has seen to every comfort.' Ferris undid the buckles and opened the trunk. The fresh, sharp odour of cedar and balsam filled the stale air of the little chamber. Aidan breathed it in. If ambrosia had a scent, this would be it. 'She sends her love.'

Aidan felt tears sting his eyes. She did indeed. Everything in the trunk represented that love, each item chosen not just for his comfort, but to remind him that she was with him still, though prison bars kept them apart. There were clean shirts, neatly pressed, cravats, waistcoats, jackets, trousers, all packed with balsam sachets. There were blankets and sheets from home, fine linen pillowcases sporting her embroidery work at the hems. When he thought Ferris wasn't looking, he held a pillowcase up to his nose and smelled the faint scent of her hair, of her, rosewater and vanilla. He lingered too long and Ferris caught him. He quickly thrust the pillowcase away.

'It's all right to miss her.' Ferris clapped him on the shoulder in consolation. 'She wants to see you.'

'No, absolutely not. I don't deserve her. I am

not worthy of her. I've tried to tell her, but she won't listen. She must think about how to distance herself from me now. Tell her not to come. I don't want her here.' Aidan busied himself with the sheets. 'Tell her to stay at Bramble.' Where she could have her beloved Christmas among family.

'She's already on her way. The ladies are coming up today.' Ferris smiled. 'Really, Fortis, do you know your sisters-in-law so little to think any of us could dissuade them from coming? She'll be at the town house with us on Portland Square. We'll take care of her.'

'Thank you.' A little band around his heart loosened to know Avaline was close by, surrounded by family. Perhaps that would be enough. He hadn't realised how much that meant to him. Aidan relented. Perhaps it would do them both good to know the other was all right.

Ferris rose to go and the two men embraced. 'She can come just once, Ferris. This is a terrible place. There's illness everywhere, everyone has a cough. She has to think about the babe.' He hoped he wasn't being selfish in relenting. He had not understood until now how love was a blessing and curse. It was a wondrous thing to love and be loved, as Avaline loved him. But it was a fearful thing, too. It reminded a man of all he risked and all he stood to lose; all that mattered in the world hung in the balance when a man loved a woman as he did.

Chapter Twenty-Two

Avaline came on Christmas Day. He was dressed and ready for her in clean clothes. He'd even shaved after discovering his shaving kit buried at the bottom of the trunk. He couldn't even fathom the amount of money Frederick had put out to have that brought in. A razor was gold in Newgate. Dressed in a dark jacket and trousers, a pristine white cravat tied about his throat and his gold-patterned waistcoat peeking beneath his jacket, he might have been going to a holiday party. It was all part of the pretence, that somehow seeing Avaline here in this dark place was acceptable, normal.

He rose when he heard the key turn and tugged on his waistcoat one last time, then she was in his arms, hugging him, kissing him, before she even set down the lidded basket. He barely heard the gaoler call out, 'Two hours.'

He helped her out of her cloak and gently set it aside. 'Let me look at you.' He held her arms out to her side, taking her in. She'd dressed carefully, too, in a cranberry silk trimmed in snow-white lace, pearls at her neck, her blonde hair piled up in a delicate collection of ringlets high on her head. Had it only been two days since he'd been taken from Blandford, from *her*? It felt like an eternity. 'You look like Christmas personified,' he whispered, stealing a kiss and drinking in the vanilla scent of her. 'You smell like a Christmas kitchen, too.'

She laughed and the room brightened. 'That might be the basket. I've brought all kinds of treats.' She moved to the table and undid the lid. 'Help me lay it out. We'll have a Christmas picnic. I've even brought a tablecloth and candles.'

He helped her spread the cloth. 'I'm surprised they didn't take them from you.' Such things were luxuries here. Men died for them.

'They have their own baskets,' Avaline said smugly, laying out plates and ham slices. 'Courtesy of Helena and Anne. They're no different than dogs and as easily tamed.' 'They' of course were the gaolers. Both he and Avaline were trying so hard to pretend this wasn't Newgate, that their circumstances weren't dire, that

Hayworth wasn't trying to destroy their lives, their happiness.

Avaline lit the candles. 'There. Everything is better in candlelight. We have a feast, even wine.'

'I'm afraid the table might break,' Aidan joked. 'I don't think it's ever seen a feast of this magnitude.' As soon as he said it, he wished he hadn't. It made everything too real. 'This is not the Christmas we planned,' he said quietly, taking his seat on the edge of the cot.

'It's the Christmas we have.' She offered him a small smile and took his hand.

'Then let's make the most of it.' He smiled back. He had only two precious hours with her. He would not ruin them with guilt and worry. He had days ahead of him to fill with that. Tonight was for happiness. 'Will you allow me to fill your plate, my lady?'

They ate and ate, and she regaled him with stories of the nephews' antics and they laughed. They finished the wine bottle, both of them pleasantly sated with good food and good company. He reached for her hand. 'It has done my heart good to see you, Avaline, to talk about things other than...' He didn't fill in the rest of it. They both knew what he meant.

'It does me good, too.' Avaline smiled tremulously, the first show of emotion beyond happiness she'd shown since her arrival.

'Don't cry, Avaline. I don't want to remember you in tears.'

She swiped bravely at her eyes. 'It's the baby. I cry over everything. Helena says it's normal.' She tried to laugh. The effort was only moderately successful. She rose from the table. 'No Christmas is complete without a present. I've brought you one.' She dug about in the basket. 'Close your eyes.' He closed his eyes, not wanting to spoil her pleasure.

She came and sat on his lap, wafting something beneath his nose, the air filling with sweet citrus scents. 'Can you guess what it is?'

Good Lord, could he guess? The most heavenly smell in the whole world. He smiled and opened his eyes, genuinely delighted. 'Did you bring me a Christmas orange?'

'Yes. Two of them. One for you now and one for you later,' she teased, beginning to peel the fruit.

'Thank you.' He kissed her mouth softly, allowing himself this small taste of her. 'But I don't have a gift for you.'

'Yes, you do.' She popped the first section

of orange in his mouth. 'All I want from you is a story. Tell me why you became a jewel thief.'

'Oh, Avaline, you don't want to know.'

She kissed him and fed him another slice. 'Yes, I do. I find it rather exotic, really. It's very exciting to be married to a jewel thief. It's like being married to Robin Hood.'

He did chuckle at that. 'Well, I assure you it's not as exotic as the penny dreadfuls make it out to be. I was desperate, Avaline. After my mother died, I lived on the streets, making shift as best I could. I ran gin and errands for crime bosses. But there was no money in that, just enough pennies to stay fed. I slept where I could, when I could. The nights I used to spend in the brothel kitchen next to the stove seemed like luxuries in those days. Then, one day, I ran an errand to a Mayfair hotel, just to the back door to deliver a message. I hung around afterwards, right outside the front door. I watched lords and ladies go in and out all afternoon, dressed in expensive clothes. I looked at the ladies and their pearls and I thought just one of those pearls would keep me in rent and food for a month. Then, a footman spied me and kicked me out. No one likes a poor boy. I was sixteen and I realised that day nothing would change unless I did.'

Avaline wiggled on his lap and fed him some more orange. 'What did you do?'

'I started hanging around the hotel, looking for errands to run, horses to hold, anything to put a few coppers in my pocket, and I started to learn how to ape my betters. I started to cultivate my speech. I studied what the gentlemen wore and how they wore it. I listened to what they said to the ladies. I figured out who had influence and I attached myself to them. I ingratiated myself to lords who needed messages sent or flowers bought for mistresses. By the time I was nineteen, I had a decent suit of clothes. People were used to seeing me. A few ladies took a shine to me. An older woman took me under her wing.' He paused there, embarrassed by the memory.

'I will leave the rest of that to your imagination. I won't say I'm proud of what I did, though. She was my first job. I took an emerald bracelet from her. I don't know she even knew it was gone. I never saw her wear it. I fenced it. The money was all mine. I didn't have to give a cut to a boss or anyone and it had been easy. For the first time, I wasn't starving. I wasn't cold. I wasn't sleeping in the rain. I was safe. Safer than I'd ever been in my life. It was a good year and then I got caught stealing a ruby tiara from the Duchess of Chichester. That was my first visit to Newgate. But that's not me any more, Avaline. Newgate was a wakeup call. I didn't like it very much. I took the offer to join the military. Best decision I ever made. The military gave me discipline, Fortis gave me a chance to rise above my station and your love has given me so much more, no matter how this turns out. If this is all I get, it will have been worth it.'

'Please, don't talk like that,' Avaline begged. 'I can stand all else, but I can't stand that.' She kissed him. 'I've missed you, the bed has been so empty. Perhaps we might…' She caressed his jaw with little kisses and temptation whispered. It would be easy to give in, but it would dishonour her.

'We haven't the time.' He sighed hoarsely.

'We have enough,' she whispered, reaching a hand between them, touching his arousal through his trousers. It was sweet heaven and oh, so tempting.

He covered her hand with his own. 'I would

not risk these bastards seeing you like that. Our intimacy is for us alone. It is not a peep show.'

She touched her forehead to his, each of them holding each other tight. Already they could hear the clank of keys and heavy footsteps at the far end of the hall. 'Shall I come again when we have more time?' She was flirting, but he could not allow it.

'No, Avaline. You must not come again. It's not safe for the babe. Promise me. I need to know you and my child are safe.'

He kissed her one last time, hard and fast, as the key turned in the lock and came to take Christmas away, but not before Avaline whispered, 'Thank you for the story. It was the best present ever.' She pressed the second orange into his hand as she stepped away and he closed his fingers around it, a tangible keepsake of today that would linger long after she was gone.

Chapter Twenty-Three

Avaline kept her word, partially out of honouring Aidan's request and partially because she could hardly do otherwise without drawing more attention to the Treshams and to herself. In the four weeks leading up to the trial, the trial grew in publicity. Hungry for entertainment in the wake of Christmas revels and the advent of the peerage returning to town *en masse*, Londoners were starved for something to hold their attentions. The trial of an impostor claiming to be a duke's son was just the drama to captivate them.

Newspapers covered the lead-up to the trial, printing sketches of Fortis Tresham and this new claimant side by side, writing up descriptions of each and speculating as to whether or not the differences between them were enough to discount the fact that no one had seen Lord Fortis Tresham in public for seven years. They unearthed details of Fortis's military career, sought interviews with his past commanders. Cam Lithgow threw an intrepid reporter off the front steps of his town house when the man came to interview Fortis's best friend. The Duke was besieged with questions from reporters who lay in wait for him and his sons outside White's. The Duchess and the ladies had taken to getting into the carriage in the mews instead of out front where they, too, could be plagued with questions. Avaline went nowhere without a veil and an escort.

'I don't see how he can even get a fair trial and an impartial jury at this rate,' Avaline complained one morning to Helena and Anne as the three sat together taking care of correspondence and other small duties. The men were gone, as usual, meeting with the barrister Cowden had engaged and meeting with Fortis to build their defence. 'The newspapers are against him.' Newspapers that could never know of the desperate boy who'd been driven to a life of thievery to survive, the boy who'd had to take for himself by whatever means necessary what society would not freely give.

'They are intrigued by him,' Helena argued. 'He is a handsome man and handsome men attract attention.'

'But the newspapers speculate he's a handsome liar,' Avaline responded. 'They don't portray him as the wronged son of a duke. They portray him as a usurper, a man who has to prove himself. The burden of proof is on him, when it should be on Hayworth. He's the one bringing the charges.'

'If Hayworth wanted a show, he's certainly got one.' Helena looked up from her letters. 'I wonder if he understands such momentum can turn back on him? I would not willingly engage the mob.'

'I just wish there was something I could do. I feel so helpless just sitting here.' Avaline sighed. That was the real issue. She had let herself become a victim, merely reacting to the decisions of others. She wore a veil because otherwise the crowd plagued her when she went out. She stayed home because the newspapers had written her into a corner, painting her either as an innocent featherbrain who didn't even know her own husband, or as a conniving whore who'd willingly conspired with the handsome impostor, depending on which paper people read, when, in truth, she was neither innocent nor whore, but simply a woman who'd found happiness after years of emptiness and guilt. Now she risked losing that happiness. She couldn't lose him. Not now when she knew what it was to be loved and to love in return. Not now when there was proof of that love between them. Blandford needed him. She needed him. The baby needed him.

Anne set aside her pen. 'Maybe there is something we can do. Helena, do you have the invitations? We have a towering pile of invites. Everyone wants us at their teas and At-Homes. Why not oblige them? Why not go and speak out on Fortis's behalf?' Avaline's spirits rose at the thought of doing something. She glanced at Helena thumbing through the invitations.

'These are gossips, Anne.' Helena didn't think much of the idea and Avaline's spirits fell.

'They are women of standing who have husbands. They will hang on every word and they will tell their husbands what we say. We can sway public sentiment.'

Avaline caught up the line of reasoning. 'By going out, we say we're not afraid, we have nothing to hide and nothing to fear. We can show Hayworth as someone making a tempest in a teapot. We can show everyone how ridiculous his claims truly are.' She looked at each of her sisters-in-law. 'Hand me the invitations, Helena. I'll write our acceptances. I think we have to try.'

Over the next few weeks, Avaline turned visiting into an art. She dressed carefully, deliberately, in the height of conservative fashion. From the delicate lace of her fichu to the subdued colours of her winter gowns, no one could find fault with her appearance or her demeanour. She was the epitome of a wholesome young bride, the wife of a war hero, the daughter of a baron, the daughter-in-law of a duke. But she was no wilting wallflower. When a woman insinuated that she'd been taken advantage of, Avaline was quick to correct her, quick to assert that the only ones being taken advantage of were those who were being misled by Hayworth. If anyone was being harmed, it was Fortis who'd been deprived of his freedom and his name maligned on Hayworth's whim, a situation made worse by the newspapers who were exploiting the situation in order to make money. Those were the papers, she'd say calmly, looking her hostess in the eye, who were deserving

of pity. Not herself. She'd hold her head high
and declare without hesitation that she was the
luckiest of women. Her husband had returned
from war and, except for Hayworth's interfer-
ence, would be, for the first time in seven years,
by her side.

Slowly, the tide began to turn. Anne was
right. These women told their husbands. Their
husbands talked among themselves in their
clubs. A new storyline emerged, making it clear
the Treshams did not want this trial. They did
not suspect this man of being anything other
than their son, restored to them at last. Since
when did a man have to prove he was himself?
If the Duke didn't question the authenticity of
his own son, what gave anyone else the right to
do so? Not because Cowden was a duke, but because this was an issue of personal liberty and
self-determination. The villain here was Hayworth, not the man locked in Newgate.

Fortis Tresham began to emerge, in the eyes
of some, as a hero, a man for a new era of justice, where no man was above the law, not even
a duke's son. Fortis Tresham was willing to
prove himself as any other man would have to
against such charges. He was willing to toler-
ate Newgate, was willing to stand trial against

these grievous charges and prove himself. It was this last especially that impressed all levels of society. If Hayworth had thought to make this trial about pitting the old guard against the new, he had failed, although not entirely, which meant, to Avaline's worry, that she had succeeded only in part. The tide had only partly turned. While that was an improvement from the original outrage Hayworth had managed to generate, she wished it was more.

By the day of the trial, Tresham v. Hayworth had become more than the questioning of an impostor. It was about an individual's access to justice. Fortis Tresham had come to represent the idea that all men were equal before the law. Heightened tensions focused on what the law would make of that idea.

Avaline played with the wide silk ribbon of her hat as she sat in the Old Bailey, observers jostling for a seat around her. Today, Aidan's fate would be decided and consequently her own. Would she be declared a widow? A woman who'd been defrauded? Taken advantage of? She would be turned into an object of pity and then an object of scorn. Hayworth had not kept the matter of her pregnancy quiet. The papers had trumpeted it about. Would she be a woman who was carrying a criminal's child?

She breathed deeply, trying to calm her nerves. She ran a soothing hand over the flat of her stomach. She wasn't showing yet, but her gowns were fitting more snugly these days. Would Aidan see her? She hoped so. She'd worn blue today on purpose. Blue the colour of his eyes, blue the colour of loyalty and truth. It had become her signature colour as she'd made her visiting rounds. Today, Anne, Helena, their husbands, the Duke and the Duchess, and Fortis's friends all wore blue as well, making quite a statement in the middle of the court room.

She was surrounded by friends. Viscount Taunton and his wife, Sofia, flanked Frederick. Major Lithgow and his expectant wife, Pavia, flanked Ferris and Anne while Sutton Keynes, ostensibly the richest man in England and his wife, Elidh, sat beside her on one side, Helena on the other. Nowhere was the Tresham family unguarded, unsupported. The jostling mass of humanity could not reach them.

They'd been assigned to the main and original court room of the Old Bailey, due to the anticipated crowds. Avaline didn't need to twist in her seat to know the spectators' gallery was full. She fanned herself. Overhead the four brass chandeliers blazed. It was warm and the session hadn't even begun. But it would soon. Hayworth and his barrister were already in place. Her pulse began to race. She hadn't seen Aidan in nearly a month. A hidden door in the wall opened and Cowden's barrister, a Mr Kenneth Wall, appeared, an older man known for his fiery rhetoric and sharp wit. He would need both today.

She had little attention to spare Wall, though, and neither did the crowd. Behind him was the main attraction. Aidan walked tall, shoulders squared. His clothes were pressed and he was neatly turned out. He'd shaved and his hair was combed into place, but he was pale and he'd lost weight despite all their best efforts to keep him well fed. There were catcalls and comments hurled in Aidan's direction as he crossed the room to the table.

See me. Don't listen to them. Just see me, Avaline willed.

She wanted just one glance, one look from him so that she could see him and he could see her and for a moment in this wild crowd, there would just be the two of them. But Aidan's gaze stayed fixed straight ahead.

The side door opened again, admitting the jury and then at last the judge. The court rose in a rustle of clothing and then sat with barely contained excitement. The judge would have his hands full today keeping order, Avaline thought. But he was a veteran of such circumstances and wholly up to the task. He banged his gavel and called the session to order with his instructions. To the jury he said, 'We are here to decide without a shadow of a doubt if this man is Lord Fortis Tresham or if he is indeed another, but not just any other, that he is particularly one Aidan Roswell. This determination is no small matter and it requires your utmost careful consideration. If that is case, that man will be arrested on charges of perjury committed in this court for lying to us about his identity and also on charges of theft for crimes committed previously. He will be immediately returned to prison where he will await trial for crimes that are deemed a hanging offence.'

Avaline pressed a handkerchief to her mouth to suppress a cry. She'd known, of course, but to hear it said out loud was something entirely different. If Aidan were unsuccessful, there would be no time to see him, to hold him. He would be dragged away in chains. On her right, Sutton patted her arm and murmured encouragement. On her left, Helena took her hand. 'Do not worry, Frederick assures me we have a very good case.'

Avaline wanted to believe that. For weeks, she had convinced herself that they did, but Clarence Montgomery was very good, very compelling as he laid out the circumstances of Fortis Tresham's return. Fortis Tresham was dead, killed in a fall from his horse at Balaclava. Major Cam Lithgow saw him fall. This man before them was an opportunist, taking advantage of the lack of a body and a grieving family's noble refusal to give up hope. But grief had blinded them, made them weak and susceptible to this obvious chicanery. He could prove that this man was Aidan Roswell. Montgomery began to call witnesses: a prostitute who claimed Aidan Roswell had been her lover; a man notorious for fencing stolen goods in St Giles and claimed to have bought jewels from Aidan before.

Wall objected immediately, discrediting them all, arguing they had no credibility, that they would say anything for money, that it was impossible to assume they would remember anything accurately from ten years ago. Roswell had been eighteen the last time any of them would have seen him. Their testimony was wholly unreliable. Wall won the objections, but he couldn't stop the damage as Aidan's past came to life before the eyes of the court in tangible colour: women he'd slept with, men he'd stolen for and then later people he'd stolen from on his own. She was not wholly unprepared for the things Montgomery revealed. She had heard some of this before, directly from Aidan, on Christmas Day when she'd begged the gift of a story.

Turn around, look at me, she pleaded silently. *See in my eyes that nothing said here today matters, nothing that I did not already know or guess and that I already forgave you. Indeed, there was nothing ever to forgive.*

But Aidan did not turn. Was he ashamed? Was he as worried as she was about how the jury would see these stories?

For her, Montgomery's stories broke her heart. They built pathos for the boy he must have been, the young man who felt he had no other choice if he wanted to survive. All she could imagine was how alone he must have been and how desperate. These people Montgomery called to the witness stand had never been his friends, had never been people he could rely on. They'd only ever been enemies. She couldn't fathom how fearful that world must have been to a small boy with no mother, no father to shelter him.

'Don't give Montgomery's words any heed,' Sutton whispered. 'It's all in the past. A man does what he has to in order to survive.'

'Will the jury know that, though?' Avaline whispered. How would they line up Montgomery's case against Wall's? They didn't know Aidan the way she knew him. Would they see the tragedy of the stories and have empathy or would they see these stories as proof that the man before them was a calculated con artist?

Sutton smiled. 'Chin up, Avaline. They will know by the end of the day. Give it time.' But it was hard to be patient when the very thing she needed was the one thing she was running out of. Time was slipping away.

It took Montgomery the better part of the morning to lay out his damning case: the exploited grief of the Treshams coupled with the opportunism of a thief known for his charisma. The judge declared a recess for lunch and the court adjourned to catch its breath. Montgomery had woven compelling arguments, so compelling that Avaline feared the worst. They were going to lose. She nearly fainted when she stood. Sutton offered to drive her home, but she refused. Before it was all over, Aidan might look for her. She needed to be sure she was there.

The courtroom filled after the recess. Aidan resumed his seat beside Kenneth Wall. Avaline was here, despite his request to Frederick that she be kept away. He could feel her eyes on him as they had been all morning, burning into the back of his head, willing him to turn and acknowledge her. It was Orpheus's own burden not to turn. She had no idea how much the thought of turning, of catching a glimpse of her, tempted him. But he didn't want to give away too much. He didn't want her to see how much the trial had weighed on him, how worried he was that they would lose. He remained stoically forward facing for her sake and for the child's. He didn't want the stress of the trial to risk a miscarriage.

If this went poorly, the child would be her comfort. He would not take that from her, too. God, he'd already taken so much from her, ironically when he'd meant only to give her so much, all that Fortis felt had been denied her. It hadn't worked out that way. No one would ever know, Fortis had argued in the cave, and besotted with the miniature and Fortis's tales of a home and family he'd never had, Aidan had believed him. They'd both been naive, both had been desperate. The past never died. He'd just hoped it would remain buried. It might have if Hayworth hadn't been intent on unearthing it. Kenneth Wall gave him a final encouraging look as the judge entered. That unearthing would be Hayworth's undoing. Despite the damaging case Montgomery had laid out this morning, Wall was still hopeful. He'd spent most of the recess bolstering Aidan's own spirits, which were woefully flagging, perhaps because Aidan knew the truth.

Montgomery was right. Everything he'd said that morning was correct except for his claim that Aidan had instigated this impersonation with malicious intent to defraud. That had *never* been his goal. His goal had been to protect a woman from a man who was indeed intent on taking her land and forcing her into a marriage she did not want. That man was the real villain and he sat across the room going unchecked. And, if Aidan was being honest, his other goal had been to claim a life he'd never had. In doing so, he'd reached too high, too far above himself, and like Icarus he was falling from the skies of his ambition.

Wall rose and approached the bar. 'I want to begin this afternoon with a question. Why would anyone do this? Why would anyone challenge another's identity? The answer, honourable members of the jury, is simple. Because something stands to be gained. This afternoon I want to demonstrate to you that Lord Fortis Tresham sits before you, wrongly accused by a man who found his audacity to live an obstacle to the land and the woman that man coveted. When I am finished, I believe you will have every reason to conclude a grave injustice has been perpetrated.' Aidan drew a breath. So it began. The beginning of the end.

Throughout the long afternoon, Wall was meticulous. First, in pointing out that despite Montgomery's lengthy arguments, there'd been no actual evidence presented that this man wasn't Fortis Tresham. Montgomery had only argued he might be Aidan Roswell, a claim only sustained by the testimony of petty fences and whores. He moved on to question Aidan about his family and things he remembered. Then, he moved to the pièce de résistance: Hayworth's motives. It was masterfully done. Behind him, the courtroom was quiet, the earlier raucousness had been replaced by silent curiosity. Everyone waited to hear Wall's next words. Hayworth was painted black indeed by the time Wall was done. Not only was intent established in regards to him preying on Avaline, a married woman, but a trend of having tried such tactics in the past had emerged as well.

Finally, Wall moved to call witnesses. 'I wish to bring witnesses forward to testify to the identity of this man.' Aidan stiffened. He'd not been prepared. This had not been discussed with him. The judge nodded and Wall began an impressive parade of witnesses. 'First, I call Viscount Taunton, Conall Everard.'

Aidan's pulse raced. He'd never even seen this man. Taunton could destroy him with a single word.

Chapter Twenty-Four

Aidan held still as Conall Everard took the stand and made his oath. Fortis had spoken of the man, of their days at school and their lasting friendship, but Aidan had never met him, never seen him until this moment. Conall locked eyes with him and smiled. Everyone in the courtroom noted that smile. A smile meant recognition.

'Thank you for your presence today, Lord Taunton, and for making the journey from Somerset. I have just one question for you, Lord Taunton. Do you believe this man is Lord Fortis Tresham?' Aidan's pulse raced.

'Absolutely,' Taunton offered the one word.

'Thank you, you may step down.' Wall nodded and then called his next witness.

Mr Sutton Keynes.

Major Cam Lithgow.

The Marquess of Brixton, Frederick Tresham, the defendant's own brother, Lord Ferris Tresham, the defendant's other brother, the Duchess of Cowden, the Duke of Cowden, all of whom were asked the same question. All of whom replied affirmatively, the noise in the courtroom rising with each testament. Aidan began to study the jury, something he'd resisted doing all day for fear of driving himself crazy with guessing and second-guessing their responses. Lastly, Wall called, 'Lady Fortis Tresham.'

Aidan put a hand on Wall's sleeve. 'No, she needn't come forward, my wife should not be put through this.'

'She wants to do it,' Wall assured him as Avaline took the stand. Her eyes never left his as she took the oath, her soft hand on the Bible. Aidan's heart surged at the sight of her, so beautiful and so strong. He wanted to leap over the table and go to her, hold her, take her home away from the nastiness of this place. The baby was growing. He could see it in her breasts, the way the fabric of her gown pulled ever so slightly across her chest, a bit too tight. Good Lord, she'd sat like that all day. She must be uncomfortable. But she'd done it for him, endured this for him, for this moment. 'Lady Fortis Tresham, is this your husband?'

She did not answer immediately, her gaze lingering on his, loving him with her eyes, letting the court see that love and the surety that came with it before she answered, 'Absolutely. This is my husband, the man whom I will love all my days.'

'Thank you, that is all.' Wall looked pleased with himself as Avaline glided quietly back to her seat, head held high and defiant, daring anyone to gainsay her. Wall summed up for the jury, reminding them of their duty and its parameters, and of the fact that had become brutally obvious to everyone in the courtroom: Fortis Tresham's family and friends had no doubts as to his identity, why should anyone else? How odd it was that the one man who did carry doubts had a most suspicious agenda that included coveting another man's land and wife.

Aidan barely heard the summation, barely heard the judge instruct the jury one last time. He was overwhelmed by the last, of the people who had come forward for Cowden, for Avaline, for *him*. Would it be enough?

The judge offered to excuse the jury, but the

head juror shook his head. 'We are decided, your honour.' He passed a slip of paper to the judge. Aidan could only imagine how awful these moments were for Avaline. All was to be decided. Was it good or bad that the jury had decided without being dismissed? He dared not look at Avaline. He hoped Sutton or Ferris, or one of the women were offering Avaline comfort. He hoped there was a plan to get her safely away if this went poorly.

'In the case of Hayworth v. Tresham, this court finds Fortis Tresham in rightful possession of his true identity. All other claims are thus dismissed as irrelevant.' The gavel came down and the courtroom erupted into noisy exclamation. There were angry shouts. Hayworth had not been without his supporters. There were cries of joy as well. But all that mattered to Aidan was that he was free. The trial was over. He could go home to Blandford.

Before he could even fully process what that meant, Avaline was in his arms, his family and friends surrounded him, the Duke's men forming a cordon about them, warding off anyone who might intrude on their private celebration. He kissed Avaline long and hard, whispering his most ardent desire, 'We can go home.'

Frederick and Ferris slapped him on the back, Helena and Anne kissed his cheek. His mother was crying. His father had his arm about him. *His mother. His father.* It would take weeks, perhaps years, for the enormity of that realisation to settle fully on him. He was Fortis Tresham now and for ever. He had a family. Brothers. Parents. Nephews. It was an incredible gift he'd been given. Had Fortis realised that? He'd once thought it was him doing Fortis the favour. But in reality Fortis had done the favour for him.

With his characteristic efficiency, Cam got the rather large group into the carriages and back to Cowden House. With his usual discretion, Cam had managed to arrange a carriage just for Aidan and Avaline.

'I thought we were going to lose,' Avaline gasped as they settled on the seat. The euphoria of victory made her breathless in her excitement. She hadn't let go of him nor he her. If he had his way, he would never let go of her again. Three weeks without her had been too long.

'I was worried, too,' Aidan admitted. 'When I think about what could have happened.'

She silenced him with a kiss. 'Don't think about it, then. It didn't happen. Hayworth failed.' It would be a while before society let Hayworth forget it, too.

'I think it was the testimonies at the end that swayed the jury,' Aidan murmured against her neck, his body starting to rapidly lose interest in the trial. 'It was an enormous risk, though. I know why the family did it, but why do you suppose Taunton and the others did it?' It had not escaped him that they'd been willing to commit perjury for him.

'Fortis was their friend and it was what Fortis wanted,' Avaline said softly, tracing his lips with her finger.

'I never had friends like that,' he mused thoughtfully, full of awe at what sort of friendship inspired such loyalty. 'I will have to thank them on Fortis's behalf, then. They discharged their duty to him honourably.'

'And me? How will you thank me?' Avaline teased, moving her hips against him.

'I'll think of something.' Aidan smiled and slid a hand under her skirts as the carriage pulled into traffic slowly. 'It's going to be a long drive to Cowden House. Traffic this time of day is a beast.'

Avaline smiled, pressing a kiss to his mouth. 'We can start the celebrations early if you like.'

'I can think of nothing I'd like better.'

'Then let me be the first to say, welcome home, Fortis Tresham.' She laughed against his mouth, a low, husky sound that brought him rapidly to attention. He was the most blessed of men. In this moment, he was cognisant of the debt he owed the man in the cave. That man had given him his life. He offered a final salute in his mind and let go the ghost. He silently toasted that man as they all had in Cowden's library over a month ago. Fortis Tresham was dead. Long live Fortis Tresham. He was ready for Avaline, ready for their future together and whatever it brought.

Blandford—August 1856

The inside of the stone chapel was cool, a welcome relief from the summer heat. Aidan shut the door behind them and helped Avaline to sit. She was huge now with child. It would be any day now. This morning, she'd complained of pains in her lower back. Walking helped, so he'd taken her on a slow tour of the gardens. Not only was the chapel a good resting place, it also served his purpose. There was something he'd been waiting to do and he could wait no longer. He wanted it done before the child was born.

'Are you feeling better?' He sat beside her.

'Yes. No.' Avaline shook her head. 'I think I won't feel better again until this child is born. He or she has taken up my entire body.' She laughed good-humouredly.

Aidan took her hand and turned it over in his, studying it. 'There's something I want to ask you.'

'All right.' She leaned her head drowsily against his shoulder. 'But don't look at my fingers while you do it, they're swollen and puffy. I'm so fat *everywhere*. I didn't even know fingers could get fat.'

'I think you're beautiful, especially your fingers.' Aidan laughed, but he didn't let go. 'I want to hold your hand while I ask you this.' He slipped to his knee before her on the cool flagstones of the chapel, the sunlight streaming in through the stain glass behind her. 'You look like the Madonna, right now, your hair golden.'

'My belly huge. Funny how they never show that in stained glass,' Avaline said grumpily.

Aidan rubbed her belly with his spare hand. 'Huge is good.' He'd loved these past peaceful months at Blandford, watching her belly grow, his child quickening with the land as winter gave way to spring and spring to ripe summer fields.

Avaline winced suddenly and put a hand to her back. 'Whatever you want to ask, maybe you could hurry up? I think I need to walk again.'

'Avaline, would you marry me?'

'Why? What?' Avaline knit her brow. 'We're already married.'

'Not really. You know what I mean,' Aidan whispered. '*I* want to marry *you*.'

Avaline's eyes watered as she took in the import of it. 'Fortis and I married in this chapel.'

'I know, that's why I want to do it here, in this place. I need to marry you, Avaline. I want to make you mine before the eyes of God.' There wouldn't be a priest, there wouldn't be a record in the church parish. There never could be. But there would be this commitment made between the two of them in a holy house.

Aidan pulled out a ring from his pocket, a plain gold band hung on a thin gold chain. 'Avaline, will you take me as your wedded husband?'

She beamed at him and his heart was full. 'You know I will.'

He fastened the necklace and let the ring

drop between her breasts. 'With this ring I thee wed.' He kissed her softly, this woman who was his everything, the sum of his world. He would spend his life making her happy.

'Aidan, might we go back to the house?' she whispered, struggling to rise.

'Yes, of course—are you all right?' He helped her to stand.

'I'm going to be.' She smiled at him. 'I think we married just in time.'

Aidan assimilated her meaning with a moment of panic. He was going to be a father! 'Now? The baby is coming now?'

'Yes.' She bent, a little groan escaping her.

'In that case, I'd better carry you.' He wasted no time sweeping his wife up into his arms. 'You seemed lighter the first time I did this,' he joked, to ease her nerves.

Avaline smiled. 'Well, back then there were fewer of us. Now, you're carrying two.' A beautiful reminder that soon there would be three. They would be a family. This was why he'd lived…this was why he'd come home.

* * * * *

COMING SOON!

We really hope you enjoyed reading this book. If you're looking for more romance, be sure to head to the shops when new books are available on

Thursday 22nd August

To see which titles are coming soon, please visit
millsandboon.co.uk/nextmonth

MILLS & BOON

Coming next month

THE LORD'S HIGHLAND TEMPTATION
DIANE GASTON

Mairi stopped and gazed across the river. 'The mountains look so beautiful. It is hard to say what time of year is the most beautiful in Scotland, but right now I'd say October.'

Lucas agreed. It had its own unique beauty. Like her.

The faint sounds of gunfire wafted in the wind.

'The hunt is still on,' she said sadly.

Lucas had heard the gunfire on and off throughout their walk. He pushed away memories the gunfire provoked. 'Maybe that is why we see so many deer on this side of the mountain. They are hiding.'

'Hide well, deer,' she murmured.

They continued walking, crossing a patch of grass. The ground was uneven and again Lucas held her arm to steady her. When he released her, she threaded her arm through his and held on to him as they continued walking.

After a while she asked, 'Will you talk to me about last night, Lucas?'

He knew instantly what she meant. He searched for the right words to say.

'To beg your forgiveness? I should not have touched you.' *Or almost kissed you*, he added silently.

'Why?' she said softly. 'It is not as though you are really a servant, are you, Lucas? You were a soldier.'

This was his chance to tell her who he really was, but the gunfire sounded again.

'I was a soldier, but I grew up in a great house.' Let her believe he was John Lucas. 'In any event, I should not have behaved as I did towards you. It was wrong of me.'

She let go of him and walked a little faster, putting herself a step or two ahead of him. He caught up to her.

'I know you are right,' she said, but her tone was sharp.

Had she wanted the kiss? He'd thought so. He'd been too familiar with her. In his father's house he would not dream of becoming so involved with—say—one of the maids. But she was not a maid and he was not really a butler. How had this become so complicated?

Continue reading
THE LORD'S HIGHLAND TEMPTATION
DIANE GASTON

Available next month
www.millsandboon.co.uk

MILLS & BOON

HISTORICAL

Awaken the romance of the past

Escape with historical heroes from time gone by. Whether your passion is for wicked Regency Rakes, muscled Viking warriors or rugged Highlanders, indulge your fantasies and awaken the romance of the past.